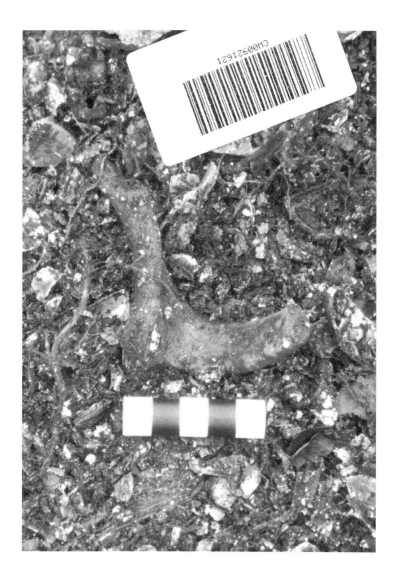

For Janine

Veneer of Manners

Francis J Glynn

Best Wishes

Frank.

XMAS 2017

The poem 'The Dead are not Dead' is from Chants d'ombre Suivis de Hosties Noires, edited by Leopold Senghor (Paris, 1949) p160.

For Shirley

Chapter 1

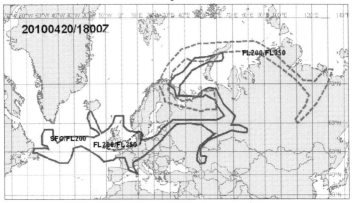

Tuesday night, 20th April 2010 10.15pm.

The Bay of Noup lies at the edge of Europe, in the archipelago that is Orkney. It was once located at the equator. To its north, there is sea all the way to the geographical North Pole where there is only the solid ice that will surely melt. To the west, the sun has set.

High above is a cloud of dust formed by the eruption of Eyjafjallajokull, four hundred and fifty miles away in Iceland. Rapidly heated glacial water has dissolved ejected volcanic matter, pushing tiny particles of pumice high into the atmosphere. The cloud is moved by the earth's rotation and the rising of air warmed by the sun. When you look into the sky, there is nothing to be seen. The cloud will be there on a cloudless day.

In 1783, after a similar eruption, Orcadians looked into a similar sky. They saw their livestock perish and they saw their crops rot. They ate kelp and resorted to unspeakable acts to feed themselves.

*   *   *

Tonight, in the dimming light, at an archaeological dig, you can see tapes that mark boundaries; cards on wooden posts, grids set out with string, shovels, mattocks, trowels, brushes, and fine and coarse screen filters. Somewhere a spreadsheet contains notes of objects found at the site with exact grid references, along with photographs and notes. This system and its procedures gives us a view of this past; a perfect example of science uncovering history. From these shards and shells and assumptions, old notions are reconstructed.

But here, here at the Bay of Noup is the sound of human labour and the percussion of rock against flesh and bone. The killer pummels against the face of his victim, Dominic Byrd, with no consideration for the historical integrity of the site. He has been beating Dominic's head with a rock for nearly a minute and a half, but the passage of that minute and a half has seemed to him as an eternity. He stops, exhausted, and rises to his feet. Looking down, he sees Dominic's face, now unrecognisable, a pulpy mess. The body is lying in a trench splashed with blood that is black in the monochrome light of the moon. The walls of the trench contain the compacted shells of limpet and mussel and scallop; shells last held in a human hand five thousand years ago, by people who ate and slept, and loved and murdered as we do today. Dominic Byrd is lying in a midden.

The killer looked down at his clothes in the poor light. He can see that he is covered in great splashes of blood. He goes down to the sea and throws the rock into the water. He leans over and vomits on the ancient sand of the Bay of Noup. Teeth chattering, he stands up, feeling suddenly quite sober, and wipes away his tears. His hands are sticky with Dominic's blood and he has smeared the mess on his face. He goes to the cold sea to wash. He returns shivering to the midden and looks again at what he has done. He sees a shovel and considers using it to cut off the hands and feet. This will slow up the process of identifying the body; but he thinks better.

"They would identify him from the DNA."

The killer is shocked at his thinking.

"Cutting off hands and feet? DNA?"

What did he know about such things? He looked around him. He didn't know where he was; he was unsure what language people spoke here. He had only the moon's light and its reflection from the white sand that threw confusing shadows; shadows that were abstruse and unreliable. The killer looked up at the stars, still visible against the light of the moon. He knew about stars, and there, without a doubt, was the pole star, right above him, but there was something wrong. The other stars made no sense. Orion was definitely in the wrong place; and why did the planets move with such speed? The very tide moved too fast, and he saw creatures scuttling off the sandstone pavement to avoid being stranded in the surf.

He was unable to comprehend the scene in front of him. The killer was a normal person with a normal life. He had a normal job of work and a wife and a mortgage. He did not recognise himself in this place. What was this carnage around him? He couldn't have done this. He was incapable of this. He was not a murderer; but, as he reflected, he realised that this *was* murder. He had carried out that act that would forever separate him from his fellow men.

He stumbled up the uneven slope back to the car which was covered in a dust made luminous in the moon's light. On the way, he felt the ground tremble. A crow called to him in the strange quiet air and there was a smell of struck brimstone.

He opened the car, started the engine and waited for the heater to warm him up. He was shivering, but he didn't feel the cold, only incomprehension. There, in the shadows, Dominic Byrd was dead, killed with a rock and with the killer's own hands.

He drove slowly without headlights about a mile up a track and parked next to a lighthouse. He couldn't rest. He had to make sense of what had just happened. He closed his eyes, but he could only see Dominic's face, the face that he had destroyed.

What had just happened? How had it come to this; from laughter and frivolity to death in the blink of an eye? All that was for later. Right now he had to make a plan, to be decisive. He would only get one chance and he had to get it right.

"I have to be methodical. Get rid of the car. It's too visible. It will lead the police to me. It has my fingerprints all over it. Get rid of the car."

He looked around at the cliffs and heard the unseen surf crash on the rocks.

"Be methodical; get rid of the car. I have to get rid of the car so I won't be identified and then I have to get off this island."

He knew he could walk to the ferry terminal twelve miles to the south and get off the island as a foot passenger on the morning ferry; but what then? No, he was getting ahead of himself. First thing first. He couldn't be sure he was thinking straight, The only way he could get back to normality was by solving one problem at a time. He had to get rid of the car.

He positioned the car, lining it up with the end of the cliff. He paused.

This was definitely the right thing to do. The half full petrol tank would ensure that the car would explode on impact with the rocks below, and fingerprint evidence would be destroyed. There would be no way that police could connect him to this place.

He backed up the car and placed a stone on the accelerator pedal. The engine raced and a startled rabbit ran for cover. The killer put the car in gear and let out the clutch. The car trundled over the heather, and stalled when a wheel became stuck in a hole in the split ground.

He grunted and cursed his incompetence. He had to focus and stop letting his mind wander. He tried to heave the car out of the hole, lost his footing and fell in the damp heather. He pushed and moved it, heaving the car back and forth, eventually rocking it out of the rut. He reversed it clear of the obstacle. He could see that the ground was smoother on the other side of the lighthouse, so he re-positioned the car. This time, he got it moving towards the drop and leapt clear. The vehicle rolled to the edge and up-ending itself over the cliff. There was silence, and then a crunch, but no explosion. He looked down and could see nothing but the empty sea. Terror washed over him. There was no chance that he could get down to set fire to the car. His heart was pounding, and he became aware of the stupidity of what he had just done.

"Shit. Shit, Shit."

He should have used the car to get further away before disposing of it. He had not been thinking straight, he wasn't as sober as he had thought. If he was to escape, he could not afford to make these mistakes. The car was at the bottom of a cliff and he could do nothing about it. He hoped the tide would wash the wreckage out to sea, and that no one would see it at this remote location.

Above his head, the beam of the Noup Lighthouse rotated and lit the night sky, warning travellers of the dangers at the cliff foot. The killer had been oblivious to the regular illumination of his actions. The light could be seen for twenty miles. Over the edge, and half way down the cliffs, ravens built nests of barbed wire where they ate and slept and raised their young. One hundred and eighty feet below, the tide followed its humdrum habit.

He walked back the way he had come, cursing his folly. After twenty minutes, he arrived again at the silent dig site; he could almost not remember what had happened just an hour and a half before. The sound of the breaking waves was constant and somewhere a blackbird sang, incongruous in the dim night. He looked around, but there was nothing to be seen, there was only the absurd sound of this bird. Was this all a dream after all? He was convinced that he would see nothing. There would be no violence, and Dominic would not be dead. He walked down to the dig and approached the midden. It was darker now. He looked hard and there seemed to be no sign of any disturbance. The tapes and tools were all in place.

Of course it was a dream. It was a dream.

He began to smile, and then laughed. Dominic was alive.

But then a cloud came away from the moon and lit the scene. There was Dominic's body as he had left it. The arms and legs straight, as if sleeping; and the head was almost invisible. It was real. The killer stopped laughing and his breath slowed. He inhaled the salty air and made a low sound in his throat, a sustained grunt. He moved slowly from side to side, shifting his weight from foot to foot; his arms hung from his shoulders. Uncontrollably, with each breath, his moaning increased in pitch and intensity, and it turned into a wailing and a keening. Anyone present would not have thought that this was a human sound. They might have thought it was a dog, or a wolf, or another creature in pain. He lifted his face to the dark canopy and wailed. He couldn't help himself. It was a sustained ejaculation, a call, an inexpressible question, asked of the silent sky. He continued to utter his cry until he exhausted himself. He fell to his knees as the cloud covered the guileless moon and the scene disappeared once more.

Out at sea, from a fishing boat blinking in the distance, a bell knolled, just audible above the sound of the waves. Our shivering killer brought himself up with a start. He realised that his mobile phone was still switched on. He could be located by the phone's signal. He took it out of his pocket but all he could see was the condensation in the partly lit screen. It had been in the sea and was now useless. He switched it off and returned it to his pocket.

He turned away from the dig site to begin the twelve mile walk back to the ferry terminal at Rapness. He walked slowly, each step an effort, but after a few minutes, he was able to pick up his pace. It was now 1:45am. He took a damp timetable from his pocket, but was unable to read it in the dim light; he was sure he would have time to get the first ferry at 9:00am. This would get him to Kirkwall, where he could get a bus to Stromness, and the Hamnavoe to the Scottish mainland, and home.

He arrived at Pierowall and walked through the unpopulated street, passing the hotel and the hostel and the homes, one or two with their lights on. It was silent and he felt he was almost invisible. As he passed the campsite, he heard the sound of tyres squealing, and a silver BMW swerved to avoid him. The pitch of the engine dropped as it sped away, sucking dust into its vortex. The killer recognised the music from the car.

'And as the skies turn gloomy'

That song. What was that song?

'…searching for you.'

Yes. What was it?

He carried on out of the village on his way south and soon all that moved were the unknown stars in the new sky.

Yes Patsy, Patsy Cline …

The clouds quickly appeared and once more darkened the sky. After about ten minutes, there was a series of thumps and he could feel rumbling in the silent ground. He looked to his black surroundings, but the little thunder continued and increased in intensity. There seemed to be grunts from all around. The moon came out again and he saw that on either side of him was a field of cattle.

'Night blooms whisper to me.'

They followed him along the fence and he could smell their grassy breath. When he stopped, they stopped; when he moved on, they followed him.

Patsy Cline. Yes, Patsy Cline.

It was as if he was being pursued by these creatures that questioned with each exhalation. There was no way he could avoid them and their innocent curiosity. His only way forward was to step slowly between them in the dark. They waited and they saw, and they breathed in the cold air. They should have been asleep in the night, but here they were, about sixty beasts pushing at each other and at their wire fence. They waited, snorting and exchanging places, taking turns to regard this individual, blowing their warm cow air. They waited, knowing that the killer's truth would arise like froth in a drink. They saw his life and his situation and his guilt. The truth became his complaint against the world. It was his plea, his claim, his bleat, his grunt.

'I stopped to see a weeping willow ...'

He stepped over the metalled road and it became soft underfoot. The cattle looked to the sky and agreed. He needed to explain. His testament could not be avoided.

The cows watched him in the meaningless moonlight. Some of them pulled at the grass. He retreated to the middle of the unsettled road and quietly walked in a straight line gasping for breath, avoiding their gaze. The ground rumbled as they followed him to the end of the field, but he was unwilling at this time to meet their demands in this dark night. They continued to breathe incessantly. There was a smell of sulphur in the air.

He carried on south towards Rapness and the ferry. He needed a shave and he was grubby. His Goretex jacket and daysack were muddy and torn from his fall. He had to think straight. His had to get off Westray.

He still felt it had been a dream. The images replayed in his head; the images of the rock smashing into Dominic's face; unendingly, again, and again, and again. He now *had* to believe it was true. In this intermittent light, where everything was apparent for a moment, and then obscured, that truth remained; but he still could not fathom out how he had come to kill Dominic. All had been well and promising and then those words came out and he remembered nothing except having a rock in his hands and feeling the hot splashes of blood on his face. It was unreal and inexplicable, but the conclusion was absolute. He had killed Dominic Byrd.

He concentrated on the walk and tried to formulate the next step of the plan.

'Out in the moonlight, just hoping.'

Patsy Cline. Yes, but what was that song?

It was obvious now that it was a stupid idea to have dumped the car, but there was no going back. He had to move on. Normality was the aim. Somehow, he would eventually turn up at his front door and the nightmare would be over. As he passed the signpost for Letto Sands, two hares slowly crossed the road in front of him. They stopped and stared at him for a full minute in the moonlight, and they went on their way, strolling.

*   *   *

On the Mainland, Roland Clett awoke and looked at his alarm clock. It was 4:30am. He had another 3 hours to get some sleep. The dram he had taken was not helping. He had a drink of water and closed his eyes.

Chapter 2

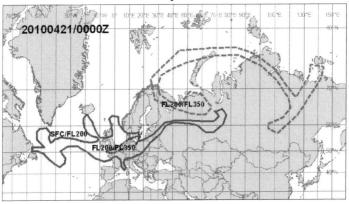

Wednesday morning, 21st April 7.15 am.

Trevor de Vries had finished his three mile run and was completing his morning yoga coordinated with ujjiya breathing, the fire breathing that he had learned from his guru in India. It warmed his upper body as he expelled the old and inhaled the fresh northern air. He would end with some meditation in full lotus position. Breakfast would be some fruit and local nettle tea that he had picked and prepared. He shaved his face and head in the cold stream next to the tent. He took his blood pressure with his portable monitor – 98/60, pulse 45 – not too bad. He felt fit and he dressed for another day at the dig.

The meeting last night had been a disaster. How did he think he could be involved in such a project, with such a man? What was being proposed involved an unwelcome link with Trevor's past and with Mexico, with all that menace that he had lived with every day. No. He was finished with all that. Last night he was able to see clearly the danger, and de Vries had walked away from it. This morning he felt he could redeem himself from all that had gone before. He could be clean again. He knew he now had to move on and concentrate on his work - his archaeology: and this dig was so special. He had done a lot of work since obtaining his permit and the data was extremely promising. He had not advised the Department about some of the oldest material he had found and had only reported vague findings to the Chief Archaeologist. He was going to make an announcement soon and he wanted it to be big, and he wanted it to be public. He didn't want to share the credit with some snot nosed office worker who didn't know a shovel from a spreadsheet.

The Bay of Noup dig was not far from the larger Links of Noltland sites up the coast. The Bay of Noup was a satellite to the Noltland site and had some of the same potential. As well as the grooved ware pottery, he had found deer and elk bones in geometric patterns. This was an unrivalled example of what used to be called ritual activity, now 'purposeful activity'. He also found interesting variations in the early shell ageing in the midden that seemed to evidence habitation 400 years prior to that of adjacent sites. If his initial test dates were correct, the Bay of Noup was inhabited between 300 and 800 years before Skara Brae. The key to de Vries' success was that he had to have enough shell samples to allow for a good statistical model backed up by accurate carbon dating. He wasn't going to get caught out again by sloppy statistics. He needed limpets, mussels, clams and scallops in proportion to their spread through the site, no less than 2,442 items to give the required data sample. This equated to around 20 items per exposed square metre of the dig. This was the magic number worked out by the bean counters to prove what de Vries could tell with his own eyes, that this was a spectacular site, unique in character and age.

De Vries had obtained the licence to work on this dig with much objection from other academics. They said his methods when he ran digs in Mexico had been unorthodox, even illegal. However, de Vries felt that these amateurs had always put up barriers in the way of his career; he knew what had to be done in the name of science. He had included justification for his methods in his book "*Archaeological Methods in Oaxaca*" (Norfolk University Press, 1999). At the time he was widely criticised in many professional journals and in the press and was considered a maverick. In particular he was criticised for his sloppy statistical methods and the lack of awareness of sample chemical contamination. The result was that his assessment of the site habitation was out by 200 years. De Vries had corrected his errors which were not about real archaeology in his eyes. They were to do with mere lab work and number crunching, a task he left to his staff. He could not be held accountable for their incompetence.

Since then he had struggled to maintain academic integrity in the face of criticism and prejudice. He had conducted tours of the Oaxaca Valley every year until the cost of the licence and travel became prohibitive. He had to deal with local anti-government groups, with government troops and with drug barons to access the dig site causing problems with the sponsors. The political situation was making it a dangerous place for visitors. In addition, De Vries' relationship with his main contact – the charismatic spiritual cartel boss 'El Santo Chapa' - was becoming increasingly precarious as well as creating personal danger for de Vries. Demands were made on him that he simply couldn't cope with. Because he couldn't keep up with current developments in Mexico, his position at the University of Norfolk was becoming tenuous. He needed to work nearer to home where the trustees would fund his archaeology. De Vries had become interested in the Orkney sites that were full of rich pickings from which he could rebuild his academic career. Norfolk University decided to fund his dig and indeed proved to be the only institution to have faith in his talent. He saw his career on the rise again.

Here on Westray he had surrounded himself with the unpolluted minds of young people who, with his guidance, saw the truth of his goals, and, indeed, the truth of his genius. This was to be his site and he needed no distractions. Speed was of the essence, but he had some of the old problems with volunteers.

Some of his boys were good; only now and then did he get a boy who had what it took, and who had an eye for a piece in a dig. But now he was wary; Dominic Byrd was cocky and de Vries had to be careful about showing his hand too early. He had to be sure the boy was right. He had made that mistake before, but now the time seemed right. He had given Dominic responsibility and praise and, he felt, his trust. Today might be the day. Trevor de Vries placed his leather fedora on his head, and turned the key, the engine of his land rover roaring in the quiet morning, and he drove to meet his team at the hostel in Pierowall.

*   *   *

Roland Clett turned up the volume to hear the news over the noise of his coffee machine. The report was of the continuing eruption of the Eyjafjallajokull volcano.

"The volcano in Iceland has been causing further disruption. The ash plume threatens to cause continuing problems for air traffic; some experts believe that this will continue for up to a year. Forecasters are worried there is a risk of further eruptions from nearby volcanoes, such as the larger Hekla, known locally as the Gate to Hell.

In Britain, revenue is being lost at the rate of £130 million per day and there has even been a suggestion of the viability of the future of air travel if the eruption continues in the long term. This would have a significant effect on the UK economy, especially considering the likelihood of recession. Now the weather…"

Clett's porridge was finished and he sipped his coffee. Outside, his view over Scapa Flow looked much the same. The conservatory, placed high up, gave him a clear outlook south over the flow with the wide sky and different clouds moving over the water. This morning the green buoy marking the site of the Royal Oak, with its thin streak of oil that continued to leak from the fuel tanks of the sunken battleship; that thin stain that would remain for ever.

Roland Clett ironed his shirt and took another buttery as it ejected from the toaster. He did not usually have butteries because of their high salt and fat content, because although separated from her, he respected his wife's concerns for his diet. However, on this occasion, he satisfied himself that any blood cholesterol created by the butteries would be consumed by the porridge – with no sugar. He would also have a macrobiotic yoghurt and an apple with his lunch for good measure.

Clett had had a promising start to his career; as a young police officer, he was involved in a high profile case of a diver from Northern Ireland washed up on Scapa beach. The diver was an ex UDA paramilitary and thought to have been murdered as part of the ongoing cycle of sectarian vengeance that was current at the time. Clett was seen as responsible for breaking the case which led to promotion and a posting to Glasgow where he worked in drugs and vice. The cost of the Glasgow posting was to his relationship with his wife Christine and his two boys, Magnus and Sandy. Christine, a teacher, was unwilling to stay in Glasgow and eventually returned to Orkney, to their house in Finstown and her family in Dounby. Clett remained in Glasgow where he saw Magnus as regularly as he could, but he saw little of his younger son Sandy who returned to Orkney with his mother. The stress on Clett in Glasgow was considerable due to the tough work culture. As a result of this, along with a case that ended badly, he was forced to take 6 months off. He returned home to work in Kirkwall as a uniformed police officer. That was six months ago and in that time he soon got used again to the cycle of drunks, domestic abuse, assaults and small everyday tragedies that made up the warp and weft of the lives of those who had not received the start in life that most law abiding people take for granted.

Finishing his coffee, Roland Clett girded his loins for the day ahead and he buttoned up his shirt. Today was his first day back as a promoted inspector. He locked the front door and started his old green Polo and headed towards the Burgh Road Police Station in Kirkwall. It was 8:10am.

*   *   *

Trevor de Vries met the rest of the dig team in front of the Pierowall hostel where the van would take them to the Bay of Noup. Ten out of the eleven volunteers were waiting.

"Good morning men. I see Mr Byrd has decided not to join us."

"Yes Professor, he went to Kirkwall last night. Haven't seen him this morning."

"I see. Well I have to say that I am disappointed and a little surprised by this unusual lack of commitment. A little out of character, wouldn't you say? Well, he will just have to catch up with us. Let us to the dig."

On arrival at the Bay of Noup, the team were getting their gear together. De Vries tried Dominic Byrd's mobile; no answer, but not unusual, given the intermittent mobile phone coverage in the area. He saw something white on the rocks. He picked it up. It was a human tooth with some pink bloody tissue material still connected to the root. He put it in his pocket. There was a shout from one of the volunteers.

"Professor, there's a mobile ringing."

De Vries stopped trying Dominic's mobile and went to investigate. "It's stopped now."

At first there was nothing amiss. The ditch containing Dominic Byrd's body faced out to sea and couldn't be seen from the path down from the van. De Vries tried Dominic's number once more.

"It's ringing again. Over there."

The team walked to where the sound of the phone was coming from and saw the body lying covered in dried blood and sandy soil. The face of the body was completely unrecognisable and was smashed to a muddy pulp. Eyes, nose and mouth indistinguishable from the general grey and brown mess that was

15

just contained within the intact part of the skull. Furthermore, seagulls had eaten some of the brain matter exposed on the faceless body. De Vries knew that it was Dominic. He had recognised the ringtone that was coming from the pocket of the dead boy's jeans and he would have known Dominic's physique anywhere. The others did not at first know what they were looking at. They did not seem to recognise that the pile of clothes and the mess in front of them was a human body. There was nothing left of the face except a blackening void and the blood had turned brown in the morning sun. Light rain was falling.

Silently, the group moved slowly, looking over each other's shoulders, gently pushing forward to see the body, touching the arm of the person in front to softly make space; giving tacit approval to make the comparison with their own condition. The individuals at the front of the group would move away after a minute, exchanging places for others to see. Then they would return, mumbling incoherently. The result was a group that appeared more animal than human, a quiet collective movement, shuffling in and out of the scene. There were no raised voices, only a murmuring and the gentle sound of their breathing. Trevor de Vries knew exactly who he was looking at.

Dominic.

He said the name softly, without realising he was making any sound.

"Dominic."

The others passed it on, whispering.

"Dominic."

De Vries analysed the situation at the dig site for himself. One or two of the younger team members' whispering had turned to whimpering and he found the noise distracting. He was instantly thinking of the dig funding and of timescales. Any significant delay, or even, God forbid, an end to the dig for the season, would be a disaster for his presentation and the conference bookings he had made. It was too late in his career to have a setback like this.

He calmed the team down and devolved tasks in order to give him time to think. How could he get the maximum amount of data from the site before the police came and stopped work? He would have to tell them of course, but for now he decided to wait. This would buy him time. He had photographs taken of all areas of the dig and he instructed everyone to get as much from their designated plots as possible before the police arrived. He convinced most of them that the police would only be interested in the area around the body. He had a bit of trouble with some of the newer volunteers who were starting to complain. They were clearly distressed and had difficulty following instructions. De Vries identified a few of his older and trusted hands and managed to get them to work on the aspects of the site he had prioritised. The others who were less reliable, who could not focus on the more sensitive areas of the site, were tasked with more menial jobs.

At 8:43 he moved to an area on the site where the reception was good and phoned the police.

"Professor Trevor de Vries here. I am the team leader at the Bay of Noup archeological dig on Westray and I wish to report a death."

He listened to the response.

"No, I am not sure of the identity. It may be a missing member of my dig team. There may be foul play given the condition of the body. The head has been badly mutilated."

He felt the chill wind on his cheek.

"Yes, the grid reference is hotel yankee four one four five zero one."

He was told to wait for police officers to attend and that this might take several hours given the remote location."

"Yes, of course I will ensure that nothing is touched."

He ended the call and crouched down beside Dominic's body. De Vries had said that he would not touch the crime scene, but he could not stop himself gently laying a hand on Dominic's bloody shoulder, just to say goodbye. Dominic would understand. De Vries took his trowel, and quickly worked around the body as

17

carefully and as respectfully as he could. He reckoned he had about two and a half hours to get the last pieces of data from the dig before the arrival of the police. He did not account for the Westray special constables.

*　　*　　*

Roland Clett sat down for the first time at his allocated desk, an old civil service office desk, incongruous in the modern police station. It was covered with the stains of old coffee cups and ink and scratches. Some of the circular marks appeared to be concentric and there were crude lines that hinted of images. He thought he could see a lion. Someone had carved the wood in the corners so that there were straight gouges on the top and the side of the desk. The surface layer of wood was starting to lift off in places, showing the chipboard underneath. The desk was uneven on the floor, so Clett took a piece of paper and folded it until it was the correct size. He bent down to place the paper under the short leg of the table and noticed more graffiti on the underside of the desk:
'Tommy fucked, Helga carved'.
He smiled. Where had this desk come from? He reckoned that it had been brought from the old Watergate police station, inherited from other days. He made the desk even, changed the seat for one with working castors and sat down. Reaching into his pocket he took a pebble from the North Wick beach on Papay and placed it on the desk. Out of the window, he looked west out over the Peerie Sea and to Wideford Hill. Behind him, to the south and east, he could just about see the spire of St Magnus Cathedral lit with strong sunshine, a sight so familiar that sometimes it became invisible. Inside there was the usual office babble. People exchanged pleasantries and congratulated him on his promotion.

The force on Orkney consisted of one Chief Inspector: Maggie McPhee, one inspector: Clett himself, six sergeants and

18

twenty three constables. In addition, there were a number of special constables scattered around the islands who were the first line of contact. There was also local admin support, and further assistance could be called upon from from Northern Constabulary in Aberdeen and Inverness. Forensic and technical support was available from SPSA, the Scottish Police Support Service based in Dundee, three hundred miles to the south. The Orkney area boasted an unusually low rate of crime and the emphasis of police activities was on community relations and support.

At 8:45 Sergeant Norman Clouston entered Clett's office. "Excuse me *Inspector*."

Clouston placed the emphasis on the last word. Both men smiled, given that they had known each other for over twenty years.

"Yes *Sergeant.*"

"Just received a report from emergency services of a possible murder on Westray."

Clett scanned the printout that Clouston handed him.

"The Bay of Noup?"

"Aye, at an archeological dig site."

"Not a 5000 year old murder?"

"No inspector, I don't think so."

Clett put the report on his desk.

"I'll give Archie Drever a call and get the Special Constables to start the ball rolling while we arrange an investigation team. So, this is what it is like being an inspector."

"Aye, an' wait 'til you see the paperwork."

*   *   *

Special Constable Archie Drever was tending his prize Charolais herd at Garth Farm when his mobile went off. He recognised his friend's voice.

"Roland; or should I say, *Inspector*."

"Thanks Archie, very kind of you; this is official."

"Ok, what's the story?"

"There has been a report of a body at the Bay of Noup."

"At the dig site?"

"Aye. Do you know anyone up there?"

"Aye well I've seen the dig leader and a bunch of young guys there. Harmless enough. They've been staying mostly in the hostel for over a month and they get the ferry back and forward to Kirkwall for a bit o' nightlife. The mannie in charge thinks a lot of himself. He camps, and runs in the morning and dresses like something out of Raiders of the Lost Ark. What's his name again, De Smet? No, sounds more Dutch; maybe De Jong, De Vries, something common."

"OK Archie, thanks. The normal procedure would be to have the local constable organise a response, so could you get Special Constables John Leask and Angela Fedotova to attend the site to secure it and keep bystanders away? We are looking for confirmation of the report and to tape off the area; take names and addresses and statements, but the main idea is to preserve the site. Keep me up to date; anything you think significant, just give me a call."

"I can be there in ten minutes."

"Just a wee word Archie, it might be messy. The body is badly mutilated. Keep an eye on Angela and on young John."

"I wouldn't worry about John. He saw his fair share when he was in Afghanistan, and Angela is a trooper. Leave it to me Roland."

*   *   *

The killer looked at the haggard face in the mirror; the red eyes hidden in pallid skin, dishevelled hair and stubble; he would almost not recognise himself. He walked out of the waiting room toilet and waited until all the cars boarded the MV Earl Thorfinn. The big red clock at the pier head read 8:58am. A vehicle swerved past him on to the ferry blaring its horn - the silver BMW that swerved to avoid him at Pierowall last night. Again the music.

That song, what was that song?

The driver cursed The killer through the open window. He felt his pulse throb in his temple and he wiped perspiration from his forehead. He avoided eye contact as he collected his embarkation ticket and went up to the passenger lounge and took a place in a corner. It was warm in the cabin and he continued to sweat. The ferry departed on time, and to his relief he saw that it was full of shoppers, young people on business, and a few other backpackers. He could keep a low profile. The purser took his money without looking at him, being more concerned with how an elderly islander sitting next to him was managing with her ticket. There ensued a long conversation about summer ferry timetables and her sciatica. It would take an hour and a half to get to Kirkwall. He only needed to avoid attention.

Patsy Cline. Yes. Something after … searching for me.

A little girl of about four came up to him:

"Why are you all dirty? Does your mummy not have a washing machine?"

He forced a smile and mumbled a response. His pulse raced, pounding in his temples. The girl's mother quickly snatched her away.

"I'm so sorry."

"No problem."

"You shouldn't talk to strangers."

"But he was all dirty."

*   *   *

The Bay of Noup came into view as Archie Drever turned a bend. The site could not be seen from the road and the immediate view was of the nearby farm. He drove through the yard and along the track to the dig site. When he got close he saw several of the volunteers on their knees working, brushing stones free of sand. He couldn't see any signs of a body and wondered if he was at the correct place. He got out of his vehicle and as he got closer, he could see a man in a leather hat and photographer's waistcoat bending over a shallow pit, working at a piece of ground. He saw a body in the pit where the man was working.

"Hoi! You! What are you doing? Get away from there."

De Vries turned to face Drever who called to the other people working at the site.

"All of you! Stop working immediately!"

"And you are?"

"Special Constable Drever; you must all move away from the area."

De Vries addressed the team.

"All right men, just carry on."

Some of the dig team moved about and Drever could see their footprints in the disturbed ground. Already he could anticipate problems for forensics. As the man with the leather hat stood up, Drever could see the body below him. He drew a sharp intake of breath. He could see part of the head with no recognisable facial features. He composed himself.

"You will not carry on, you will all stop work immediately or you will face charges of obstruction of justice."

The team started moving away from the site, whispering amongst themselves.

Archie approached the man with the leather hat.

"Are you Mr de Vries?"

"Professor de Vries if you don't mind."

"What do you think you are doing? Come away from there. What are you doing next to that body?"

"How dare you take that tone with me. Don't you realise …"

Drever reached out to take the arm of the man in the leather hat and direct him away from the body. De Vries avoided Drever's grip, but grunted and slowly moved away from the shallow pit.

"Professor, the main team of officers will arrive from Kirkwall as soon as they can get here. It *was* you who reported the death to the police?"

"Please don't waste my time. I shall wait until someone in authority arrives."

"Do you know the name of the young man whose body lies over there?"

"I decline to comment."

He lifted his head and looked away from Drever and towards the team.

"Why are you still working in this area around this body? Professor …"

De Vries continued to talk through Drever.

"I will not respond to such questions from a junior officer. I want you out of my way so my team and I can carry on this crucial scientific work."

Drever raised his voice just a little.

"Professor, you must not carry on any further work until you are authorised by the Senior Investigating Officer."

"And when will I see the Senior Investigating Officer?"

"Whenever he gets here from Kirkwall."

De Vries rolled his eyes.

"And until then?"

"Until then nothing is touched."

"This is not good enough. This is holding me back. Out of my way; I am going to carry on with my work."

De Vries turned to the team.

"Men, we shall continue with our allocated tasks."

The members of the team looked at each other; one or two stood. Drever addressed them once more.

"You will remain clear of this crime scene. I repeat, anyone further tampering with evidence at this site may be charged with interfering with evidence and wasting police time."

He turned to de Vries.

"Professor you will sit down now and you will not attempt to carry on work at this site or you will be arrested."

"You, and what power do you have, junior constable?"

De Vries sneered and some of the team members sniggered.

Drever lowered the tone of his voice and stood an inch away from de Vries' nose. He spoke slowly and deliberately and there was a menace in his voice.

"I am instructing you to sit down and let me do my job. You will be interviewed by senior officers when they arrive and I suggest you adopt a more helpful tone; and I do have the power of arrest."

De Vries sniffed and turned away, lifting his tablet computer.

"Just damned incompetence!"

Some of the team members whispered to each other.

Archie Drever was joined by Special Constables John Leask and Angela Fedotova. Leask, 22, a local man, recently out of the army, was new to the job, and was committed and conscientious. Fedotova was English born, and had lived in the community for many years. She had been a special constable and had experience in traditional rural policing matters. They had all seen death at various times in their work; ordinary deaths in homes or farming accidents, and Leask had seen bodies in Afghanistan, but they were not prepared for the scene in front of them. At the sight of the body, they both struggled to control their nerves.

Drever took the lead.

"C'mon, let's get on with it."

Fedotova and Drever cleared the dig team from the area and began the interviews. Leask started to unwind a red boundary tape that read:

'POLICE DO NOT CROSS'.

Drever found a spot with decent reception and called Clett.

"Roland, this is a mess. There is the body of a young man, possibly in his twenties, badly mutilated. The face has been bludgeoned and no facial features remain. The remains of the head have been exposed to the elements. It rained last night and seagulls have been busy."

"Thanks Archie. Definitely a murder site then?"

" Aye, but there's more. The archaeological dig team have continued work around the body and have severely compromised the site. Forensic work will be a nightmare. The area surrounding the body has been contaminated by the dig activities. As well as the damage caused by the seagulls to the body, there are footprints everywhere. Some of the blood and body matter has been stepped on and spread around, and it will be a job to separate out which site traces were from the time of the murder and which were caused by the dig team. The dig team are still here but we have moved them away from the site of the body. There are ten young males between sixteen and twenty-five and some are fairly traumatised. The team leader is Trevor de Vries. Doesn't half fancy himself. He might be trouble, but he's out of the way for now."

"Looks as if we have our work cut out for us."

"Aye. When do you think you will get here Roland?"

"Norman Clouston is arranging transport right now. I'll let you know. How are Angela and young John?"

"They are a bit shaky, but they are getting on with it."

"Ok Archie. Thanks. Talk later."

Clett shouted through to the sergeant's desk.

"Sergeant Clouston, could you assemble the duty team please, and I think this might require the use of a helicopter. I need to see if the Chief Inspector will approve it. In the meantime, can you see if one is free at Kirkwall Airport? Also, give Forensics and ICT support a call at SPSA to get a Scene Examination team here. Call Northern Constabulary in Inverness."

"Sure thing, Inspector."

"Forensic support and the CID team at Inverness will take a few hours to arrive, but we can get started with the initial non-intrusive measures using local resources."

*   *   *

Drever turned to one of the team members who appeared to be the most composed.

"Hi, I'm Special Constable Archie Drever. Can you tell me your name please?"

"Rodger McMillan."

"How are you feeling Rodger?"

"Pretty shaken up. You don't see one of your mates killed every day."

"No you don't. You're doing ok. Rodger. Can you tell me whose body that is?"

"It is Dominic Byrd."

"B – Y – R - D?"

"Yes."

"Ok; and how long has he been at the site?"

"We all started at the same time, about five weeks ago."

"Do you know where he is from?"

"No, down south somewhere in England."

"Can you tell me anything more about him?"

"He was great. At the beginning, we didn't rate him. The rest of us are either studying archaeology or have got our degrees. He was a beginner, but he took to it like a duck to water."

"And how did you find the body?"

Rodger told Drever about the phone ringing.

"It was horrible. Professor de Vries instructed us to carry on working."

"Hmm. Thanks, and can you tell me when was the last time you saw Dominic alive?"

"He was here the day before yesterday, but he didn't come to the pub that night. He took yesterday off, so I haven't seen him since the dig activity stopped at about 5:30pm the day before yesterday."

"Do you know where he has been?"

"Some of us get the ferry to Kirkwall for a bit of a change, so maybe he was there."

"And do you know if he had any particular friends there?"

"Not really. I didn't know him that well outside the dig."

"OK Rodger, here is my mobile number if you need to call me. Do you have Dominic's number?"

"Sure, can I text it to you?"

"Yes please. Thanks for the information; some other officers will take a statement from you later on, and you might like to take it easy over the next while. You and your friends have all had a significant shock and you may experience flashbacks and other symptoms. There will be counsellors here who will tell you more."

Drever could see the significant features of the site despite the contamination, in particular the position of the body which did not appear to have been moved. The fingerprint and forensic team would clarify any possibility of evidence collection. He photographed the fresh tyre marks around the scene. Forensics would do all this again, but they might take time to get on site and there was the danger of material attrition. Further contamination was still possible. Fresh crime scene data was crucial.

Drever was getting a feel for the site – the lie of it. In the salt air he could still smell the blood and the faeces that had emitted from the body post mortem. He saw the splashes of the body matter on the rocks, clear despite the contamination. This was a scene of uncontrolled violence. Drever felt that there was little point in looking for a murder weapon. A gun or a knife would be out of the question. He could see where the assailant had stood or kneeled in the hint of a shadow in the blood and body matter spray pattern. The attack was from a very close position. This act was personal and not that of a calculated killer. They would have seen each other's eyes in this interaction, they would have smelled each other's breath and fear before the blow that would have taken away the victim's senses. It was likely that a nearby rock was used, or perhaps one of the dig tools. Drever, a volunteer special

27

constable, was not qualified to make any of these assessments, but he had an instinctive perception despite lack of rank or formal training. He knew from previous experience what a murder scene looked like. But now he had to put his thoughts in the background and follow procedure. If a court case was to come of all this, it was the procedure that they would query. The scene was contaminated enough without some unqualified volunteer improvising, which in the eyes of his superiors he was.

Drever called Fedotova and Leask together.

"That's the boundary tape in place Archie. Is the zone large enough?"

"Looks ok John. The full time officers might move it later, but it's fine for now. Angela, we will need a list of the tools on site and get photographs of each one. The full time officers will do it again. We want to capture the positions of any possible evidence as soon as we can. Be careful not to touch anything. It will be up to the Crime Scene Examination Team to assess the actual viability of any of the tools as being the murder weapon. Feel free to photograph anything you see fit."

"What about this weather Archie? It could rain at any time."

"So tell me something new Angela. This is Orkney."

The three special constables smiled for the first time since they arrived on the site.

"We will need an awning to cover the body."

"Of course Angela."

Leask spoke up.

"My Mum has a large awning we used at a party at the weekend."

"A party? Outside? in Orkney?"

"I know. My Mum's nuts."

"Ok. Thanks John, The awning would be great, but I don't think you should leave the site."

"No problem. I'll see if she can bring it."

"Thanks John. I think we should get the list of names and addresses and make sure these lads are ok."

Chapter 3

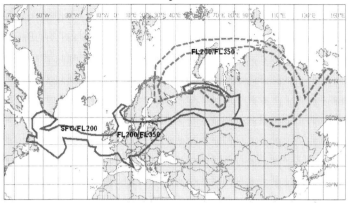

Wednesday, 21st April 9.20 am.

The green and blue tapes and posts of the dig were overlaid with another series of black and yellow tapes laid down by the special constables. The competing sets of markers offered a confusing scene to anyone passing, like layers in time reflected in sedimentary strata. These markers signified a separation of the different activities of the investigation of living and of death; the investigation of new death and of old death.

*　　　*　　　*

Sergeant Norman Clouston called Anna McDonald at Kirkwall Air Traffic Control.

"Good morning Anna. Are you enjoying this fine morning?"

"Ah, It's yourself Norman. Yes it is indeed a lovely morning. What is it that I can be doing for you?"

"Well I could start by just listening to your beautiful Lewis accent."

"Och away with you, you old devil. I have a job to be doing, and I don't want you to be wasting my time, Norman Clouston."

"Oh well I'll just have to tell you my business and look for another opportunity to waste your time."

"Ok Norman, what is it that you would be wanting?"

"Tell me Anna: is the helicopter available this morning? We need to get a team out to Westray urgently. Or are we going to be affected by the volcanic ash situation?"

"Well Norman, the short answer is yes, you are most definitely going to be affected. The current forecast will not allow for any traffic in or out of Kirkwall for the next 6 hours at the very least. As you will be aware, there have only been intermittent opportunities to fly in this area since Saturday."

"Ah, Anna, that is not great news. No flights at all? What about the scheduled Twin Otter?"

"No flights at all Norman. I'll fax you the latest transmission from the MET Office."

"That would be great. Can you let me know when aircraft are flying again?"

"Of course I will Norman."

"Ok Anna, thanks for your help. I'll just have to call another time to listen to your dulcet tones."

"Away with you, Norman Clouston."

Clouston read the transmission from the fax machine:

"The continued presence of volcanic ash in airspace around Shetland, Orkney and Northern Ireland has led to the cancellation of all services to and from Sumburgh, Kirkwall and the Northern Isles."

Clouston logged on to the Met Office ASHTAM website and could see the coverage of the volcanic ash plume over northern Europe. It was clear that there would be no flights from Kirkwall today. With the helicopter grounded, he had to consider water transport. The next scheduled ferry to Westray would not leave until 10:45. It would in any case be a 90 minute crossing. He phoned Harry Stout, the harbour master.

"Harry, it's Norman Clouston here."

"Hello Norman. What's cooking?"

"Nothin' much. I'm calling on official business."

"Ok shoot."

"You know this ash cloud, well we can't get air travel to Westray and we need to get an incident team out there toute suite."

"What's happened?"

"I can't say just now, but it is serious."

"Ok, so you want a fast boat. For how long would you be wanting this boat?"

"A few days, or until this ash cloud clears."

"Aye, if it clears."

"Aye well, we have to take it a day at a time. I was thinking about the RNLI Margaret Foster."

"Well Norman, there is a new water taxi, the Celtic Voyager, faster and ideal for getting in and out of the smaller island piers. The sea trials are now complete, but it is not due to go into commercial service until June."

"That sounds ideal Harry. Is it available?"

"Give me a few minutes."

Harry Stout made his enquiries. From his window, he could see the Celtic Voyager moored in the harbour with its engine running.

*   *   *

At the SPSA Forensic Services headquarters, Sanja Dilpit and Irene Seath walked across the car park in the Dundee sunshine carrying coffee in large cardboard cups. Irene showed her electronic pass to the reader and Sanja raised her voice to be heard over the noise of the Marketgait traffic. Irene held open the door.

"Bayern Munich last night. Shite!"

"Whit?"

"Well they wur, wur they no?"

Irene pressed the button on the lift for the third floor.

"How can you say that. Whit dae ye ken aboot it? How many times hiv Ah said, ye canny compare oor fitba' tae European fitba'."

"Bollocks darlin'. We've got African and who knows whit nationalities playing in oor teams noo. These urny wee boys frae the Dundee estates onymair. This is like global capitalism like. This is fitba' as a symbol o' the dominant narrative o' the planet, ken."

"Here look, keep it in the park doll, Hae some mer o' yer coffee."

Sanja drank a mouthful from the sharp hole in the plastic lid as they went into the lift.

"Christ that's hot."

She sucked in air to cool her mouth and continued.

"Listen darlin' Ah'm tellin' ye. Fitba' is a macro representation o' the world as we know it."

"Naw, naw, naw Fitba's just entertainment; just a bunch o' overpaid wee boys running aboot efter a ba'. Some o' them ur just better at it than the rest o' them. Yur theory is pure fallacious. It is bollocks. Just 'cos we share wan particular domain o' understandin', disnae mean that we will underston' and mutually share the concepts that each o' us think valuable."

"Whit ur ye talkin' aboot hen? Ah'm talkin' aboot fitba'."

"Naw, yer no. That's exactly ma point. Yer makin claims fur fitba' that ur purely spurious like."

"Spurious? Who dae ye think ye ur talking tae hen?"

"Come on, there's nae link between fitba' an' global capitalism. That's jist argument by example. Two parallel but unconnected domains. If situation X happens in wan, and situation Y happens in the other, then they ur the same. Naw; sorry, it's bollocks."

"Yeah, yeah, yeah, but whit aboot the money? Ye canny say that money hisnae hid an effect oan the game. You yersel' said that players were overpaid. Onyway, Ah'm no talkin' aboot any kind o' causal connection. Ah'm talkin' aboot Fitba' as a metaphor fur the human condition."

The bell in the lift rang and they went out towards the open plan office.

"Aw, here we go. Even if it is a metaphor it his tae hae substance. Whit dis fitba' as a metaphor say aboot the state o' the world – nuthin! Ye canny say it is a metaphor withoot justification; it is still spurious. Fitba' is aboot a buch o' wee guys runnin' aboot efter a ba'."

"Ye jist dinny get it. The beauty o' the game is its ain justification. Ye dinny need onythin' else."

"But, even if it is beautiful, there's still nae validity in the claim that it is somehow linked tae some phenomenon in the greater world. There's nae connection hen. Truth is wan thing. Beauty is another thing. Fitba' is wan thing, the movement o' world macro narratives is another. Full stop. Jeeze."

As they arrived at the desk they shared, Irene's phone rang."

"Scene Examination Team, Irene Seath speaking."

Irene was silent for quite a long time.

"Who is it?" Sanja mouthed.

Irene shut her eyes tight and put her finger in her ear and listened intently to the call.

Sanja did not offer further interruptions.

"Ok. Thanks. I've got that."

She made notes on a pad.

"Can you email details as they come available please? We can pick them up en route. We will leave as soon as we book out our car and the site kit."

Irene hung up.

"That wis a request for Forensic and ICT support. A suspected murder on Westray in Orkney. No much information jist noo except mobile phone photographs o' the body. Available data is bein' emailed. The ash cloud has grounded flights, so we have to drive up there. We'll hae tae catch the 4:45 crossing at Scrabster."

"Naw we canny."

"How no?"

"'Cos o' the volcanic ash business, the Hamnavoe is away tae pick up UK citizens in Bergen."

"How do you know that?"

"'Cos Ah like, listen tae the news, ye ken? John Swinney made an announcement in the Scottish Parliament."

"OK, we will have tae make other arrangements."

"Does Keillor ken?"

"He is talkin' tae the Kirkwall Station jist noo. We huv tae sign oot the forensics and pathology site kit frae stores. Huv ye got yer jammies an' yer toothbrush?"

"Always darlin', always."

Sanja took Irene's cereal bar and gulped it down.

"Look hen, that's ma cereal bar."

"Aye, I'll buy ye anither oan the road tae Scrabster."

*   *   *

Inspector Roland Clett scribbled notes as he held the phone between his ear and his shoulder.

"Understood Dr Keillor, we will talk later when the situation is clearer."

Clett put the phone down and took a sip of now lukewarm tea. The cup dripped tea on to the desk, adding to the patterns of rings and stains created long before. He looked at the blank whiteboard with the words 'Bay of Noup' written in red marker. How would this board be filled?

> '...information which is obtained in
> the course of a criminal investigation
> and may be relevant to the
> investigation is recorded'

Clett brought to mind the standard methods enshrined in the Criminal Investigation and Procedures Act (1996). This board, all the photographs, videos, interview records –

> *'...any material which is obtained in the course of a criminal investigation and may be relevant to the investigation is retained'.*

This making of a history of the investigation had already begun. All these artefacts would evidence the story that would be told. The story that would end in someone going to prison for murder.

Clett saw this systematic approach to an investigation as a siege; it was inelegant. As a result of this approach, much of what would be retrieved, certainly the early information, would be useless, but experience and practice showed that inconsequential pieces of data could turn an investigation around. Clett had mixed feelings about this method. He knew it was necessary to show an objective methodology, and he would never admit to reacting to a hunch, but privately he relied on the subtle connections in a case that would usually become apparent when daydreaming, or when near to sleep. At these times, he would experience insights relating sometimes diverse pieces of information that were not obvious to him in a more alert state.

Now, though, at the start of an investigation, information was in short supply. Every scrap of data was collected. Through repeated sifting and analysis of what was in front of them, there was an organic process where the narrative of events would rise through the noise, like the developing of photographic film, the picture would appear through the chemical murk. The question was always whether the resulting image was truly grown from the evidence or whether it was drawn by virtue of the implicit assumptions and wishes of the investigating parties.

Chief Inspector Maggie McPhee's window looked out over the Peerie Sea. Clett and Clouston knocked and entered. "Gentlemen, what have you got for me? Before you start, Inspector Clett, you will be the SIO. Interesting first day on the job wouldn't you say?"

"Yes Chief Inspector."

Clett caught McPhee's eye and smiled.

"Can we talk about resource issues?"

"Go ahead Roland."

"We should use the incident room."

"Agreed."

"… and we will need a facility for the Forensics Crime Scene Examiners and local information gathering. Do we really want it on Westray? Transport will be difficult."

Sergeant Norman Clouston leaned forward.

"We could get the mobile incident unit from Inverness. It could be here in a few hours."

"Not really; not until the Hamnavoe is back in service."

"What about the short Pentalina crossing to St Margaret's Hope?"

"Right enough Norman, but even that's going to hold us up a bit, and we would still have the problem of where it would be sited. It would have to be the car park at Pierowall."

Maggie McPhee looked at both men.

"I don't see a problem. First floor incident room for all information gathering and site management and send kilo two and kilo six or seven to the site - the large transit should accommodate site activities and Crime Scene Examiners, and the 4WD for general transport. Don't bother with the mobile unit from Inverness. Back this up with on line evidence sharing, conference calling and that should sort it."

"And Press?"

"Use the Watergate steps as usual."

The Sheriff Court steps next to the old police station was one of the traditional locations for public press meetings that required television cameras when weather permitted. McPhee carried on.

"…or use my office if you like, or our car park. Anywhere that suits. We will cross that bridge when we come to it. You were asking about a helicopter?"

"Yes Chief Inspector, but it seems that all air traffic is grounded for the meantime due to the Volcanic Ash situation."

"Good. I won't have to worry about funding that. Do you have another transport option?"

"Yes Chief Inspector, I have just got the ok from the owners to use 'Celtic Voyager', a new fast water taxi that should do the trick."

"Thanks Norman. I take it that ICT and SPSA support is in hand."

"I'm on to that Chief Inspector."

"Thank you. Let me know what you need from me."

"Will do Chief Inspector. Thanks."

*   *   *

The killer went out on the deck of the MV Earl Thorfinn. He leaned against the painted handrail and shivered in the still air and the sweat cooled on his body. The smoke from the funnels lifted vertically into the sky as if the boat was at rest. The sea was like glass, reflecting the frozen clouds. He moved about on the deck and there was no wind. As he settled with his thoughts, there was a quiet singing just beyond the rumble of the ships engines. He looked out to sea. There, not twenty yards away, was a pod of about twenty seals sunning themselves on a rock. They were looking at him and he caught the eye of two bulls. They turned to each other and roared.

*   *   *

Clett stood in front of the empty whiteboard in the incident room to give a short telephone conference briefing. As they connected, Constable Nancie Keldie ticked off their names.

"Good morning everyone. Forensic Scene Examiners Sanja Dilpit and Irene Seath here."

"Good Morning, I'm Inspector Roland Clett. I am the designated SIO for this case. Already connected are your manager Dr Keillor and Detective Inspector Tony Nelson from the Inverness CID. As you all probably know, the body of a young man has been found at an archaeological dig site at the Bay of Noup in the north of Westray. We do not know the time of death, or the cause of death. There is currently some confusion regarding the condition of the crime scene. Special Constables on site are controlling access as we speak. We have just become aware of this body. We do not yet have a suspect.

Our initial task is to preserve the site for the SPSA team who may not arrive for some time. We will have to photograph and document any aspects of the site that may deteriorate in the period up to their arrival. We will take witness statements and names and addresses. We will set up an incident room on Westray to deal with local needs, and another here at Burgh Road for press briefings and strategic planning. Any queries from the press or the public should be directed initially through Sergeant Norman Clouston.

The SPSA team will be delayed because of the restrictions caused by the Volcanic Ash Cloud situation. We will have helicopter and fixed wing flights via the scheduled Loganair Islander service when allowed to do so by Air Traffic Control. In the meantime, we have the use of a water taxi called the 'Celtic Voyager' that is available now at Kirkwall Harbour.

Have I missed anything? Norman? Chief Inspector?, Dr Keillor in Dundee?"

"Yes, Dr Keillor here. Two of our Crime Scene Examiners, Sanja Dilpit and Irene Seath, are driving to Scrabster with the standard forensic murder scene kit which should be relayed asap to the murder scene. With the Hamnavoe out of service, I wonder if you could arrange some other transport from Scrabster?"

Norman Clouston spoke up.

"Don't see a problem. I think we can get the Celtic Voyager to Scrabster. Can we get their contact details?"

"Aye, this is Irene Seath here. Sergeant, we are able to pick up emails to the SPSA support address. If you email it I'll get our mobile numbers to you."

Keillor continued.

"Thank you. Returning to the forensics issues, obviously there is a possibility of the attrition of forensic material. We will be available for any remote forensic or IT backup that is required. The protocols state that site activity by non SPSA staff is not normally permitted and can lead to evidence corruption. However, because of the special nature of this situation, site deterioration and the remote location, some intervention may be sanctioned with advice from this office. Please discuss with us if any such intervention outwith the SLA parameters is being considered. Our immediate response e-mail address and emergency helpline is available as per standard procedures in the Support Level Agreement documentation. Please use these to send us any relevant photographs or other data where you require specialist assessment. A secure server will be made available for evidence sharing. Please email myself or one of my colleagues for secure access giving your warrant number and the approval reference from your senior officer. We will also facilitate web conferencing. The on-site team will be trying out a new technique of spatter radius analysis that will supply more detailed physical information about the assailant as described in my recent paper that I can email to you gentlemen."

Clett looked at Maggie McPhee, raising his hands in question. She shrugged.

"Thank you Dr Keillor."

"Inspector?"

"Yes Chief Inspector."

"Inspector, as you said, Sergeant Clouston will be in the role of local liaison, but I would like to be appraised of any information given to the press. It also may be appropriate to get other officers from Northern Constabulary in Inverness involved."

"Detective Inspector Tony Nelson here. We would of course be happy to offer any support we could to our friends in Orkney."

Maggie McPhee looked to Clett for a response, but he remained silent.

"Thank you DI Nelson", said Chief Inspector McPhee.

Clett responded:

"Thank you Chief Inspector. Anyone else?"

Norman Clouston spoke.

" Inspector, the Airwave radio reception is patchy on Westray. I think we should bring the repeater."

"Thank you Sergeant. Ideal. Is that about it?"

There was silence.

"OK. There are reports from Special Constable Fedotova of distressed young people from the dig team that might need some support; Norman, could you please ask the local medical centre and social work office to prepare to supply some counselling?"

Clett directed an operational hazard analysis discussion with notes taken by Clouston. They considered transport, scene movements, health and safety and victim support issues. No firearms were involved to their knowledge, but other weapons were considered. This live document would be updated as the investigation evolved and only be closed once the case was closed.

Having collected the necessary hardware, laptops, Airwave comms repeater, and sample kits, the team drove to the Harbour, a few minutes away. They boarded the Celtic Voyager and left Kirkwall Harbour at 9:38.

*   *   *

" Whit aboot poetry then?"

Irene was sitting in the passenger seat, knitting.

"Whit ur you oan girl?"

"Poetry is by its nature extended metaphor and surely ye are no gonny tell me that it disny tell us onythin' aboot the world."

"Ye're never goin' tae put fitba' on the same level as poetry."

"That's exactly whit Ah am de'in doll. Fitba' is a sublime statement of human endeavour; the operation o' the individual within a set of boundaries, how they must enter intae a dialogue with the gemme, with their team mates, and wi' the opposing team. It is the quintessence o' the human struggle. Look at Beckham in the England Greece game in 2001 when he equalised in injury time. He kicked the ba' wi' his right foot frae a free kick and bent it intae the top corner o' the Greek net. Pure poetry. Ye cin look it up on YouTube."

"An' yer sayin' that Beckham is a poet."

"He is. No wi' wurds, but wi' his fitba'."

"Ah'm tellin' ye, jist a bunch o' wee boys."

"An' that is called argument by repetition."

"Whit's that ye said?"

"Ah said it's argument by repetition."

Both girls laughed.

"Time fur a coffee Sanja?"

"Aye, an' ye owe me a cereal bar."

Chapter 4

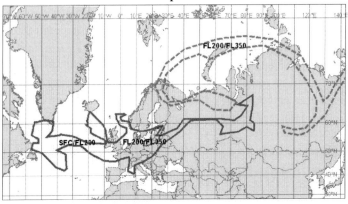

Wednesday, 21st April 10.02 am.

The engine noise of the 'Celtic Voyager' competed with the roar of the wind. Clett could just about make out his boss's voice. He shouted into the old Nokia.

"Maggie. There's a lot of confusing reports just now and it's difficult to see the wood for the trees. There is one report that the body had been washed up in the sea, another that there were two bodies, and that a silver car had been seen speeding away last night at Pierowall. We are going to have to keep the press advised to stop speculation."

"Ok Roland, leave the press to me. Just keep me up to date."

"No problem Maggie."

He looked into the sky as they headed north, skimming along on the smooth sea. High above, transported by winds caused by a mix of the rotation of the earth and the complex sea of rising and falling eddies of warm and cold air, the ash cloud moved, blown by vortices of warmth and fate. People wondered, in these clear blue skies, if the ash was really there; this invisible cloud that was causing so much havoc. Would it ever come to earth? Would everyone wake up and find cars and crops covered in this invisible ash; would the world be changed, or would it remain as a persisting threat high in the atmosphere?

Since returning to Orkney from Glasgow, Roland Clett had spent time in the Orkney Room at Kirkwall library, transcribing the memoirs of Archibald Clett of Canmore (1721-1799), an eighteenth century Orkney improver. Archibald Clett had attempted to write an Encyclopedia Orcadiana, a compendium of all things Orkney, based on the ideas of the French philosophes and encyclopédistes. All that remained of Archibald Clett's writings was in a collection of letters that were held in the Orkney Room archive. Clett carried photocopies of these letters for transcription. None of the responses from the many correspondents have yet been found.

He took out one of the letters and read it against the motion of the boat. The script was consistent, in an even hand, and to save paper had been written first from left to right, and then overwritten from top to bottom. Some of the letters had even more text written diagonally. When Clett first read these letters, he had difficulty deciphering the layered lines of text, but now he was able to interpret them and was building up a picture of a liberal and travelled man with interests in science, philosophy, the arts and in the development of Orkney. Clett had not yet worked out why Archibald Clett, a wealthy landowner with his own library, who wrote to Enlightenment luminaries Denis Diderot, David Hume, Benjamin Franklin and Adam Smith, had to resort to saving paper. He made a note to investigate the availability of paper on Orkney during this period, around 1783, the date of this current communication: when Orkney had experienced famine and its weather was then also affected by a volcanic eruption in Iceland.

The photocopy fluttered in the wind:

To Mr B. Franklin Esq.
Rue Raynouard, 66
Passy
France
August 23rd 1783
Dear Mr Franklin,

I should like to pursue the recent notions of your last letter to me regarding the current climactical anomalies. Here in these islands of Orkney we have seen reports of the tragical consequence of this meteorology. For some years we have lived with a famine that has caused the direst of consequences for the lives of the inhabitants of my islands. So when this most recent of disasters has befallen us, my countrymen have become desperate. Crops have failed and the poor beasts that were to have fed the people have died. Some of the souls on these islands have been reduced to eating kelp. The Norse language of older people is heard no longer, and the folk tell tales of children stolen by seals while they played. What tragedy that my lands, my Scapa, my little Mediterranea, has come to this.

There is a fear of Armageddon in the heat and dry fog. A pestilence of the throat has been visited on my people. The sun, although hot, does not dissipate the fog. Its rays do not appear. The countryside appears whitish grey, and the fog emits a strong odour. The fog is so dry, that it does not tarnish a looking glass and liquefying salts, it dries them.

My barometric glass has indicated an unusually high pressure of the air during this last summer, and a haziness has prevailed, such that our Hoy Hill is not discernible; and the appearance of the sun has been like a faint red ball of fire without a ray darting from it. I have read that travellers returning from Rome and other areas report similar effects.

Some of our natural philosophers have speculated upon the cause of this misfortune and there is a wide agreement that the origin is of a vulcanic nature, but the geographical source of this location is not agreed. Some say it originates upon the islands of Samoa, or indeed from southern Italy. I do not concur with these explications and I would assert that there is no satisfactory exposition of the translation of vulcanic matter from these southern areas of the globe.

I should like to propose another source upon the following reasoning. Consider that the earth rotates such that the sun rises in the east and sets to west. Thus any vapours created at a point on the earth and had flown high enough into the sky would wish to remain there while the earth rotated beneath it. To our position on the rotating earth, these vapours would appear as but a wind, high above us. This wind coming from the east would carry smoke and vapours until they fell again to earth. Furthermore, the latitude of the source of the vapour would stay the same since the earth rotates around a singular axis. Thus by examining the globe, we would look to a source of vulcanism to our east, and at a latitude close to our own. I have found three such sources. The first is in the region of Kamchatka, and the second is the far western regions of North America where I have heard are vulcanic mountains. One other place where such mountains exist is in Iceland, but it is further north and the smoke would have to travel almost around the globe. Is it possible that this dust has been lifted by the high winds over such an immense distance and fallen again to earth? If similar observations were to be reported from your country, this would provide evidence for this speculation.

I look forward to reading any thoughts you have on the matter.

I remain your Most Humble and Obedient Servant,
Archibald Clett of Canmore.

Roland Clett's own research had identified the Icelandic volcano Laki as the source of the eruption in 1783. It had had a significant effect on the crops and on parts of Orkney. Furthermore, the resulting death of livestock exacerbated the outcome on the population. Famine conditions were already causing profound misery to Orcadians.

The Celtic Voyager crashed in the waves and Clett was brought back to the present. He looked up and saw the colours of the homes of Pierowall over the prow. Over his right shoulder, he looked across the water to the nearby island of Papay and could see the western parks of his parents' farm lit momentarily by a shaft of sunlight.

Clett and his team arrived at Pierowall harbour on Westray at 10.05, leaving the Celtic Voyager to return to Kirkwall to pick up the psychological support team from the medical centre. Special Constable John Leask was waiting at the harbour.

"Hello Inspector, we've not met, I'm Special Constable John Leask."

"Hello John, I'm Roland Clett."

"Yes sir, I know. I'm very much looking forward to working with you."

"Yes John, it is nice to have you on the team. You've been three months on the job?"

"Yes sir"

"And before that?"

"Well, in the army and then as a paramedic in Aberdeen, and then a year helping out at my Mum's bed and breakfast."

"Your Mum is Jean Leask?"

"You know her?"

"Not personally. She was a few years behind me at school."

"I'll tell her I met you."

"Aye, say hello for me."

"The car is this way. The Bay of Noup is only a five minute drive."

When they arrived on site, Clett walked straight up to Archie Drever.

"Ok Archie, what have you got?"

"Well, according to the dig team, the body is that of Dominic Byrd, aged about twenty. He was a dig team member and arrived about five weeks ago. He's from England, possibly from a public school background and was well liked. There were no known arguments with other team members. No immediate indication of a motive. There is a mobile phone on the body – we left it there, but we have the number."

"Good Archie. We can pass it on to forensics."

The young people from the dig team were huddled together as the special constables spoke to each of them In turn. The team leader was away from the group and could be seen using a tablet computer.

Clett was offered a cup of tea by Mrs Jessie Sclater, who lived at Noup Farm, just a few yards from the dig site. Clett looked around and saw people in the group holding mugs of tea. Jessie was doing well with her thermos and tupperware box of biscuits, but Clett would have to ask Clouston to get some catering at the site. Clett politely declined the tea and thanked Mrs Sclater for her hard work.

"It's nae bother son. Jist look at these young things, they're a' in sic a state. Somebody his tae look oot fir them. Are you the mannie in charge then?"

"Aye Mrs Sclater, I'm Inspector Roland Clett."

"Aye you'd be Bill and Vera Clett's laddie. Ah ken you and your brother Russell fae Papay. How are your Mum and Dad? They are such a nice pair. Do they still run that farm? Whit are they keeping noo?"

"Thanks, Mum and Dad are fine; and Russell has the farm now and he has about ninety Jerseys."

"Aye, he his two bonny lassies his he no?"

"Aye, Sarah is fifteen and Carol is thirteen. They are at high school in Kirkwall."

"Fifteen and thirteen, eh; well, I remember them when they were born, peedie wee things. My they were bonny. Aye well his coos and his girls will be keeping him busy. But you have two boys as well. They'll be fine strapping laddies noo, I'll say."

"Aye, Magnus is working with computers in Glasgow, and Sandy is studying at Glasgow University."

"Computers is it, well they say there's good money in that business."

"Aye well, he does all right."

"Look son, Ah'll no keep ye. Ye've got important work tae dae. This is jist sic a terrible business. A murder on Westray. Whitever next? Mind me tae yer mum and dad, son."

"Aye Mrs Sclater, I'll do that. Oh, by the way Mrs Sclater, did you see anything last night?"

"Ah well mibbe son. I thocht there was a car engine, a petrol engine — no, a diesel engine. It wis late on when I went tae bed, but Ah looked oot the windae and Ah couldny see naethin – an it wis skyare moonlight[1], bright as ye like."

"What time was that?"

"Oh aboot quarter tae twelve. But that's no a' son. It might o been a nightmare, but there was an awfi scream. Ah'v never heard sic a sound. Ah thocht is wis a wild animal, it wis like a howling. Ah'm sorry son, but Ah didny go oot lookin' fur onythin'. Ah certainly wisna going aboot in the cauld in ma nightie efter hearin' somethin' like that."

---

[1] Skyare moonlight – bright clear moonlight

"Would you describe it as a human scream Mrs Sclater?"

"Ah couldny right say, but Ah suppose it could hae been son. It wis jist like a bad dream."

"And do you know what time this was?"

"Aye son, Ah woke up and looked at ma clock. It wis twenty tae twa. Dae ye think that wis the poor laddie being killed son?"

"I couldn't say Mrs Sclater."

"Ah hope it wisnae. It wis an awfi sound."

"Thanks very much Mrs Sclater. Will you be all right?"

"Aye son. Dinna fash."

"Ok Mrs Sclater, that's all I need to ask just now. A police officer will take a statement from you later on."

"Aye son, that's fine wi' me."

Clett nodded across the site to Drever who was talking intently with a few of the young dig team members, some clearly distressed. He would talk to one young person, and when they became embarrassed, or exhausted, or just out of information, Drever would place a hand on their shoulder. There would follow a minute or two of silence, and quietly, the young person would open up again and offer more information, or Drever would simply comfort the person he was talking to, not moving on until the person was settled.

Clett walked around the site and considered the different layers of archaeological and criminal evidence. He looked carefully again at the body. Like everyone else who saw the scene, he was shocked by the sight in front of him; the seeming everyday figure of a young man wearing jeans and a sweatshirt lying with his hands by his side, his face mashed to a pulp with visible bits of bone and peck marks left by the seagulls. He had an involuntary image of an empty crash helmet in his head, but he put it aside. There were no immediate moments of inspiration for him, only a deep sense of the pathos and unreality of the scene. He had seen murders many times in Glasgow, in flats with bare electric light bulbs, mattresses on the floor, and empty bottles or syringes lying

49

on the stained carpets; or in the ditches and scrubland on the estates among shopping trolleys and discarded vehicles. He had also seen the victims, young men and women who were destined for their end, and others who had a promising future stolen from them in a moment of madness. But this was his first such experience on Orkney, on the land where he was born. He felt the unsettling insult to his home deeply; here was an act that brought upset and horror. Of course there had been murders before on Orkney, and the sagas tell of drink fuelled slaughters that left the soil steeped in violence, given a peculiar kind of dignity with their implicit claims of honour and valour. But this death had no dignity. In no way could this death be associated with any distorted sense of nobility. It was squalid and sordid and pathetic.

Clett suited up in a disposable overall and gloves and approached Dominic Byrd. He lifted the mobile phone from the body and placed it in an evidence bag. He operated it through the clear plastic. There were two calls to someone called Patrick yesterday. He scanned the handwritten list of team members given to him by Drever. There were no Patricks on the list. There were numerous texts and emails, including a lot from 'Trevor'. Clett switched off the phone. A correct analysis by the forensics team would take some time.

Clett looked at his watch. It was 10:21.

"Bugger."

He called Norman Clouston.

"Norman. The Earl Thorfinn!"

"Sorry Inspector?"

"The Westray Ferry! The Earl Thorfinn! It will arrive at Kirkwall at 1025. We must get officers and a car to the ferry as it moors at Kirkwall. We need the list of passengers. The killer may be on the ferry. You have less than five minutes"

"Of course inspector. Right away."

*　　　*　　　*

The MV Earl Thorfinn arrived early at Kirkwall harbour at 10:22. The killer was able to see that there were no police officers checking the traffic or passengers. As he made his way along the deck, he heard the music from the silver BMW.

"Patsy Cline – Walkin' After Midnight! Of course!"

First off the ferry, the killer, whose name is Patrick Tenant, handed back his embarkation ticket. He walked quickly away along the main road just as a police car raced up to the disembarkation ramp with its blue lights flashing and sirens blaring. The driver of the BMW glared at him. He disappeared into the Kirkwall shopping crowd to look for a quiet place to think through his next move.

As he walked through the people in the street, the pigeons made way for him. He was followed by a stray mongrel.

*   *   *

Clouston was kicking himself; the ferry. When Clett called, he knew immediately what they had failed to do. He had already lost track of a number of foot passengers. They did get details of the remaining passengers and vehicles, none of whom reported anything suspicious. It appeared to be a normal, uneventful crossing. The embarkation cards going out matched those boarding the ferry, but this didn't mean much. They were not identified by name. The credit card transaction record was obtained from the purser to be traced, but many of the tickets were bought with cash, and the purser did not remember any faces or unusual features of any passengers. Clouston arranged for all the available passengers to be interviewed. To his count, fifteen had disembarked prior to the police arrival. He advised the interviewing officers to focus on, and try to get any information about them. While scanning the list of car number plates on the MV Earl Thorfinn, Norman Clouston saw the registration RUS5. Clett would be interested in that.

Clett looked up to the morning clouds that were now moving faster.

"It's blowan up."

He thought of his father's voice and how he would describe this weather. He looked back to the scene in front of him. He knew how he had processed these scenes in the past; he would merely observe and assimilate as much detail as possible on a slow walk around the site. It would be later, sometimes in the middle of the night, when he would awaken with images that would be out of place or suddenly related and they could be the factors that might matter. The persisting question was always Why? The How was someone else's job mostly. What would have led someone to carry out such an act? What was the sequence of events that led to such an outcome? It was seldom clear why people committed such crimes, but it is a given that a story would be told that explained the motivation. In the meantime, however, it was the plodding procedural work that mattered. Clett knew fine that this was much more likely to come up with results. The telephone number obtained from an otherwise unimportant interview, the colour of the scarf observed by a witness, or the sound of a car. These all assisted the building of a case. The hunch had very little place in respectable police work, but Clett knew that connections might come as a result of time spent just observing. He allowed himself ten minutes walking around the crime scene. He looked at the colour of the upturned stones that were stained brown with blood; the interaction of the dig team members; the attitude of the dig leader. He looked at the tools and the marks they made resting in the sand, and he saw the line of the outgoing tide that had come to within twenty five metres of the dig site. He also saw the debris of the murder, the smell of faeces and salt and seaweed, and the damp from the still present morning dew.

After ten minutes of his observations he found the distractions, the questions from witnesses and officers overwhelmed his efforts at concentration. He passed Constable

Nancie Keldie holding a video camera. She had been silent during the briefing and during the crossing. She shivered inside her police issue fleece jacket.

"How's it going Nancie?"

"Sir, this is jist awfi. I canny stop my hands shaking."

"Don't worry. You will be fine. Just stick to the procedures. Remember your training. Don't enter the actual crime scene until the Crime Scene Examiners get here. Focus on the procedure and don't be distracted."

"Yes sir."

"Don't forget if you need to talk to someone, that can be arranged. Are you sure you are ok?"

"I'll be fine sir."

"Ok. Let me know if you need me for anything."

"Thank you sir. Oh sir?"

"Yes Nancie."

"Eh, well, I'm sorry but your shirt is sticking a bit oot yer troosers."

"Oh. Eh, thanks Nancie."

Clett flushed.

"Can't have the SIO wi' his shirt sticking oot his troosers."

They both smiled.

Clett tucked his shirt in and walked towards Drever. They had first met at a seminar for special constables in training at Tulliallan Police College where Clett was giving a lecture about vice and drugs activities in Strathclyde. They immediately made a connection because of their Orkney background. When other officers and trainees met in the bar at night, Clett and Drever separated off and talked about the families they knew and who was married to whom; what jobs they were doing; which farms were doing well; who was healthy, who had died, who had had children, and what school they were going to; the kind of dialogue that is the currency of human interaction in Orkney. They soon become friends. Drever was interested in Clett's career, and Clett was fascinated by Drever's intriguing history. Drever had been secretive about his past, even with Clett, but he told him that he had been a successful diamond dealer in Antwerp in the large and thriving market for precious stones. Clett was curious to hear the stories about the diamond trade. Transactions of millions of Belgian Francs were agreed on the shake of a hand, or the nod of a head. This system, without an overt policy of checks and balances, relied upon the good name or the word of a particular dealer. This contrasted with the ways of the modern workplace where individual's actions are so governed by procedure.

During their time together, they shared experiences without divulging specific personal details. Things were communicated by exchanging information about their families or friends. They related to each other by recognising the shared life in each other's stories. They did not mirror or repeat the stories back to each other, but accepted each other's explanation as recognisable in their own experience. No specifics, no overt declarations were required, but a silent acceptance that their lot was in some way equivalent.

The two men had kept in contact since the course and Clett had recommended Drever for the post at Westray despite objections from the other assessors. Drever was perceived as a loose cannon who would not follow orders or stick to procedure. He came out with top marks, and along with Clett's recommendation, got the position. They had become closer when Clett returned to Papay to stay with his parents, and they had spent more time together when Clett had been at his most vulnerable.

"Archie, could you keep an eye on Nancie Keldie. She's a bit twitchy."

"We all are Roland. Angela and young John Leask were both upset, but everyone is settling down now into the interviews and just keeping people calm."

"I'll get everyone together for a chat in a few minutes. How are the dig team doing?"

"Fine Roland. I think they are fairly calm now, but de Vries just winds them up again. The man's a fool."

"Speaking of which ..."

Chapter 5

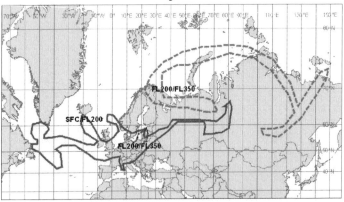

Wednesday, 21st April 10.50 am.

"You there! Officer!"

"Ah, Mr Trevor de Vries I believe. I'm Inspector Roland Clett."

"Professor de Vries if you don't mind. I believe I am entitled to the courtesy of my title."

De Vries was tall and he used his height to assert himself. He boomed in his baritone voice.

"Look there, you have to understand how important this work is. I have crucial data to collect and my funding and academic timetable dictate a strict timescale for this dig. I will leave the area of the body alone for you to get on with your tasks and we can work together on the site. Agreed?"

There was a moment of silence. Clett spoke slowly and evenly.

"Professor, all activity will stop until the end of the crime scene analysis. This may take several days. Any further obstruction from you and your team will result in a charge of tampering with evidence in a murder inquiry."

Indeed, Clett was considering this charge there and then, but it could wait.

"What! This is outrageous. Who do you think you are? Do you know who I am? You will be hearing from my ..."

Clett cut him off.

"Mr de Vries, you will not cause any further disruption to this site. It is a crime scene and it will be preserved for analysis despite the contamination you have brought to it."

"Contamination! My God man, what is it with you people, why can't you listen to reason? Do your worst, you have no idea of the real damage you are doing."

"Mr de Vries ..."

"I've told you, it is Professor."

"I am formally instructing you to return to your team and follow the directions of the police officers. If you do not, you will be arrested and charged immediately with wasting police time and obstructing the course of justice."

"Arrested? Why I've never been so insulted..."

De Vries was suddenly aware that the site had become silent; all eyes were on him. He turned away, mumbling, and strode towards the rest of the team.

"Damned impudence. Outrageous."

He took out his tablet computer and made some notes. One of the young men in his dig team approached him.

"Boss, would he really have arrested you?"

"I don't know George. You can't take chances with these sorts. I came across this in Mexico, you know. It is the scientist's job to rise above such squalid distractions. Let this be a lesson to you all."

"Boss will you put this in your blog?"

"Yes, and it will certainly appear in my memoirs."

Another young man from the team spoke up.

"Boss, you can only rationalise with these country types so much. They think they are above everything."

"Yes Alan, one tries to assist them, but authoritative intransigence is a common theme in dealing with these uneducated enforcers of blind rules. As I said, I saw it in Mexico, and it is prevalent everywhere from Africa to the Far East, and we have now seen it in Orkney, supposedly part of Our Great Britain. Gentlemen, learn from this. Value and protect your academic integrity. It is a bastion against such prejudice. Remain above it at all times."

The boys in the dig team made notes and nodded earnestly.

Clett collected the other officers around him.

"Right. This appears to be the body of Dominic Byrd, aged twenty; popular; currently no known individuals who stand out as suspects. We don't expect the SPSA Crime Scene Officers for quite a few hours, so it goes without saying that what is left is to be preserved intact. I can't believe that the dig team carried on working, contaminating so much of the area. I have to say I'm not optimistic about getting a lot of forensic evidence here. The site is forensically compromised, but we'll follow procedure. Constable Gunn, here's the victim's phone, could you pass it on to ICT forensics for analysis please?"

"No problem inspector."

"Constable Keldie, constable Gunn, could you get DNA sample retrieval on all witnesses present and collect all footwear samples and fingerprints?

Archie, Angela, and our new special constable John Leask have made a good job of containing the site and a list is available of all present."

"Yes Inspector, we are waiting for the arrival of a canopy over the body."

"Thanks Archie, we don't want any more evidence washed away. As to a murder weapon, we shouldn't jump to any conclusions. We might be talking about a rock, but a firearm may have been used. We can't confirm without forensic analysis. It might be that the destruction of the front half of the head is a deliberate attempt to mislead us. There may be a bullet buried in the rest of the brain matter. Any suggestions? Yes Angela?"

Angela hesitated, and then spoke up.

"Sir, there are a lot of archaeological tools around the site. Any one of these mallets, pick-axes or trowels could have been used."

"Thanks Angela. Nancie, could you please organise an audit of all the tools on site and tag them for forensic examination?"

"Yes sir. If it was a rock, it could have been any of the rocks around here. It would be amazing luck if they found it. It might be identifiable from embedded body matter, but it's more likely that it would have been thrown in the sea."

"Thanks Nancie, we might have to organise a fingertip search. Also, I would like some door to door interviews. Find out if anyone has a car missing or anyone has been behaving strangely. Archie, John, Angela, tap into the local knowledge."

The special constables nodded and scribbled in their notebooks. Clett continued;

"Archie, you wanted to show me some tyre tracks?"

"Yes inspector, back at the road."

"Ok, we'll have a look in a minute. It might be worth emphasising that the amount of damage to the victim's skull indicated a long and sustained assault. Even if a rock was not what caused the victim's death, it was probably used to cause the damage to the frontal skull. This might indicate that the assailant would have had to be strong and fit, or highly emotionally charged, or possibly under the influence of drugs. Nancie, have you got all this?"

"Yes sir."

Nancie Keldie continued filming for the case records.

"Anyone else? No? Well, can we please see if we can organise some catering? Maybe from the Pierowall Hotel – tea and sandwiches? We have a lot of traumatised people here. Poor Mrs Sclater must be out of milk by now; and I don't know about you lot, but my porridge was a long time ago."

*   *   *

The very large amount of blood had now dried in the morning sun to just another shade of brown. It would soon merge with the colour of the soil and soak into the ground along with the 5000 year-old shells and bones. Only on the stones would the spatter radius be clear, and that would soon fade.

*   *   *

Drever showed Clett to the track where he had seen the tyre marks.

"These look fresh and quite different from the other vehicles around."

Clett bent down to look closely at the tracks.

"One hundred and ninety five mill radials, domestic standard fit."

"It looks like the car took off in a hurry, given the amount of wheelspin on the track."

"He has gone west, away from Pierowall and out to Noup Head. It's a dead end."

Drever nodded towards the west.

"I had a walk along the track and it looks like there is only one set of tyre tracks."

"You think the car is still up there?"

"I can't see any sign of tracks coming back."

"And there is no road back?"

"Just the lighthouse and the cliffs."

"Let's get up there and have a look around."

Clett and Drever drove towards Noup Head. They skirted along the side of North Hill and the track deteriorated at the Loch of the Stack. All along the way the same tyre marks were present, more or less distinct dependant on the surface. When they arrived at the end of the road they parked at the lighthouse. Noup Head was an exposed promontory on a one hundred and eighty foot cliff with nothing but the North Atlantic to be seen on three sides.

"So, no car. He's driven the car off the cliff then?"

"That would be a logical conclusion."

"Look at all this disturbed ground surface. Over there too."

Clett pointed to the other side of the lighthouse.

"Lots of wheelspin here. He's got himself stuck in a rut. Look at this bald stump of turf."

"No sign of footprints on this side, Roland, only crushed heather and reeds around the tyre marks. Has someone fallen out of the vehicle?"

"Aye, jumped more like, before the car went over. The tracks go right to the edge."

"Yup, looks like he got stuck on this side of the lighthouse, got it out of the rut, and then drove around the other side and tried again from there."

"He must have wanted rid of the car badly. Why didn't he just keep it and use it to get away?"

"Aye, if he had alternative transport, there is no sign of it here. He must have walked back."

"To the Bay of Noup, or to Pierowall..."

"Or even to Rapness?"

"Really? You mean to get the ferry? He walked?"

"He would want to get as far away from the crime scene as possible."

"Without a car?"

"Hmm…."

"A local?"

"Can't see it Archie. We don't have anyone local that would so something like this, But you never know."

"Could be a newcomer."

"I think you guys would have picked up any dodgy newcomers on the Westray radar."

"Aye, right enough. So; an outsider, maybe connected with the dig."

"Possibly."

"If it was an outsider, why did he dump the car?"

"Don't know Archie. Any chance we can see the foot of these cliffs?"

They peered over the overhang to the roaring surf, one hundred and eighty feet below.

"No chance Roland."

Clett looked at his mobile phone. There was no reception. He called Norman Clouston on the Airwave radio.

"Romeo sierra one three from romeo india seven. Over."

"Romeo india seven, this is romeo sierra one three, go ahead."

"Drever and I are at Noup Head. It appears that a vehicle has been driven off the cliff. Can you get some fishing boats in the area to check out the base of the cliff for a car wreck, and possibly obtain an ID.?"

"Understood. Colour and type?"

"Vehicle is domestic saloon. No further information at this time. We are going to need the forensic team up here. We need something that might place a suspect at this site, maybe pollen samples."

"Understood, romeo india seven. Your mate Janie Shearer from *The Orcadian* has been in touch asking to confirm a story about a body on Westray."

"Received, romeo sierra one three. I'll call her back; and she's not my mate if you don't mind."

"Aye, sure thing romeo india seven."

Drever looked away from Clett and smiled.

"Romeo sierra one three, how did you get on with the Earl Thorfinn?"

"We got there in time to catch most of the passengers disembarking, but we missed a few. I'm checking the list of vehicle registrations and I'll let you know what turns up. There's one number that I have to confirm. I'll text you in five minutes."

"Understood, romeo sierra one three. Any more information?"

"Negative, romeo india seven. Out."

"Romeo sierra one three out."

Clett and Drever made their way back to the Bay of Noup. In the background could be heard the network background chat on the Airwave radio. Drever tutted.

"I don't know how you put up with those radios."

"Why."

"Because they are no good to man nor beast. You can't even hit anyone with them."

Roland looked at Archie and nodded his head from side to side. Drever looked out at a pair of bonxies gambolling in the wind.

"The old radios, now they were the thing. If you threw one of the old radios at someone, that really did the job."

"That is the kind of attitude that will put a stop to your meteoric rise in the Northern Constabulary. And it is probably why they don't let you have one."

Drever smiled. He stopped the car and they looked down to the Bay of Noup, at the farm and the dig site.

"If only we had access to a helicopter."

"I know. That car has been washed out to sea."

"It could turn up anywhere in a 40 mile radius."

"Aye, and it might not."

"Aye, it might not."

Back at the dig site, Clett found a place with mobile phone reception and called his parents on Papay. He felt they should know that he was close by. They were preparing to go on a caravanning holiday to Whitby the next day. He had wanted to visit them beforehand, but with exams and interviews leading up to his promotion he could not make the visit.

Roland's brother Russell answered the phone. Russell had taken over managing the farm about ten years ago. Their relationship had always been mutually supportive, but their different journeys in life had sometimes been a source of disagreement. Russell had always had a yearning to work away from the island while Roland wanted to stay. Despite this, it was Russell who couldn't resist life away from Papay. Like all island children, they both had to deal with leaving home at the age of twelve and the disruption of boarding at Kirkwall High School. Roland found that he could cope and went on to get his qualifications and a career, but Russell couldn't resist the magnet of home and returned to Papay to work on the farm. Their parents were aware of their boys' abilities and desires and had encouraged the courses of their present work. Bill and Vera Clett knew their children and their strengths, and if the question had been put to each of them, they would have agreed that when all was said and done, their parents had directed their choices to best suit their characters.

Russell passed the phone over to their mother.

"Roland, son, why don't you pop over for lunch? Your Dad has just made leek and potato soup. You can leave all the bothersome details of the investigation to the people who work for you. You do know that we are so proud of you and your new important job."

"It is not really like that Mum. This is a murder enquiry and I have to ensure all the procedures are followed."

"A murder enquiry. That's just so exciting. Come over for lunch and tell me all about it."

"I can't really Mum."

"But Roland, you are in charge. What is the point of getting promotion if you can't get the people under you to do some work? You don't have to do everything. Anyway, this new job will give you more time, and you and Christine can be with the boys. Aren't you seeing Christine tomorrow?"

"Yes Mum, we are meeting for lunch."

"Well that's just lovely Roland. She can help you put all that horrible Glasgow experience behind you. But come over for lunch with us today Roland. Just come over. No-one will miss you."

"Mum, you know I would like nothing better than to come for lunch."

"But it is just a half an hour on the ferry. Dad will collect you from Moclett pier. You could even time it to get the Loganair flight back and that will be only a few minutes."

"Mum, all flights are grounded because of this volcanic ash business."

"Roland, you are just making excuses now."

"Mum, you don't understand."

"No I mustn't understand. I mustn't understand why our son can't just take an hour out to see his parents. What is the point of having seniority if it does not come with some little extra time off when you need it? You know we are taking the caravan to Whitby tomorrow and we won't get another chance to see you for weeks."

"I'm sorry Mum, but this is really important. I really have to stay and run this investigation."

"For goodness sake, Roland. It is just an hour. I have to say, I feel a bit let down."

Clett's phone buzzed. It was the text from Clouston.

"I'm sorry Mum, I have to go."

Clett knew that he had disappointed his parents. He would make amends later. Clouston's text contained information about a silver BMW on the MV Earl Thorfinn. The registration was RUS5. Clett recognised the number immediately. He would need to make enquiries back at Kirkwall as soon as possible.

*   *   *

Patrick Tenant stood outside the Victoria Hotel. Cars squeezed past each other in the narrow flagged street and he had to keep moving to avoid them. It was starting to rain. He was trying to think clearly. He had killed a man and he couldn't remember why. He had not slept and he was exhausted. Could he risk getting in to his hotel? He could get a change of clothes and clean up and think through the next step. He had to get home; to where things were ordinary and normal and where the last twelve hours would be as a dream; to where there was no blood and no terror and where there was peace. A funny kind of peace nonetheless. His wife would want information and he would need to have answers. She would, as always, score points on him and belittle any efforts he made. In her eyes he was useless, and she took every available opportunity to point it out. However, it was his normality, and it was better than the situation he was in now. But now, right now, he had to think of what was the next step and not to look at the big picture. One step at a time.

He decided to get in to the hotel and check out as if nothing had happened. He waited until a large group of tourists arrived and entered with them. He got to the hotel room unnoticed. He showered and allowed himself fifteen minutes sleep. He changed and packed. He was glad he had brought a small rucksack. He left his main suitcase behind a stairwell on the top floor. It would never be found there.

He checked out of the hotel with little comment. He tried to control his breathing and looked around. He was starting to sweat and then he saw the girl behind the desk staring at him. How did she know? Did she know his heart was pounding? What did she know? Of course she couldn't know anything, but she carried on staring as he turned and tried to walk calmly out of the hotel with shaking knees. He came out into the cool air and went to a bank machine. He took as much cash as he could. He could not risk his credit card being traced and he would have enough for the journey home as a foot passenger.

"A foot passenger."

He realised that he would have to explain the missing car to the insurance company and to his wife.

As he turned from the cash machine, a man nodded a greeting. Patrick Tenant looked away, flushed and embarrassed. His first reaction was confusion. Why was this stranger acknowledging him? Who was he? He knew no-one in Orkney. Then he realised that he had passed him in the nightclub two nights ago; did he know who he was? He turned away not wishing to be recognised.

"Was it only then, the night before last, when everything was so different? God. How did this happen?"

Patrick Tenant had arrived on Orkney three days ago. His company was engaged in a large contract with Orkney Islands Council to dispose of old cars left lying around the islands. They specialised in scrap metal and vehicle disposal and saw this as the first in a series of lucrative contracts in the other Scottish islands. The meetings went well with the council and Patrick had two days to enjoy his small break. He became entranced with the Orkney Islands and visited the well-known sites: Skara Brae, Maes Howe, the Italian Chapel. He fell in love with the place. The landscape, the air and the peace gave him a sense of freedom he had not known for a long time. He felt himself again. He came to realise that reality that was the years of imprisonment in an uncommunicative relationship, along with the worry of debt and the daily grind.

After his tour around the Mainland he was to attend a post contract social event. He and some members of the OIC team went for a meal and a few drinks and then to a nightclub. That is where he met Dominic Byrd.

Patrick was immediately attracted to Dominic. He found his presence electric. Here was someone he could relate to; someone who was interested in him. He looked at him when he spoke and didn't interrupt. Dominic was engaging and athletic, and Patrick felt they had so much in common. The sudden and open nature of their relationship reflected Patrick's new sense of freedom and belonging.

Patrick was fascinated when Dominic described the dig at the Bay of Noup. He accepted when Dominic invited him to the site. They would meet the next day and get the ferry to Westray. Patrick offered to drive. Dominic told him about his enthusiasm for the dig and its history, and amidst the din of music and chatter and lights of the nightclub, Patrick saw this as an unmissable opportunity to experience more of this new world. They talked further into the inebriate and inevitable night.

Chapter 6

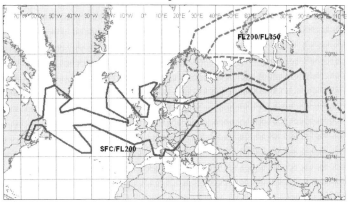

Wednesday, 21st April 11.25 am.

Norman Clouston pressed the PTT button on his Airwave radio. He was calling Roland Clett.

"Romeo india seven from romeo sierra one three."

"Sierra one three go ahead."

"India seven. More data on victim."

"Go ahead sierra one three."

"Victim, Dominic Byrd; verified aged twenty from Little Gidding, near Cambridge. Mother lives at home with father - serial bankrupt. Nothing else is known about parents at the moment. Victim attended a local public school and reported to have a charge of credit card fraud two years ago."

"Understood sierra one three. Please advise nearest police station to send officers to inform Mr and Mrs Byrd about their son?"

"Already done india seven!"

"Good; ... and can you request they obtain more information about victim's movements and recent lifestyle? Get their telephone number and I'll give them a call myself."

"Understood india seven. There's one more thing you should know."

"Yes sierra one three?"

"Constable Keldie reports that one of the dig team saw Byrd in an animated discussion with a man of about thirty on Tuesday night at the Fraction nightclub."

"Fraction? Ronnie Rust's place? Confirm."

"Confirmed india seven. Fraction nightclub. They were not arguing and seemed to be enjoying each other's company."

"In Ronnie Rust's nightclub?"

"Yes inspector."

"Understood. We might be getting somewhere here. India seven out."

*   *   *

the timetables at Kirkwall bus station. The rows of times and places were a blur. It had been a while since he had used a bus and there were so many possibilities for error and each one had the potential for him to be caught.

He decided that he would catch the 11:35 bus to Stromness where he could get the Hamnavoe crossing back to Scotland. That would take thirty-five minutes. He would miss the next crossing to Scrabster at 11:00, so he would have to wait for a few hours. He would have to keep out of the way in Stromness for a while. Would they raise the level of security? Everything he did would have to be with the aim of leaving no trace. Boarding the ferry presented another problem, but he might be able to get on while the staff were diverted; but that was a consideration for later. The only way to tackle these problems was to take them one at a time.

Tenant's eye was drawn to a paragraph at the bottom of the ferry timetable.

> **PASSENGER NOTICE: All passengers aged 16 years and over are required to be in possession of photographic ID at check-in.**

How would he get past photo ID? If he had to, he could just show his driver's licence. He hoped that it was unlikely that he would be associated with the murder at this stage – unless they had identified the car at the bottom of the cliffs. God, he had to be right. Could he rely on this kind of thinking in this world where each person, each creature, and the very elements seemed to conspire against him? He thought through his options once more. He had to minimise the record of his movements. Flying was out of the question: he would be clearly traced if he chose to fly. Anyway, all aircraft were grounded because of the ash cloud. On the other hand, witnesses might still identify him on the ferry, and records of his presence on board would put him in a particular place, at a particular time. Was he making the right choice? He had to be disciplined and be methodical. He had to be as invisible as he could be. He had to think of a way around the problem of photo ID.

As he settled at the rear of the heated bus to Stromness, he became drowsy. The bus cradled him in warmth and the rhythm of the engine rocked him into an unwanted but inevitable state of sleep. His eyes closed and he was back on Westray. Dominic was there and they were laughing together. Then it was darker, and in his dream he saw him in the moonlight. He saw himself kneeling over Dominic's body, with its face black and featureless. Tenant felt the sweat on his forehead. Slowly, like a doll moving seamlessly between poses, Dominic stood up and turned towards him with his eyeless face, a hooded void surrounded by dripping patches of skin and scalp. Dominic was singing, but the singing was a single note increasing in volume, and the sound came out of a gap in the black that was once his mouth. The single noted song was a powerful intense scream that tore through Tenant's head. He could only look into this black space. He was breathless to the sound of the continuing scream and he jolted out of sleep, gasping for air. He was frozen with the power of this nightmare noise; he was dizzy and his vision blurred. He felt sucked into the vortex that was the abyss surrounding him; the unknown way forward from a bewildering past and a confusing present.

Awake now, he looked around the bus and saw nothing unusual; but still the scream continued. He was awake and the sounds from this shocking dream insinuated into his consciousness. People on the street were going about their business silently despite the terrifying noise, and children still played. The piercing sound continued. Was he going mad? Was he really awake? Slowly, he came to be aware of his situation. The bus passed the post office at Finstown. The sound was a siren. People were going about their daily lives as if nothing was happening, but still the wailing continued. It was like an old Second World War air raid siren; Tenant was in a cold sweat. What was this sound and of what danger did it warn? Could nobody else hear it? Was it for him alone? Why didn't people react? The sound continued as the bus carried on west past the houses and an old pub that said 'Pomona Inn'. The sound appeared to come from the hills to the south and faded as the bus left Finstown. It skirted the Bay of Firth and cruised past the green tree-filled cleft at Binscarth. These were the first trees Tenant had seen since arriving on the island. His breathing became more normal and then there was a thump and a familiar, low rumble in the ground, like a quiet thunder. But the sky was clear. Again, this place impacted directly on Tenant; its disconnected images affected his senses, like watching a television when the sound is out of sync. Events were occurring, but their expected causal connection to other things was not clear. He breathed in short breaths and began to sweat. He looked again at his surroundings. What was it about this place? Nothing seemed normal. He desperately needed to return to the world he knew. Despite the warmth of the bus, he was cold and shivering and he felt his shoulders tight and solid against his neck which made his head ache. He looked around at the people in the bus. No-one seemed to notice him, but he knew deep down that he, Patrick Tenant, was answerable to them all.

At 12:20 the bus came into Stromness and as he expected, Tenant could see the Northlink Hamnavoe ferry berth was empty. The bus pulled in at the Ferry terminal.

From his seat, he noticed the elderly lady from the Westray ferry slowly getting off the bus. She glanced at him and looked away. He tried to think it through. Could she have seen him? Had she seen him in the queue getting on the bus? Did she recognise him? Yes, she was staring at him as she walked away. In his fatigue with all the problems he had to solve, he was finding it difficult to concentrate. He had to think of the photo ID problem. He could try to get on to the ferry by climbing on to the side of a container lorry or other large vehicle. However, the ferry terminal was too quiet just now. He had to disappear until closer to the time of the later 16:45 crossing. Tenant turned away from the ferry terminal trying to think through his next step and saw a notice that read:

Due to a request by the Scottish Government, the MV Hamnavoe is being deployed to Bergen to repatriate UK citizens currently displaced due to the current Volcanic Ash Emergency. Consequently, there will be no sailings on the Pentland Firth route on Wednesday 21st and Thursday 22nd April.

Outside the Stromness ferry terminal it was raining heavily. Tenant thought through the new information. No sailings today. Jesus God, how can I get back home? I need to get off this island. How do I get home? He desperately needed to return to a place where he understood the landscape, to where the very ground under his feet did not conspire, and where trees and strangers and dogs and birds did not sneer at him and his misery. But he knew that people must not see his reactions, he would only escape if he appeared normal.

"Appear normal; that was the secret."

He went into the ferry terminal and looked at the brochures next to the tourist office. The staff were dealing with a German tour party who were also trying to get off the island. He picked up a leaflet about the Pentalina, a catamaran ferry that operated between St Margaret's Hope at the other end of the islands, and Gill's Bay, on the Scottish mainland. He looked again at the bus timetables. He discovered he could get a bus to St Margaret's Hope, change at Kirkwall and, he reckoned, get the 17:00 crossing. The only problem was more buses and more exposure to witnesses; it was likely that the same problem would await him on the Pentalina. He would have to deal with that later. This was the only choice open to him now.

He caught the 12:30 bus back to Kirkwall. He paid his fare and was grateful that it was not the same driver. The bus ride was bringing him back towards the place he was trying to escape.
"Will I ever get off these islands?"

Tenant felt destined to be subject to this movement backwards and forwards, between past and present, an eternal return; like pushing a rock up a hill, only for it to fall down, where he would have to push it up again. In his dreams and in his seeming waking state, this appeared to be his reality.

Once more, he was exhausted through lack of sleep and, drifting off in the warmth, he thought that the bus was bringing him to the Bay of Noup and Dominic Byrd's body. The bus was somehow back on Westray and he looked out north to the past. He was hanging in time between the pole and the tropic, between the south, his future, and his old action in the north, suspended in sounds half-heard in the stillness between two waves of the sea. There was no smell of the earth. The time was daylight and Dominic was standing and waving silently to him with no face. Tenant woke as the bus braked. Again, he was sweating and shivering in the warmth. The bus was returning through Finstown, but this time it was silent. There were no other passengers.

Through the window Tenant could see people walking. People at their business. Seagulls swooping; and the clouds, the clouds slowly dancing in the blue sky. Above these clouds was another cloud he could not see; one that offered danger to those who flew too high. There were no sirens now. The bus sailed quietly through Finstown.

*　　*　　*

Volcanic ash clouds are normally composed of particles of the chemical emissions from a volcano, the cooled products of a pyroclastic cloud. Eyjafjallajokull was different. It had erupted below a glacier. The rising magma coming into contact with the ice resulted in a thermal shock that created hundreds of thousands of tonnes of tiny particles of very hard material. This made the ash different from that of other eruptions. The cloud would rise very high in the atmosphere and it would be blown into the jetstream to be transported huge distances. The dangers were many. To any aircraft flying through the cloud, the ash could be ingested into engines where the small particles would turn to glass, shutting them down; any aircraft flying through the cloud would be effectively sandblasted, rendering the windows opaque, blocking any vision. To animals and humans on the ground, there was a danger of inhalation and respiratory illness. The added danger of damage to crops that was part of the cause of starvation in the 1783 eruption would not be as great a danger in 2010, but it would still affect the livelihoods of many farmers.

*　　*　　*

Clett telephoned Mr and Mrs Byrd in Little Gidding.
"Mrs Byrd, I have to tell you that I am so very sorry for your loss."
Mrs Byrd was crying.
"Do you mind if I ask you a few questions?"

She sniffed.

"No."

She blew her nose.

"It's all our fault you know."

"I'm sorry."

Clett paused.

"Did Dominic live with you?"

"No we hadn't seen him for about two years. After the credit card fraud at school, which wasn't his fault you know – it was so tragic, such a waste of a young man's talent. You see, he was asked to leave and he travelled for a while – to Holland, and to Thailand and to Scandinavia. He had lots of friends you know; all over the world. He talked with them by email all the time. We are so proud of him. But you must see, really when it came down to it, he didn't really care about us. We have had our own problems, getting the extension finished and all that trouble with the builders; well, Dominic never showed any interest. He was a lovely boy and so good looking. He was very clever, but no-one in authority could see it and that's why he couldn't get a job. His older brother Nathan could have set him up in business, but no, no, no. Dominic had to go his own way."

"Did you know Professor Trevor de Vries?"

"No inspector, should we?"

"Professor Trevor de Vries was the archaeological dig team leader."

"Yes, and that was another thing. What was he doing on an archaeological dig? He had never been on one before. What did he know about archaeology? He was always welcome at our beautiful home – we have a beautiful cottage, but he never visited. That's the thanks you get. We've never been to Scotland. Why did Dominic go there?"

"We know that Dominic had been on Orkney for about five weeks and we are trying to locate his movements prior to this. His phone had been used in Holland and Sweden in the previous month. The technical support people are trying to identify his contacts. When was the last time you saw your son?"

Silence.

"Perhaps last September? He phoned at Christmas, but no, definitely September because it was the flower show, or was it October?"

"Was Dominic ever involved in drugs?"

"Oh no, Dominic would never be involved in anything like that."

Mr Byrd coughed in the background and took the phone away from his wife.

"Inspector, Simon Byrd here."

"Hello Mr Byrd. Once again, can I say how sorr …."

"Yes, yes, yes. Look inspector, I always knew Dominic would come to a bad end. He wasn't as pure as the driven snow and, frankly, he was a disappointment."

Mrs Byrd wailed.

"The credit card fraud was all him and nobody else, and he has ploughed his own furrow ever since. This is where it has come to a stop. Why couldn't he have been a success like his brother Nathan? He had the intelligence and God knows we spent enough on his education. Ungrateful little shit."

There was a moment where nothing was said.

"Thank you both for your time. It is likely that your son's body will not be released for a few days. It will have to be approved by the Procurator Fiscal, the Public Prosecutor in Scottish Law."

Mrs Byrd sniffed as her husband returned the phone.

"We've never been to Scotland you know. Isn't it just so cold there?"

Clett left his number with them; he thanked them once again and hung up.

*　　*　　*

Tenant's bus arrived back at Kirkwall at 13:10. The connection from Kirkwall would not depart until 16:15, arriving at St Margaret's Hope in time for the ferry at 17:00. He had three hours to wait so he decided to hide in a museum. He wandered bemused through the artefacts and information boards and read short extracts about old Orkney, the Sagas, and about the death and the violence that told the story of Orkney's past. He saw the pictures of the inscriptions and the translations of the runes.

'Old stones cannot be decyphered'

He read about Earl Thorfinn. How do I know that name?

There was Thorfinn the Mighty who went to Rome on a pilgrimage to atone for a life of piracy and sin; and there was Earl Haakon who went on pilgrimage for the murder of Magnus, and he read about the drunk Earl Erlend Haraldsson murdered by Earl Rognvald and Earl Harald.

'Coming at night like a broken king'.

What was it about this place? Was there murder in the earth? Was he caught up in some kind of wind that drives human action? He still could not believe he had killed Dominic. He would not harm a flea. Patrick Tenant just couldn't recognise himself in these actions. Were Magnus and Erlend Haraldson's killers driven by the same force? Were they also caught up in a sequence of events over which they had no control?

Nonetheless, he knew he had killed. The disturbing world he was experiencing would somehow be the cause of the retribution that was due to him, and that somehow was his desire.

*   *   *

"Sanja, Dr Keillor here."

"Hello Doctor."

"Where are you?"

"We're at Berriedale Braes, so we're making good time."

"Good Sanja. I've decided we should use the spatter radius analysis techniques as I described in my presentation last week. Will you have any problems with the directions for measurement and the definition of the spatter threshold?"

"No Dr Keillor."

"Good. That should give us a height and build of an assailant within an error field of ten percent. Remember, the more measurements you take, the more accurate will be the outcome. And don't forget that we must eliminate the imponderables."

"Yes Doctor."

Sanja stifled a giggle as Irene poked her in the ribs.

"We will be in touch if there any problems. Thank you Doctor."

Sanja ended the call.

"Whit a load of bollocks."

"Him an' his bloody spatter radius."

"Have ye no seen the latest draft o' his paper?"

"Aye, but only 'cos he's bent everyone's ear aboot it since forever."

"Did ye ken he stopped me on ma way tae the lavvy and kept me fur ten minutes on the boundary threshold definition? Ah wuz burstin so Ah wuz."

"Well Ah don't know aboot you, but Ah canny wait tae see it published."

"Whit? You sneaky cow. That's only cos he is sure tae get his professorship and he'll be oot o' your hair."

Irene paused, knitting needles in mid air.

"Well, aye, and Ah like ma job. It's no as if you're gonny tae tell him it's rubbish."

Irene cleared her throat and mimicked Dr Keillor's delivery:

"The application of spatter radii analysis at the locus and its use in the assessment of the height and build of an assailant."

Both girls laughed.

"Rubbish isnae in it. You and I hiv seen enough blood and guts tae ken, ye canny make a mathematical model tae fit. There are too many variables."

"Aye, the imponderables".

"The imponderables", they said together, imitating Dr Keillor's Broughty Ferry accent.

Both girls collapsed in laughter.

"Watch where yer driving ya silly bitch."

*   *   *

On Westray, Clett's Airwave radio crackled. It was Chief Inspector Maggie McPhee.

"Romeo india seven from charlie india three. Over."

"Charlie india three. Go ahead."

"India three I need you to hold a press conference tomorrow morning."

Clett paused and took a breath.

"Understood charlie india three. A press conference? Confirm you want me to take it?"

"Affirmative india seven. You are in the best place to give answers at the moment."

Clett paused again before pressing the transmit button.

"Understood charlie india three. I will take it at the steps of the Watergate Sheriff Court Building at 9:30 tomorrow morning. I have a meeting with the Procurator Fiscal at 8:30 after the teleconference."

The thought of a press conference terrified Clett, but it was his responsibility as SIO. He would merely read a prepared statement and that would be that.

"Romeo india seven out."

*   *   *

Above, the sky was being blown along and around. It would not stop. The ash and the clouds mixed and separated and the whole constituency moved not to a pattern but was an invisible maelstrom that tore at Patrick Tenant's world. He remembered Dominic telling him that here on Orkney they could never forecast the weather in any accurate sense. Local people learned to live in this world where the conditions would change from hour to hour; where the weather could be so different at locations only a half mile apart. Here strong sunshine in a blue sky, and there, pouring rain from which you had no choice but to shelter.

Here, the ash cloud would rise and fall and be blown from east to west and north to south. It's presence and its unpredictability were absolute.

Chapter 7

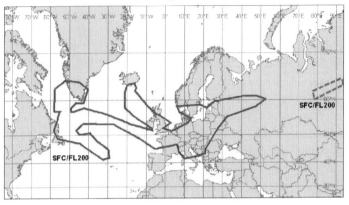

Wednesday afternoon, 21st April 4.20 pm.

The bus headed south from Kirkwall. Tenant looked back towards the big red cathedral and its spire, and he recognised the distillery and the long straight road south to the Churchill Barriers. He had been there just two days ago as a tourist, but this time, as he left the town, the beauty of the landscape was tempered with unreality. Tenant was living in a dream world where everyday signs were unreliable. He had flashbacks to the image of Dominic's faceless head screaming at him; he didn't know if he was asleep or awake, or which direction was north. Here, at four o'clock in the afternoon, he thought he saw a sunset. Was that the west? He looked out and saw a bright light in the dull sky' but it was not the sun. It was the gas flare from the oil storage plant on Flotta.

As the bus crossed the first of the Churchill Barriers, the man-made causeways linking the islands, he saw that the sea level on either side of the road was different. He looked again. Yes, but how could that be? The level of the water was different on the right and left of the barrier. He could only put it out of his mind. His confusion with everything he was experiencing was becoming overwhelming.

*   *   *

Tenant looked west across Scapa Flow towards the foggy calm horizon with the light of Flotta hanging in the sky. As the bus slowed and the engine revs fell, he heard crows calling. He turned to his left and saw in a field about thirty of the birds formed in a circle with a single individual in the middle. The crow at the centre appeared to call to the surrounding birds and they took it in turns to hop into the middle and peck at the accused with their large powerful beaks. This was a crow's court. The victim did not try to fly off and stayed where he was, waiting for the next call and the next peck. The conclusion was inevitable and horrifying. The field was already strewn with feathers. The crow stooped, exhausted.

The barbarous interrogation with its mysterious questions carried on relentlessly and the bus continued on its way; on its way through a beautiful landscape deformed by Tenant's perception. Each thing twisted into a parallel with death and suffering. He was aware that other locals and tourists on the bus were observing the same scenes he was, but he could not but choose to focus on the suffering and on pain. Given the experience of the last few days, what choice did he now have? How else could he now see the world?

As Tenant Arrived at St Margaret's Hope and the harbour came into view, he saw the huge bright red catamaran dwarfing the other vessels and the terminal. He was expecting a state of the art facility with waiting rooms and cafes, but what he saw was a queue of cars and a portacabin. There was no police presence.

He had been thinking about the photo ID problem. He had two choices. He could just show his own passport and take his chances. The better option was to look out for a group of passengers who would be likely to attract attention and use them as a diversion and get on to the ferry while they diverted officials; or again, he pondered the option of climbing on to the side of a van or lorry. He was looking for a group and a possible vehicle when he became aware how melodramatic this all was. He picked up a ferry brochure and looked for any mention of photo ID notification. He read the pamphlet over and over. No Photo ID! The company did not have a photo ID rule! All he needed was for the police not to be present. He allowed himself to relax a little. This was another step towards home and its predictable realities.

At three minutes to five, Patrick Tenant walked on to the Pentalina ferry to Gill's Bay. He took his embarkation card and felt himself let go a little for the first time. He relaxed in the passenger's lounge away from the busy cafeteria. There was now an end in sight.

*　　*　　*

Sanja Dilpit and Irene Seath climbed out of the Celtic Voyager at Pierowall pier at 17.05.

"You will be Irene and Sanja. I'm Roland, sorry, Inspector Roland Clett, and this is Special Constable John Leask."

"Hello Inspector, Hello John."

"Afternoon ladies" said Leask.

Seath and Dilpit looked at each other and rolled their eyes. Clett smiled and Leask flushed.

Clett and Leask helped them with the equipment cases.

"How was your drive up?"

"Och the usual, no problems really. It wis just a guddle unloading the equipment cases at Scrabster."

"And the crossing?"

"That wee boat is the business. A bit bumpy, but got us here in no time. Great fun."

"Ok, the Bay of Noup is 5 minutes away. Jump in."

John Leask deftly negotiated the single track road heading west.

"We are just coming to the Bay of Noup and there's the dig site past the farm."

They passed through the farm yard. Sanja nudged Irene and pointed to a dead sheep behind a gate. Leask continued:

"You can see the awning where the body is. Without the awning, the body wouldn't be visible from the road or from the farm."

Sanja and Irene saw the site. It was quiet now with no volunteers and only three officers present. They left the car and walked down to the dig site and the body of Dominic Byrd.

"Jeeze what a mess. You can't tell the ancient crap from the new crap."

"Aye and the mess of that body. The heid's like a crash helmet filled wi' muck."

Leask looked at Clett who smiled and shook his head.

"You've seen the e-mails with the initial information?"

"Aye Inspector. It looks as if yon team leader mannie his made a right mess."

"Sorry about that. How much information do you think you will get from the site?"

"Canny say the noo. We'll jist hiv tae take it wan step at a time."

Irene handed Sanja a pack with blue disposable overalls and surgical gloves. Clett carried on talking as they suited up.

"Okey dokey. You are booked into the Pierowall Hotel. You'll have to check in. John will be your local liaison, supported by the other officers and special constables. You have my number and you can call me if you need to. If you have any preliminary comments, voice them at the telephone conference tomorrow morning."

"Aye, Inspector, nae problem. Talk tae ye in the morning. Cheery!"

*   *   *

The Pentalina picked up speed as it headed south out of Scapa Flow. Tenant felt that at last he could look forward. Normality was within his grasp. He could escape from these islands and on to the more predictable, and firmer terrain of the Scottish mainland. He breathed more easily.

He looked out of the port side and identified the Cantick Head lighthouse from the chart on the wall. Further on and out past the island of Swona, the water was behaving strangely. It was as if the whole body of water was rotating in a hypnotic spiral, as if it was disappearing down an enormous plughole. He couldn't take his eyes from the sight. It was yet another disturbance in his cosmos. His breath quickened again and he gasped for air. The whole world was spinning. Would it never end? The ferry carried on, but Tenant again felt helpless in the face of the events that limited his actions. This demonic contingency that conspired and now permeated his life. His choices were being made for him whether he liked it or not. The whole world was forming a funnel through which his options were being filtered. The pitch of the engines dropped and Tenant looked away from the whirlpool and out of the window. Gliding abeam the ship, a seagull turned its head and directly and purposefully, saw into Patrick Tenant's heart.

*   *   *

Clouston was reconsidering the extra security precautions he had put in place on all the Orkney inter-island ferries. He did not need to worry about the Hamnavoe, still in Bergen ferrying holidaymakers stranded by the volcanic ash emergency. However, he had not yet received an answer from the Pentalina booking office. He tried the office again and this time there was a familiar voice.

"Ah Jessie, how's my favourite girl?"

"Norman Clouston. You don't call in months and now I'm your favourite girl. You must want something."

"Now Jessie, don't be like that. You know you love me really. Don't you remember our special weekend?"

"Aye, but Norman, you didn't phone."

"I know Jessie, but you know how it is at work."

"What, like catching criminal masterminds in Orkney? Yeah, Right."

"You would be surprised Jessie, but look, I was going to ask you if you fancied a weekend in Aberdeen; you know, some shopping, a nice meal."

"Norman Clouston, you have the cheek of ...."

"Now Jessie, you know you want to."

"I don't know, Norman."

"I happen to know Jessie that you have taken a weekend off in June, so what about that?"

"How do you know that Norman?"

"Well, while catching criminal masterminds, I bumped into your brother Jack at the new community centre at Burray."

"Aye, he works there for Ronnie Rust. Ronnie is opening it on Saturday"

"Aye. Well Jack told me you had a weekend off. Why don't you come to Aberdeen with me. You know it will be fun."

"Well, I don't know Norman."

"Great. That's settled. Now to some business."

"Business. Norman, I knew you wanted something."

"No Jessie, you know it's not like that. The two things are not connected, they are separate conversations."

"Well get on with it."

"Jessie, we have to ask you to increase your security level because of this Westray murder. We are sending two officers down to monitor all foot and car passengers leaving Orkney on the Pentalina. I take it we have missed the 17:00 sailing and the arrival at Gill's Bay?"

"Yes Norman you have, but I'll see if James at Gill's Bay knows anything."

"I would say he does; I've requested some officers attend there."

"Ok Norman, leave it with me. I'll sort it before I close up this evening."

"Thanks Jessie, and I'll go ahead and book a hotel in Aberdeen."

"We'll see Norman, you are going to have to be especially nice to me."

"Jessie, of course I will."

*   *   *

Clett stepped off the Celtic Voyager at Kirkwall Harbour and turned left along Shore Street, past the marina, to the Olfsquoy estate. He called his wife.

"Hello Christine."

"Hello Roland."

"Have you time to speak?"

"Aye Roland. I'm just at Mum's in Dounby. We are going to have tea together and then I've got fifteen class reports to complete."

"Sorry Christine. Will I call later?"

She eyed the pile of reports in front of her.

"No, now's fine. How's the investigation?"

"Och it's early days Christine, you know."

"Did you eat lunch today?"

"Aye, I had a sandwich from the Pierowall Hotel."

"Did you call for something in particular?"

"Well Christine, it's about nothing really."

"Aye..."

"Well, I was thinking..."

"Yes Roland?"

"Do you remember the wee carving of a wren that we missed buying from that gallery out at Birsay?"

"The wee wirren? Of course I do."

"Well the person that bought it might sell it to me and I wanted to know if you were still interested."

"Interested? Of course; but even second hand it will be expensive."

"Don't worry about that. I've got that sorted."

"Are you sure it is our peedie wirran, the one that was sold before we could get it?"

"Aye, it's ours."

"Roland, that would be lovely."

"Ok, let me make a phone call."

Christine looked at her Mum making the tea, and at the paperwork in front of her.

"Roland, I have to get back to work."

"I know Christine, so do I."

"Ok."

"Still ok for lunch tomorrow?"

"Aye. That'll be nice. Will you still be able to get away from work?"

"I'll give you a text if there is a problem. Ok?"

"Okey Dokey. See you then. Bye."

Clett pressed 'end call' on his old Nokia and looked up at the house in front of him. He stood at the bottom of the drive of the gaudiest bungalow in Kirkwall. In a town where the dominant tones were muted and understated, Ronnie Rust had a house that was painted bright blue. In the garden at the front, there was a huge ornate fountain, complete with cherubs, and there was a pair of horse's heads on the gateposts. In the drive were two identical silver BMW's with the number plates RUS5 and RUS6.

People said that Rust had interests in the building trade, but no actual building projects appeared to have materialised in his name. In reality, his wealth was from various illegal sources such as tobacco smuggling, and he was suspected of drugs dealing. Clett knew there was much more. Clett and Rust went back a long time.

Clett pressed the doorbell and was rewarded with a very long and loud rendition of the Big Ben chimes. Rust opened the door.

"Hello Ronnie, how are you?"

"Ah, Inspector Roland Clett, I believe. How are you enjoying your promotion?"

"News gets around fast I see."

"Aye, Roland, as you well know nothing gets past me on these islands. Come on in. Would you like a dram?"

"No thank you Ronnie. How is your Auntie Brenda?"

Brenda Rust had looked after Ronnie after he returned from the list D school as a teenager and all the time he lived in South Ronaldsay.

"She's fine. She is round the back. Want to say hello?"

"No thanks, just tell her I was asking after her."

Clett cleared his throat.

"Actually I'm here on official business."

"Aye, and it will be to do with that body on Westray. You don't think I had anything to do with it?"

Rust changed his tone with a glint in his eye.

"Do I need my lawyer again Roland?"

"No Ronnie, you don't need a lawyer. I'm just here to ask a few questions."

"Okey dokey Inspector Clett, what can I do for you? Are you sure you won't have a dram?"

"No. As you said, a young lad was killed on Westray on Tuesday night and he was seen in your nightclub that evening talking to somebody we would like to speak to. The murdered boy's name was Dominic Byrd, and the person he was with may have been called Patrick. We would like to get some statements from people who were there, starting with the bar staff. Can we see the roster please?"

"Well Roland, old mate, there are one or two problems there. You see I don't own Fraction any more. I've just sold it to some Norwegian investors. The contracts are being exchanged as we speak. Anyway, I haven't been involved in the actual running of the club for a year or so now. I leave that to my manager

Geraldine, Geraldine Work. That leaves me free to deal with more, eh, strategic concerns."

"Aye Ronnie, strategic concerns."

Clett breathed deeply.

"Ok, can I have Geraldine Work's number?"

"No problem Roland."

Clett entered the number into his phone as Rust slowly read out the digits.

"Thank you Ronnie. Were you at Fraction on Tuesday?"

"No, I was not."

"Can you tell me where you were on Tuesday?"

"Since you ask, I was at a trustees meeting for my new community centre at Burwick."

"And who else was there?"

"You could start by asking my good friend Sheriff Charlie Sinclair."

"Ah, the Honorary Sheriff…"

"I take it you do not have a warrant."

"No Ronnie, it is not necessary at this time."

Rust looked past Clett to the view out to the bay and sucked on his cigar. He motioned inside to the open plan lounge.

Clett saw a thick hardback business biography on Rust's coffee table. It was called 'Chasing the Model' by Sam L Winker and showed the author, a tanned square jawed blond man in a blue suit sitting at a desk.

"So how do you explain the presence of your car on Westray on Tuesday night and Wednesday morning?"

"Wasn't me."

"Your car was observed on the Earl Thorfinn on Wednesday morning."

"So?"

"What were you doing on Westray?"

"Told you, it wasn't me."

"You were seen."

"No I fucking wasn't. Listen to me. I have two fucking beautiful motors. I can't drive them both, so I sometimes let my employees use them. Geraldine had the car on Tuesday night. I don't know where she went with it."

"We'll check that out."

Rust stepped out to the porch and sucked on his cigar. His earrings glinted against the yellow sodium streetlights. He nodded back towards the lounge. Clett breathed slowly.

"Do you like my new television Roland? It is a 65 inch plasma screen with wireless internet streaming."

"Oh aye, but does it get the football Ronnie?"

"Aye, but are you taking the piss Roland?"

"Do you think I am Ronnie?"

Rust's voice quietened again and dropped in pitch.

"You just be careful *Inspector* Roland Clett, or you'll be back in a fucking uniform before your feet touch. I'm a powerful man in these parts. Don't you forget that."

"No Ronnie, I won't forget that."

Clett turned to leave and he let himself out. As he got past the horses' heads, his phone buzzed.

"Sanja Dilpit here Inspector."

"Sanja, what can I do for you?"

"We have just bagged the victim's hands and feet and we would like authorisation to move the remains to Balfour Hospital for a post mortem."

"You know that the usual procedure is to have our undertaker remove the body to Inverness to the pathologist."

"I hope you don't mind sir, but I have made some enquiries and Dr Sinclair is actually on Orkney just now and has agreed to carry out the post mortem at Balfour Hospital if that is ok with you."

"Certainly Sanja. No problems. If he's happy, I'm happy."

"And I'm not stepping on any toes?"

"Not at all Sanja. It is a big help. Do you want to use the Celtic Voyager?"

"Yes please, if you are ok with that."

"Certainly. Are you still ok for an update at tomorrow's telephone conference?"

"Yes Inspector. No particular surprises, but we'll give you a full assessment tomorrow morning."

"Thanks Sanja. Goodnight."

"Goodnight inspector."

From the Olfsquoy estate, he walked in the dull light back to his battered desk in the Burgh Road Station. It was late and he was exhausted and he still had his report to write.

An hour later, Clett started his Volkswagen Polo and drove back to Scapa. The remaining light from the late sunset over the graveyard at Tofts almost illuminated his thoughts, but Clett was just too weary. He arrived and opened the door of the house. Rented from an old school friend, it was an out of season holiday home next to the Scapa distillery. He microwaved a meal and lit a fire in the small stove. He moved a pile of ironing from an armchair and sat with his paperwork, looking out from the glazed balcony, protected from the cooling night. He gazed out over Scapa Flow towards the bright candle of the oil terminal on Flotta. He called Christine.

"Hi. Were you asleep?"

"Aye, but I'm pleased you called. Busy day?"

The microwave rang and Clett removed the hot meal.

"You could say that. I'm exhausted."

"Did you have something to eat?"

"I'm sitting with a microwaved meal just now."

"At this time of night?"

"I know Christine, it is just the day that it has been."

There was a moment of comfortable silence that punctuated the small talk.

"What time are you up in the morning?"

"About half seven. That Anna Shearer is becoming a pain."

"Is that Janie Shearer's wee girl, Janie Shearer that works for *the Orcadian*?"

"Aye."

"I remember her from school."

Another silence.

"Lunch tomorrow?"

"Aye, I'll text to confirm. Depends how the investigation goes."

"OK Roland. You get some sleep now."

"OK, goodnight Christine."

Chapter 8

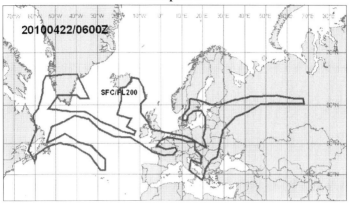

Thursday morning, 22nd April 2010, 7.45 am.

Sanja Dilpit and Irene Seath were finishing cooked breakfasts at the Pierowall hotel.

"Kenny Dalgleish."

"Whit? Nae bloody way, yeh silly bitch."

"Who would you hiv then?"

"Jock Stein."

"Jock Stein? Rubbish. He would always be fighting wi Matt Busby aboot Manchester and Glasgow, you know, how big the fatty bits in the black pudding should be?"

"By the way, this is spectacularly brilliant black pudding."

"Aye, but they would be rock solid on 4-4-2 formations."

"Pass the toast please darlin'."

"Ok Ah'll gie yeh that, but I reckon Kenny Dalgleish as manager is the dog's bollocks. If he takes over Liverpool they will take off."

"Rubbish, as soon as he took his boots off, he was finished."

"No. This gentleman was much misunderestimated."

Irene smiled. Sanja carried on.

"He runs a team with sensitivity and gets the best out of the players when he is their manager."

"Merr coffee?"

"Aye, please."

"How's yer knittin'?"

"Fine. It's a bunnet fur ma new neice."

"Nice colour."

"Left over fae a wee blanket Ah made her."

Sanja's phone rang.

"When are you going to change that bloody ring tone?"

"What's wrong with bagpipes? That's real music."

"Ma phone disnae get reception here."

"Mines is ok. Different network."

Sanja retrieved her phone from her handbag and read a text message.

"It's the number and PIN code for the teleconference. We better get going."

"Here are you sure ma mascara isny a' clumpy?"

"You and your bloody mascara, Ah'm sure you've got OCD."

*   *   *

Clett logged on to a computer. While he was waiting, he looked down and observed some of the marks on his desk. In the morning light, you could make out concentric circles scratched in the veneer. He lifted his head to the whiteboard, covered with a growing amount of information, photos and written names with lines between them, indicating connections. He took a marker and underlined Rust's name and placed a question mark after it.

He turned to his colleagues who were waiting for the teleconference to start. There was some small talk as everyone connected and introduced themselves. Clett began.

"Morning everyone. Can we start with Sergeant Clouston, what is the ash cloud situation?"

"Thanks. Yes, the SIGMET Volcanic Ash advisory communication indicates that it is still causing problems with air transport in the lower airspace around Orkney. However, I've confirmed with Kirkwall ATC that there may be some flights. Aircraft will fly dependent on the continuing six hourly ash cloud forecasts. We still do not have full timetables. I believe there may be an incoming flight from Glasgow this morning. Basically watch this space. In the meantime, the Celtic Voyager is still available."

"Thank you Sergeant. I believe that there has been some light rain overnight at the Bay of Noup, but there is now an awning covering the crime scene which will protect it against further disruption or contamination. The body was removed last thing last night and the post mortem is being carried out as we speak by Dr Sinclair at Balfour Hospital. Perhaps our SPSA colleagues could say some more about the current forensic situation."

"Aye, Sanja Dilpit here. We carried out as many on-site forensic tests as we could and Inspector Clett approved the body's removal to the morgue at Balfour Hospital last night. After the full post mortem and subject to the Procurator Fiscal's approval, we think the body can be released to Mr and Mrs Byrd."

"Thank you Sanja."

Clett returned to the whiteboard and pointed to Dominic Byrd's facebook picture.

"The victim has been positively identified as Dominic Byrd, aged 20 of Little Gidding near Cambridge. Irene and Sanja are still waiting for the lab to confirm this with a DNA test. DNA samples were taken from Mr and Mrs Byrd by Cambridgeshire police yesterday. Dominic Byrd arrived on Westray in mid March as a volunteer member of the dig team. He was reported as being a popular and a flamboyant member of the team. No motive has currently been identified. Once Byrd's movements and connections have been discovered, perhaps this will become clear. There is an unconfirmed report that the victim was seen at the Fraction nightclub on Tuesday with an unidentified man aged around thirty. There were calls made on the same night from Dominic's phone to someone called 'Patrick'. The man in the nightclub might be Patrick."

Clett continued.

"In terms of suspects, there is one candidate that we are interested in at the moment, Professor Trevor de Vries. He was disruptive in regard of obstructing the investigations at the crime scene. At the very least he will be charged with tampering with evidence. In addition, I think that there is another possibility that we might include. Ronnie Rust's car was on Westray at the time of the murder."

Clett paused to look at Chief Inspector Maggie McPhee. She shook her head from side to side. Clett cleared his throat and continued.

"According to the current reports, there have been no significant arguments at the dig site. Trevor de Vries is a charismatic leader who appears to have a close knit team. All are male and under 25. None had – to date - any significant previous convictions, except one who has a charge of possession of cannabis. No witnesses have been forthcoming. Mrs Jessie Sclater of Noup Farm hadn't seen anything, but she placed the sound of a car at around 23:45. Tracks were found at Noup Head that seemed to show that a car had been driven off the cliff. This may be the same car that Mrs Sclater reported. She also heard a scream at around 1:40. If it was the victim, it would suggest that Dominic Byrd was alive at 1.40am. Sanja and Irene, have you any more you can give us?"

"Thanks Inspector. We would reckon the time of death as between ten and eleven o'clock on the evening of Tuesday 20th April, so that differs from the time of your scream."

"Thanks Irene, we will have to figure that one out."

Irene continued.

"The victim had been assaulted by multiple blows to the head with a rock. The head had been pulverised from the front and brain and facial tissue and bone matter had become amalgamated due to the impact of the blows. There was no retrievable dental data. No traces of any bullets within the skull area were found, and no traces of any shell cases have been found in the surrounding area. We have also been able to assess other aspects of the body despite the site contamination. There were no incisions on the body caused by any blade, but some particles of matter were found under the fingernails. These are being analysed for viable DNA content. The body material spatter radius was around 2 metres with a 'shadow' where the assailant stood. From this 'shadow', we could say that the assailant was around 6 feet and of slim build. I would like to remind officers that the technique used for this estimate is still in its infancy and cannot be fully guaranteed.

To have carried out a sustained assault with perhaps up to one hundred blows standing up and striking down over a height, the assailant would have had to have been very fit. The repeated and precisely struck area of Byrd's head indicates that the blows were struck in a single sustained attack. Assuming that the blows were continuous we estimate that this may have taken about a minute and a half to two minutes from start to finish.

Today we will examine tyre and shoe tracks. We have the photos of the footwear of all members of the dig team and we should be able to identify or eliminate them as suspects as appropriate. We will examine the tyre tracks at Noup Head and confirm or otherwise whether they were from the same vehicle. To finish our work on the site, we will collect and examine other DNA, hair, and bone fragments both within the spatter radius and around the wider site. We will also prepare a 360 degree software presentation which will give a virtual display of the murder scene and of the damage to the body itself. This can be emailed and used by officers remotely for further analysis and also for actual presentation as evidence in court. The computer generated images can be used instead of photographs in court. Lastly, the office at Dundee is preparing a forensic telephony presentation which will offer an evidential display of all the telephone and data traffic between Byrd and any other relevant parties. This is under way and some data is forthcoming which appears to connect Dominic Byrd with drug contacts in Norway who in turn appear to have separate connections with Trevor de Vries. The data will be available on the secure drive. Anyone who doesn't yet have the permissions for this drive, please let us know."

"Thanks Irene. You have done a massive amount of work. Did you two get any sleep last night?"

"Jist gie us fags and coffee Inspector, fags and coffee."

"Ok. One or two final points. Fishing boats have been alerted to look out a wrecked car around the coast. It may be that the car driven off of Noup Head is washed up. A car was reported speeding south, out of Pierowall between two and three o'clock in the morning. Nancie Keldie and Jamie Gunn are still on Westray with Special Constables Drever, Fedotova and Leask and will carry on a second tranche of interviews with all dig team members and local residents. They have also been carrying out door to door enquiries but are not coming up with any substantial information. Relief officers will take over this morning and give the Westray officers a break. The counselling team from the Kirkwall medical centre are also on site and have carried out critical incident counselling for the members of the dig team and others. I'll be giving a press conference this morning. Ok that's it from me. Anyone else?"

There were a few grunts of 'ok for me'.

"Ok we'll have another telephone conference tomorrow unless something comes up. Please get back to me any time."

*   *   *

"Roland?"

"Yes Chief Inspector."

"What was that about Ronnie Rust?"

"Sorry Maggie, I should have warned you he was in the frame."

"In the frame? What do you mean Roland? What's got into you?"

"Ronnie Rust's car was on Westray on Tuesday night and there is an unconfirmed report of a car racing through Pierowall later on that evening. Also, the victim was seen in his nightclub on the night of the murder."

"Was the car in Pierowall Ronnie Rust's car?"

"We're working on that."

"Ok Roland, you can follow this up, but be very careful. He has a lot of power and you have to look out for yourself. You can't afford to be humiliated by him again."

"Thanks Maggie, but I know Rust. He is absolutely capable of this level of violence. He fits the profile one hundred percent."

"Roland, I'm serious, you are too close to him and he can hurt you, and he can hurt this department. He is held in affection all over Orkney as a generous businessman."

"Aye and we know how he became successful don't we?"

"Nothing is proven Roland, and remember, even if he doesn't work within the law, we do. Right, are you ready for this press conference?"

"No, well, I mean, yes of course Maggie."

"You will be fine Roland."

*   *   *

Sigurd Rostung ran his fingers through his bushy moustache and scratched under his wig. There was a knock on his door.

"Come."

Roland Clett entered the Procurator Fiscal's Office. The two men shook hands warmly and Rostung clapped Clett's shoulder with an expansive gesture which made his gown billow like a sail.

"Roland, my dear friend. Good morning. Congratulations on your promotion."

"Thanks Sigurd. You could say it's been something of a baptism of fire."

"A busy first day then?"

"Absolutely. We have a murder on Westray."

"Really. How interesting."

"Yup. Body in an archaeological dig, among the old bones and stones. Couple of suspects."

"I'm intrigued."

"Well, you will need the information soon anyway."

"Whenever you like Roland."

Rostung looked at the clock on the wall and the files in front of him.

"Actually I'm in court at ten o'clock."

"I won't keep you Sigurd. I have a press conference on the steps at 9:30. I'm meeting Maggie McPhee in a few minutes. I was hoping for some peace and quiet."

Rostung looked up.

"Really? A press conference? Will you be all right with that?"

"I have to be."

Rostung shifted his large frame on his leather seat and looked at Clett, who moved from foot to foot.

"Have you heard from Christine?"

"Aye, we are hoping to get together for a chat over the next week or so."

"That's just fine Roland. That's great news."

Clett looked at his watch.

"Roland; look, why don't you just have a seat here. I have to collect a few more files."

"Thanks Sigurd. Five minutes is all I need."

"Absolutely no problem Roland. Take as much time as you want."

Rostung gripped Clett's shoulder firmly and left him alone in the office with its view dominated by the spire of St Magnus Cathedral. Clett sat down and placed his elbows on the desk and put his head between his hands. He breathed slowly as he had been taught.

Clett went out to the steps of the Watergate Sheriff Court as Maggie McPhee came up behind him. This was the traditional meeting place for television interviews and press conferences going back to the time when it was the main Police Station.

Five journalists stood in the rain, holding their phones and voice recorders in the air. Clett knew Janie Shearer from *The Orcadian*, and there was one other face he knew, but he could not put a name to it.

"Gentlemen, Miss Shearer."

He nodded to Janie.

"You have the printout of the police statement which I will now read."

"A body was found at the Bay of Noup on Westray yesterday morning Wednesday 21st April. The body was that of a young man of twenty years who was volunteering on an archaeological dig on the island. We currently have no suspects, but we are continuing our enquiries. We will not release the name of the dead man until the body has been formally identified and the family are fully aware of the situation."

"Inspector. What can you say about the condition of the body?"

"I can't release that information at the moment."

"Isn't it true that the body is unrecognisable and the head has been beaten to a pulp?"

"I can't comment."

The familiar face spoke up.

"Inspector, isn't it true that you are not long back from sick leave, and this is your first week as Inspector? Are you up to this investigation?"

Clett felt his head swim. He stuttered.

"Eh, I, em, that is not for me to say."

Maggie McPhee interjected.

"Inspector Clett is a highly proficient officer and brings to this investigation many years of experience and judgement. I have total confidence in his abilities. That will be all."

The journalists moved away in the rain talking among themselves. Clett and McPhee turned in to the building.

"I'm so sorry about that Roland."

"It's ok Maggie, you weren't to know they were going to ask about that."

"No Roland, but I wish I hadn't said I had confidence in you."

"I beg your pardon?"

"Of course I do have confidence in you, but I wish I hadn't said it. They will read into it the exact opposite meaning. They are probably going to find out about your history."

"That doesn't matter Maggie. I will just stick to the facts. I will not allow my circumstances to become the story."

"Hmm. I think we should be careful about this Roland."

*   *   *

Clett was sitting behind the wheel of his old green Polo. As he gave the key its second turn, his old Nokia buzzed. It said 'DREVER' on the screen.

"Archie."

"Roland. How was your press conference?"

"Nerve wracking. I hated it. Anyway, how's things? I should be over this afternoon to check on arrangements. I'm meeting Christine for a fast lunch and then I'll get the Celtic Explorer over."

"You know Roland, there really is no need to. It is all running smoothly. Those girls from Dundee are absolute stars. They are totally running the show."

"Aye, they were impressive at the telephone conference this morning. Have they found any more?"

"Well they have been up at Noup Head and are taking pollen samples that can be used to identify whether anyone has been in the area."

"Any luck with the car?"

"No Roland, it could be anywhere now."

"Assuming it was driven off the cliff."

"Oh, Sanja and Irene have no doubt about it. They identified the 195mm radials as possibly coming from a 2004 Toyota."

"What? How in God's name did they do that?"

"Don't ask me. They have access to some database that identifies information within the tread patterns."

"Jeeze, new one on me too. Archie, what do you think about de Vries?"

"The man's a fool Roland. He's all bluster and hot air. There's no way he killed that boy."

"That's not the way other people see it."

"The man would run a mile if you said boo to him."

"That's my feeling. What about Ronnie Rust?"

"You're not serious. What is there to link him?"

"His car was on Westray and he is certainly evil enough to have done this. He could have driven the car off the cliff and made his escape in the silver BMW."

"That would mean he would have had two cars to start with."

"I'll have to think that one through."

"Look Roland, be very careful. Do you have any real evidence against him?"

"Well the car on the ferry …"

"Yes, but anything more substantial?"

"Rust owns the nightclub where the victim was last seen alive."

"Ok Roland, you've got to step back a bit here. What motivation would he have? what are the connections? The Bay of Noup is a bloody long way from a nightclub in Kirkwall. Be very careful Roland. You don't need this kind of diversion."

There was a moment's silence.

"Roland, did you say you were having lunch with Christine?"

"Yes I did. I'm a wee bit nervous, but I'm looking forward to it. I could do without the distraction of the case, but we organised it a while ago, and I'm not letting an opportunity like this go."

"Absolutely Roland. That's good news. I hope it works out for the two of you."

*   *   *

"Anna Shearer, stop your blethering. If you want to talk, you can talk to me about your numbers. Would you like to do that?"
"No Mrs Clett."
"No. Well get on with your work please."
Christine Clett did not want any interruptions this morning. She was anxious about meeting her husband. She wanted it to go well and it appeared that they both wanted to get back together. It all seemed right, but she still worried. Glasgow had changed Roland and he was of a more melancholy frame of mind since coming back to Orkney. He had stopped drinking, and he was more predictable, he had been seeing a counsellor for the post-traumatic stress disorder he had experienced and he was now off the medication. Had he taken the re-promoted post too soon? So many questions: what would their boys say? How would he deal with the stress of a demanding investigation?
Anyway, the arrangement was made and she knew she could make it a positive experience for them both.
The babble of 8 year olds' conversation rose again.
"Anna Shearer, that is enough. Come to my desk please."

*   *   *

Chief Inspector Maggie McPhee walked smartly up to Clett's desk.
"Inspector Clett. This is Mr Simon Byrd, the father of Dominic Byrd."
"Oh. Mr Byrd, you should have called and we would have met you at the airport. We didn't expect you."
"Mr Byrd has just introduced himself to the desk sergeant, Inspector."

"But how did you get here? There are still flight restrictions, and the Hamnavoe is out of service."

"You don't have to concern yourself with that detail Inspector. Let's just say that I'm tired after a long drive and that I had to push some people at Gills Bay. I got the ferry to St Margaret's Hope."

Clett looked at Maggie McPhee who raised her eyebrows.

"So you are Clett. I spoke to you on the phone."

He put his hand out to be shaken.

"Yes Mr Byrd, how is your wife? Is she with you?"

Clett took Byrd's hand. Byrd was wearing light tan kid gloves. His handshake was overly strong, and he gripped Clett's hand tight for a moment too long.

"I suppose you could say she was grieving; too taken up with her affairs. In modern terminology, she could be said to be in denial."

"Everyone has their own way of coping."

"Quite."

Clett eyed Byrd lift the stone from his desk and roll it between his gloved fingers, examining the colours nearly present within the small rock.

"It's from Papay."

Byrd looked over the top of his glasses at Clett.

"Won't you sit down? Will you have a coffee?"

McPhee caught Clett's eye.

"Inspector, Mr Byrd wants to see his son's body and visit the bay of Noup."

"I see. Chief Inspector, would you like me to continue with this?"

"Yes please Inspector. It was nice to meet you Mr Byrd. Once again, I would like to express my condolences."

"Thank you Chief Inspector."

"Oh Inspector, are we on for another press conference tomorrow morning?"

Clett looked at McPhee.

"Tomorrow morning?"

"Yes. I think so. Lets talk about it later."

Clett took a deep breath as Maggie McPhee turned away and left the two men alone. He looked at Simon Byrd.

"Mr Byrd. How much do you know about the manner of your son's death?"

"I know he was murdered and his body is badly mutilated and that you have not yet apprehended anyone."

"Yes. I can bring you up to date on the investigation so far. As to viewing the body, I would really not recommend it."

"For God's sake man. I'm his father and I've seen a dead body before."

"Mr Byrd, he's unrecognisable. We may only be able to identify him positively from his DNA. The blows that killed him destroyed all facial features. There are not even any dental remains."

"Nevertheless, I still want to see him."

"If you insist. We can go now if you wish."

*   *   *

Clett and Simon Byrd drove the short distance in silence to the small morgue at Balfour Hospital.

"Mr Byrd, this is Dr Sinclair, the pathologist who carried out the post mortem on your son this morning. Dr Sinclair, this is Mr Byrd, Dominic Byrd's father. He would like to see his son's body."

"Really? Mr Byrd are you aware of the condition of your son's body?"

"Inspector Clett has told me."

"I see. I have to say that it is possibly the most mutilated body I have seen."

"Yes, I know doctor. Can we get on with it please?"

Sinclair directed them to the cold storage room and slowly removed the cover from the body of Dominic Byrd.

As the cover was lowered from the body, Simon Byrd gasped.

Clett and Sinclair saw Byrd's face turn white.

Clett directed him to a chair. Byrd snapped -

"I'm all right."

"Would you like a few moments alone with your son?"

"Yes."

As the door closed, Simon Byrd stood still with the body of his son below him. That idiot Clett was right. He would not have known his own son. There was nothing left that was recognisable. Of course, they hadn't seen him in nearly a year, and then only for a few minutes.

"You little shit. You have fucking let me down yet again. Ungrateful spoilt little runt."

As Byrd reflected on his disappointment in his son, he became more angry. He was breathing in short breaths, his fists were clenched and his shoulders and neck were taut. He turned and punched the tiled wall three times. His hands hurt and he let them hang down. He felt hot tears on his cheeks. He sniffed and wiped them away and composed himself. He turned to the door.

"Inspector, I have finished."

On the way back to the Burgh Road Station, Simon Byrd had not responded when Clett spoke, not a single word since viewing Dominic's body. Back in the office, he glared at Clett.

"Right I want to know why you haven't arrested that bastard de Vries. Your colleague Detective Inspector Nelson said his arrest was imminent. I want to talk to him. He seems to know what is going on."

"You seem well informed."

"Yes I have been following the local press on the internet and I have been briefed by Detective Inspector Nelson, your superior, I believe. It was he who said I should come up and that I would be expected."

"I see. Well, Professor de Vries is being investigated along with others, but no arrests have been made. In addition, DI Nelson is not my superior. He is the same grade as myself, he is merely attached to CID. I am the SIO in this case."

Clett bristled at the assumption that Nelson was superior.

"Look, I don't care. When can I see this chap de Vries?"

"I would not advise talking to Professor de Vries."

"Nelson assured me that there would be no problem."

"I'm sorry, but DI Nelson had no authority to say what he said to you. I am the SIO. I cannot stop you speaking to Professor de Vries, but I would strongly advise you not to do so. It may damage any case that will be brought."

"I see. So that's the way it is. Nelson warned me about you people. No matter. I'll simply get my lawyer to make the necessary arrangements."

"I think you will find that your lawyer will not be able to help you with this."

"Right. I want to visit, what is the ridiculous name of this place, the Bay of something."

"Yes, the Bay of Noup."

"I want to go there, as soon as possible if you don't mind."

"It will take us several hours by ferry and car."

"Look you are starting to irritate me. I want to see where my son was killed."

Clett paused and lifted the phone.

"Sergeant Clouston. I have Mr Simon Byrd with me. He wants to visit the Bay of Noup. Can you see if there are any flights to Westray?"

Clett listened to Clouston's prolonged response.

"Thank you Sergeant."

Clett replaced the handset.

"Mr Byrd, As you will be aware, there are still no flights in or out of Kirkwall. We have the services of a water taxi that can get you to Pierowall on Westray, which is about a five minute drive from the Bay of Noup. The water taxi will take about forty-five minutes. Would that be satisfactory?"

"If that is what it takes. Let's get on with it."

"Ok Mr Byrd, Sergeant Clouston will be here in a few minutes and he will accompany you to the harbour."

*   *   *

Clett finished his tomato and basil soup and was sipping his coffee. The lunch was going well and the ordinariness of the situation was a distraction from the case. He was pleased to have this interlude with Christine and the prospects it held, but soon he had to get back to the office.

"One other thing, Roland. Why did you steal my coat?"

"Sorry?"

"In Glasgow when I came down when you first got your posting there, you stole my beautiful grey coat. I know you stole it."

Clett was embarrassed. He remembered perfectly well that he had taken it, but did not want to explain. Also, this was not a conversation he really wanted to have now.

"I didn't want to come to Glasgow, but we went anyway, and when we stayed at the flat in Bearsden, you stole my coat. One day it was in the wardrobe, and after the first day, it was gone. Were you trying to keep me there?"

Clett said nothing.

"Why did you do that, Roland?"

"I don't know."

"No Roland, I would like to know why you took my coat."

"I don't know. I couldn't stop myself."

There. He had admitted it."

He had taken her favourite coat and put it in one of the suitcases and stored it with the pile of cardboard boxes in the attic.

"I knew you had taken it."

"But you said nothing."

"I know. I knew you would give it back sometime."

"I gave it back when you stopped talking. I knew you had to go back to Orkney. I didn't want you to go back."

"Yes."

There was a pause and they smiled at each other. Clett's phone buzzed in his pocket and he looked at it with the intention of ignoring it.

"Sorry Christine, it's Russell. Should I take it later?"

"It's ok Roland, you speak to your brother."

Clett pressed the green button on his old phone.

"Hi Roland, I know you are busy, but I've got really bad news. I know this is not a good time and there is no easy way of telling you this; but, well, Mum and Dad are dead. They died in a car crash this morning."

Roland paused for a moment.

"No Russell, I spoke to them yesterday. There is some mistake."

Christine put her glass down, aware something was amiss.

"They were driving down the A68 and had a head-on collision. They were killed outright."

"But they were going on a caravan holiday to Whitby."

"Yes, they were towing the caravan at the time."

"God Russell, I spoke to them yesterday. I was a shit and didn't see them for lunch."

"I know Roland, but they would have understood."

"I should have taken time off and gone to see them."

"Roland, I'm sorry. Look, I know you are up to it with work just now, so let me and Margaret do the organising. I can keep in touch with Christine. Call me when you can."

"I don't know."

"Please Roland. Let us help."

"Well, ok Russell."

There was a moment while both men waited for more words to say.

"Russell,"

"Yes."

"How are you?"

"Och, you know how it is. This is awful, but we have to get on with stuff just now and deal with how we feel later. Margaret is strong and the girls have been great, but they are young, you know. Margaret is going to Kirkwall today to pick them up. Thanks for asking."

"OK Russell, keep in touch."

Clett put down his phone. Christine waited for him to speak.

"Christine, Mum and Dad are dead. That was Russell."

"Oh Roland. Bill and Vera. Oh no. I'm so sorry."

She reached across the table and held his hand, quite tightly.

"Do you know what happened?"

"They were towing their caravan and there was a head-on collision with another vehicle. They were killed outright."

Killed outright, Clett repeated the phrase to himself. What does that mean? He tried to imagine what their last moments were. A lorry coming straight at them. Was this better than some lingering death? In all his dealings with death in the past, he was able to place a boundary around it. Somebody else loved those people, but these were people he loved, and they were his parents, and Russell had told him they were dead.

There was silence for a few moments.

"God, what a time for this to happen."

Clett felt guilty as soon as these words had left his mouth. He felt guilty that he had not visited them yesterday; he felt guilty he had not phoned them more; he felt guilty he had not been a better son.

"Why didn't I visit them yesterday? I could have, but I thought this bloody investigation was more important. I'll have to call Russell back to deal with details."

"No Roland, let me do that. I'll let you know what you have to do. You will have to be involved with the investigation until someone else can take over. I'll let you know how it's going. People will understand."

"But they are my mum and dad, how can I leave them, there is so much to do. I'm the oldest. It is expected of me. Let me tell the boys."

Clett's phone buzzed again. Clett looked at it, expecting Russell. It was Clouston. Clett hesitated. His head was swimming. What does Clouston want? Clett looked at Cristine. As she held his hand, he answered.

"Hello Inspector, I have some information for you. The telephony and data analysis has been released and Dominic Byrd was found to have had text and e-mail connections with individuals with a history of illegal drugs activities in Scandinavia, Holland and England. Some numbers on his mobile were those of some heavy suppliers. Inverness are interested and DI Nelson wants to speak to you."

"Tony Nelson?"

Clett hesitated before answering. Nelson's presence in this investigation was unwelcome. He had been Clett's supervising officer in Strathclyde when things went wrong.

"Surrey police also wanted to talk and the Chief Inspector wants a word as soon as you can."

"OK Norman, I'll get on to it. Thanks."

He looked at Christine. She got up and helped him on with his coat.

Clett stood up, confused. He turned around looking for his jacket, unaware that he was now wearing it. Christine turned down his collar and smoothed the shoulder of his coat. Outside the café, people walked and talked and carried on engaging in ordinary day to day activities. They pushed prams and bought stamps and tried on shoes and chatted together as if nothing had just happened.

"Do you want to carry on with the investigation Roland?"

"Aye, for a while Christine, but keep an eye on me will you? I don't want to be doing anything stupid."

"Of course."

As they left the tearoom, they hugged.

"Be careful Roland, and keep in touch. I'll call Russell in a wee while."

"Thanks Christine."

Chapter 9

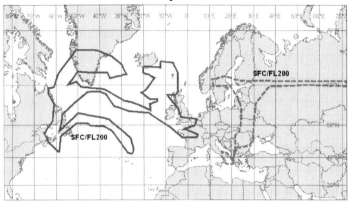

Thursday afternoon, 22nd April 2010 2.15 pm.

Simon Byrd stepped off of the Celtic Voyager and looked around at Pierowall. It was silent except for the sound of birdsong and the quiet rumble of the boat's idling engine. Lobster pots were piled high against the harbour wall and some sheep walked down the street.

"What on earth did my son see in this Godforsaken place?"

John Leask walked towards him.

"Mr Simon Byrd, I'm Special Constable John Leask. Inspector Clett has asked me to escort you to the Bay of Noup."

"Special Constable? What is this? More incompetence. What kind of message boy are you?"

"Here is my warrant card sir."

Simon Byrd brushed it aside.

"For goodness sake."

Leask drove Dominic's father to the site in silence. They were met by Archie Drever. Sanja Dilpit and Irene Seath were wearing white disposable overalls; Irene examining a substance in a test tube and Sanja typing at a laptop.

"Mr Byrd, your son was found just over here."

At the dig site, they lifted the yellow and green tapes and went down to the midden. Simon Byrd looked north to the sea and back to Jessie Sclater's farm, and then down to the depression where Dominic's body had been found. There were small pinned numbers at various points in the site that identified where pieces of evidence had been located. He bent down and reached out his arm. John Leask spoke.

"Sir, I don't think…"

Drever stopped him.

"It is ok sir, go ahead."

Dilpit and Seath looked at Drever, but said nothing.

Byrd lifted a scallop shell from the midden.

A voice behind him shouted.

"I say. You there. What do you think you are doing? Get off my site."

Shit, thought Drever. He recognised the voice of de Vries.

"I say, You there."

Byrd stood up and looked towards the person shouting at him.

"And you are?"

"I might ask you the same question. You there, junior constable, whatever your name is, why are you letting people on my site?"

"Professor, please leave immediately."

"I'll do no such thing."

"Professor, would that be Professor de Vries?"

"It most certainly would. Who are you?"

"I'm the father of the boy you killed."

"What? What nonsense is this?"

Both Drever and de Vries were surprised with the speed that Byrd moved. He was out of the ditch and had leapt on de Vries, striking him three blows to the head before Drever could do anything. De Vries fell to the ground, Byrd fell on top of him and gripped his windpipe between his fingers and thumb and squeezed viciously. Byrd was grunting.

"You bastard."

De Vries couldn't breathe. Unable to speak, his arms were flailing like a child's, trying to push Byrd out of the way; his wide open eyes were popping with the increased pressure in his head, his tongue protruding from his mouth. Leask got to Byrd and put his arms under his shoulders from the rear and up and around his neck, clasping his hands behind the back of Byrd's neck. Byrd couldn't escape Leask's grip and he was forced to release his hold on de Vries. De Vries tried to get to his feet, but stayed kneeling on all fours gasping for breath. As he recovered, he grabbed a rock and raised his arm to place a blow to Byrd's head, but he fell to the ground in exhaustion. Drever by now had reached de Vries and kept him down. Byrd was screaming at de Vries, and de Vries croaked at Byrd in protest, each demanding immediate release, and that they would be filing for police assault.

Drever guided de Vries, who was shaking and bleeding from the blows to his head, away from the scene and locked him in a car. Leask spoke to Byrd, lessening his grip slightly.

"I am sorry for your loss sir, and I understand your anger, but you must not attempt to approach Mr de Vries again. If you do so, it might harm any case that might be brought against him. Also, I might have to restrain you. Is that clear?"

Simon Byrd nodded.

"I am going to release you now. Are you calm?"

He nodded again.

Leask released his hold on Byrd. Byrd turned around and glared at Leask. He pointed a gloved finger in his face.

"Look sonny, don't you ever lay a hand on me again. Make no mistake, I will be making a complaint against you. Now, I want you to get me away from this pathetic place."

Byrd rubbed de Vries' bloodstains from his tan kid gloves until they were no more than smudges.

As Drever returned to de Vries in the car, he could see him trembling in the back seat.

"Are you all right Professor?"

There was no response, just a small whimper. De Vries' left eye was swelling and blood trickled down his cheek. He was forcing his breath through his damaged windpipe.

"Perhaps we can get Irene and Sanja to look at those wounds. They are trained medical professionals."

De Vries regained his composure. He croaked.

"No thank you."

There was also a tremble in his voice.

"I have some arnica back at my tent and I can apply a poultice if I need to. I have no need of your help. Just get me away from that madman."

De Vries turned away from Drever and blew his nose.

"Interesting wee bit o' rough and tumble there don't ye think Irene?"

"Aye, yon laddie Leask can handle himsel'. Kind o' a surprise. Ah thought he wis like kinda weedy."

"Weedy is it Irene?"

"Sorry John. Ah didn'y ken ye were listenin'."

"Aye, well, you never get used tae that stuff. It is always horrible. I had to do it a few times in Afghanistan, and it is worse with guns and everyone stressed up. To think I came back to Orkney fur some peace and quiet."

"Naw John, ye did yersel' proud there."

"Thanks Sanja. Do you want me to help move some more of your test kit?"

"Naw John. We want tae jist crack on. If ye could jist gie us a hand wi' the lighting, that'd be dandy. Irene his some brilliant coffee in her flask if ye want some."

"Aye, well maybe."

*   *   *

Sandy Clett had another sip of lager and looked out of the bar to the crowds milling on Byres Road. He was getting used to the faster pace and rhythm of Glasgow life. He was on his way back to the library. This time of year, study places were at a premium and he didn't want to work in the flat. He shared it with three mates, two bicycles, four stereos, five laptops and no food. His phone rang.

"Hi Sandy, it's Dad."

"Hi Dad. How's it going?"

"Fine son. Is it ok to speak?"

"Aye I'm just on my way to get something to eat and then I'm back to the library."

"Ok, well I'm afraid I have some bad news for you."

"What's that Dad?"

"Well… I don't know how to tell you this, but Granny and Grandad Clett; they are, well, they are dead. They were both killed in a car crash."

"Granny and Grandad? Both of them?"

"Yes. They were taking the caravan to Whitby and had an accident on the A68."

"What? My God. That's terrible Dad. When did it happen?"

"Early this morning. Uncle Russell called to tell me at lunchtime."

"What do you want me to do, how can I help?"

"Well nothing just now. The funeral might be on Monday, but Mum and I want no pressure on the two of you."

"You've spoken to Mum about it?"

"Yes we were having lunch together when Uncle Russell called."

"Really? You and Mum?"

"Yes. As I was saying we don't want either of you..."

"And have you had lunches together before?"

"Aye, once or twice."

"Well that's great, but it would've been nice to know."

"What, that we were having lunch?"

"Well yes."

"Well ok Sandy, Mum and I've had a few lunches, and we've talked about some things. I know the two of you will have feelings about us and our future."

"Aye, feelings we have."

"Look Sandy, I'm sorry you're finding out like this. I had to tell you about Granny and Grandad. I didn't want it to turn into an argument. I'm sorry. I had not planned this."

"No. It doesn't look like it, does it?"

"Look, I'll call later and we can have a proper chat."

"Aye. When did you say the funeral was going to be?"

"Well we're not sure, maybe Monday, but I was saying that you don't have to come if you have too much studying."

"And why wouldn't I want to come to my own grandparent's funeral?"

"I wasn't saying that Sandy."

"Bloody hell, Dad."

Silence.

"Sorry son, maybe we should talk later."

"Aye let's do that."

Sandy hung up and immediately made another call.

"Margarita, I've just had a call from that bastard father of mine,"

"Oh, what did he want?"

"Well. He basically told me that my grandparents have been killed in a traffic accident."

"What, both of them?"

"Aye. But then he goes on to say that I shouldn't go to the funeral."

"I'm sure he didn't say that Sandy."

"He bloody well did. He said I would be too busy with my studies to attend the funeral of my own grandparents. And he is seeing Mum again."

"But surely that's a good thing Sandy?"

"Aye well maybe, if the bastard hadn't dumped her in the first place."

*   *   *

Clett composed himself and dialled his other son, Magnus.

"Hi, it's Dad here."

"Hi Dad, how's it going? How's the new job going?"

"Hmm, well, it's very busy just now, but I've phoned for something else. Do you have a minute?"

"Aye Dad, on you go."

"Well its very bad news actually."

Clett went on to tell his son about the accident.

"What? that's terrible. They were going to Whitby weren't they. What happened?"

"They had a head on collision with a truck somewhere on the A68."

"God, I don't know what to say. Are you sure?"

"Yes Magnus."

"Sorry Dad, what a stupid thing to say, sometimes I …"

"Don't worry about it son. It's ok. No-one knows what to say at times like this."

"How are you taking it Dad?"

"Thanks Magnus, I'm ok, but work is a real problem just now so Uncle Russell and Aunt Margaret and Mum will be doing a lot of the arrangements."

"So Mum knows."

"Aye, we were having lunch when Uncle Russell phoned with the news."

"Lunch? You and Mum? That's great news Dad. How long has this been going on?"

"Oh we've met once or twice now."

"That's brilliant; I'm really pleased for the two of you. Tell Mum for me will you?"

"Ok son, I'll do that. However there is one thing you might be able to help me with."

"You mean Sandy?"

"Aye, I tried to tell him about the funeral arrangements, probably on Monday, and I told him about mum and me. He has got it into his head that I don't want him at the funeral."

"What?"

"I know. I'll try to call him later, but if you could have a word, it'd be a big help."

"Ok Dad I'll see what I can do."

"I'll get leave for Monday, shouldn't be a problem, I'll talk to you later."

"Bye Dad."

"Bye son."

*   *   *

Christine and Roland looked out over the Ouse, the small tidal estuary near Finstown. The clouds were red-tinged by the setting sun. The cold evening air blew through them and they quickened their step.

"Look at those waders. They have a lovely gait."

"Aye."

Christine placed her arm in front of Roland's chest.

"Stop Roland."

They stopped in their tracks. Christine whispered:

"Lutra lutra."

"Sorry?"

"An otter."

Roland whispered back.

"You and your Latin. Just call it a bloody otter."

Christine smiled and placed her finger over Roland's mouth. The otter glanced at them and continued rummaging in the shallow water. It put its head below the surface for a few seconds and came up again with a trout in its teeth. It turned and disappeared into the reeds.

Roland and Christine looked at each other and smiled. They walked on in silence.

"Roland, I'll support you all through this. You know that, but I do feel you shouldn't have to do another press briefing tomorrow."

"I know Christine, but I really can't avoid it. I'm the SIO. I'll just get it over with and start to back off afterwards."

Chapter 10

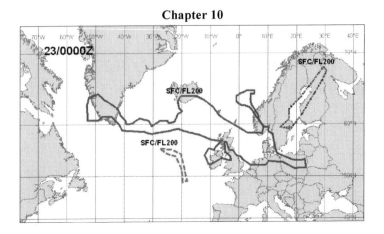

Friday morning, 23rd April 2010 8.45 am.

"Good morning everyone. For this teleconference I'll give an outline of the progress and people can add contributions as they see fit. We have more support now and we have had contact with the drugs section at Northern Constabulary and Strathclyde. Relevant emails are available on the secure drive. No progress with the door to doors on Westray, but there has been communication from Cambridge police who want to follow up possible leads. I have approved the release of the forensic draft report to cleared officers. The raw telephony and data evidence has just been distributed. Initial information seems to indicate that Dominic Byrd has been found to have drug dealing connections in Scandinavia, Holland and England. We know that his family live near Cambridge, his father, Simon Byrd is a serial bankrupt and that Dominic himself has been charged with credit card fraud on two occasions. The main suspect is still the dig team leader, Trevor de Vries. He's been acting strangely from the start and he's been responsible for major crime scene contamination. If not charged with the actual murder, he'll be charged with obstructing the course of justice and tampering with evidence. He was observed by other dig team members to be somewhat obsessed with Byrd."

Clett continued:

"Dominic Byrd's father arrived here yesterday and insisted on seeing his son's body. He also visited the Bay of Noup and I believe there was an unpleasant set-to between Mr Byrd and Trevor de Vries. Apparently, young John Leask gave an excellent account of himself."

Maggie McPhee spoke up.

"The press are showing interest in this case, and it won't help matters if this fight was to become headline news."

"DI Tony Nelson here, what about that press conference Inspector Clett? Any comments? Bit of a farce wouldn't you say? Have you not seen the story? 'Investigating Cop Not Up To Job' I would suggest that that is not a good headline, eh?"

"I'll continue to run the investigation as long as Chief Inspector McPhee sees fit."

Clett looked at the *Daily Record* on the table. It was opened at the half page spread, an old photo of Liam Tumelty smiling and holding a tin of beer.

"So are you?"

"Sorry?"

"Up to the job then?"

"Of course."

"Great, because I'll be arriving in Kirkwall at lunchtime."

Clett closed his eyes and stretched his neck; the bones of his vertebrae clicked in his head. He looked at Maggie McPhee and she nodded.

"We decided this morning."

"Ok", said Clett, "We have another press briefing in the next few minutes and then we get on with the investigation; more forensics and data analysis and another interview with Trevor de Vries. Keep me informed of any further information please."

Clett and McPhee arrived at the Watergate entrance with seven journalists.

"Good morning ladies and gentlemen. I'm Inspector Clett. I'm the SIO in this case. I will read out the prepared statement.

'The body found on Westray on Wednesday morning has formally been identified as that of Dominic Byrd, twenty years old, of Little Gidding in Cambridgeshire. He was assaulted and died sometime late on Tuesday night, 20th April. The next of kin have been advised. Forensic specialists continue to retrieve evidence. As yet no suspects have been identified.'"

"What is your interest in Professor Trevor de Vries?"

"No comment. Our investigation is continuing."

"Why are you harassing Ronnie Rust, who is a well-known pillar of the community? Isn't this just a personal grudge you bear him because you wrongfully arrested him before?"

"He was not wrongfully arrested, he was found not guilty in a court of law, which is a different thing."

"But you still bear him a grudge?"

"No."

"So you are friends, then?"

"I wouldn't say that."

"It sounds like you bear him a grudge. What about your record while in Strathclyde police? Isn't it true you were responsible for the death of a drug addict?"

Clett paused and gasped for breath.

"I, eh,…"

"Inspector isn't it true that you have mental health problems? Isn't it true that you are entirely unfit to run this investigation?"

"I will run this investigation to its conclusion. I, eh, … em,"

Clett flushed and turned to Maggie PcPhee.

"Thank you Inspector. Whatever difficulties Inspector Clett may have had in the past bear no relevance to this investigation. I would urge the press to report on the facts of the case. Northern

Constabulary will have no hesitation in prosecuting any slanderous reports about its officers. Briefing over. Thank you."

Some of the journalists shouted some more questions, but Maggie directed Clett back in to the Watergate building. They found a quiet waiting room.

"God, that was a disaster."

"I don't know what to say Roland. You have to respond to these comments in a more robust manner. It will help you and it also makes it look as if we are more in control. I don't want to take you off the case, but I think we are going to have to manage the press briefings differently. Your past is becoming the story."

"It's that reporter from the *Daily Record*, I know him, he's Terry O'Brien. I had dealings with him before. It was to do with the murder of Liam Tumelty."

"You mean that boy that was your informant in Glasgow?"

"Yes."

"That settles it. We have to take you out of the loop as far as the press briefings go."

Clett sat down opposite his boss and put his forehead on his palms.

"What about your progress with the evidence against de Vries? Is there any forensic evidence?"

Clett remained still supporting his forehead with his hands.

"Roland?"

"Come on inspector. Do you have evidence that implicates De Vries in the murder of Dominic Byrd?"

"Eh, no. Not yet. Anyway, I eh; I feel this might not be our only avenue of enquiry."

"Oh?"

"Yes. Special Constable Drever and I have spoken about this and we feel this might not lead to a safe prosecution."

"Ah, Drever. I wondered when he would come to the surface. A Special Constable is not exactly qualified for in depth case analysis, and we all know his past."

"Please. Chief Inspector, Special Constable Drever may have history, and his file may very well indicate unreliable aspects of his character, but, I really think he has a feel for de Vries that is relevant to this case."

"OK, go on."

Clett took a deep breath.

"Drever and I are both of the opinion that de Vries's character is inconsistent with this murder. The murder was committed by someone who has made serious mistakes. Why would he have got rid of the car? This killer is a person who is out of control."

"But if de Vries has deliberately compromised the crime scene, and if he has indicated an obsessive relationship with Byrd, then this is surely worth following up."

Clett nodded; he was getting exasperated and irritated with his boss's questions.

"Yes Chief Inspector. It is, and we will, especially with reference to this new telephony evidence. We have some possible common telephone traffic between Byrd and de Vries and some figures in the drug dealing community in Holland, Norway and England. I will be discussing this aspect of the case with DI Nelson."

"Yes Roland, DI Nelson's role will be to liaise with agencies in relation to the drugs connections. He has a large amount of experience in this field. He and you are to share intelligence and report to me. My information is that the telephone numbers you refer to belong to suspected high level drug dealers who have been on Tony Nelson's radar for some time. This link opens the whole case up as regards motive for the murder. I would also suggest that it raises very significantly the level of suspicion over Trevor de Vries. However, I recall that up until now, there has been no identifiable motive."

Clett placed both his hands on the desk.

"Motive? Motive, Why is....Why is everyone fixated on motive? Christ Maggie. People don't kill each other for a reason. We both know that irrationality is the very nature of murder; it is what makes it … it is what makes it unique. It cannot be a calculated act because to murder someone for rational reasons makes us irrational. Kant said that we treat people as ends, not as means to ends."

"Roland. Stop, stop, stop. What is the matter with you? All this is armchair philosophy. Our job is to find a killer. That is what we do. Focus and get on with the process."

"I'm sorry Maggie. You're right."

Clett stopped and breathed. He listened to the little sounds around him. Outside, the Kirkwall traffic gently rolled by; a teacup clinked as it was placed on the table. Children were playing and shouting and birds were squalling to each other. The plethora of everyday engulfed him. All these tiny events, this wonder in the ordinary, slowly settled him. He closed his eyes.

"Roland, are you ok?"

"I'm fine."

"Do you want to carry on?"

"Yes Chief Inspector, there is one, or maybe even two more possible suspects."

"Yes?"

"There is the unidentified man who met Byrd in the Fraction Nightclub."

"Ok, does anyone know who he is?"

"Not yet, so far we have no leads."

"Ok, you said another suspect."

"Yes."

Clett paused again. He was anticipating his boss's reaction.

"Ronnie Rust."

"Roland, no. You still think Rust is a suspect? You couldn't make a case against him before. What evidence do you have?"

"I'm in the process of building a case, and you know about his BMW being on the island, and the victim being in his nightclub on the night before the murder."

"And? Motive? Witnesses?"

"Motive again. Sorry, no, nothing to add."

Clett noticed the photos around McPhee's desk, of her husband fishing, of her and him at a dance; happy, ordinary. He carried on. He was nearly finished.

"There may be some more links in the data and telephony analysis. I will keep you up to date."

"Just be sure you don't give Rust ammunition for a harassment charge. I don't need to tell you, he is an upstanding member of this community and has many friends. You are the only person who appears to think badly of him and any investigation of him might be seen as victimisation. It would not reflect well on this department."

Clett's phone had been buzzing during the meeting. He looked down and found that Russell had been trying to get in touch and he had missed two calls. He felt short of breath and he gasped for air.

"Roland, are you sure you are all right? Do you need to answer that call?"

"Not right now Chief Inspector I will call back, but there is something else you might need to know that is unconnected with the case."

"Go on Roland."

Clett stopped and breathed slowly. There was a cloud outside Maggie's window. The shape was of something, but what? What did it remind him of?

"Go on Roland"

"My parents were killed yesterday in a car accident down south."

Maggie put her hand to her mouth.

"God, that's awful Roland, why didn't you say something earlier?"

"Sorry, but I felt the investigation had to carry on. To be honest I kind of feel as if none of this has actually happened. It doesn't feel real."

"And to think you took that press conference. God, Roland, you must be devastated. You know, if you want time off, that's no problem. Now that Nelson will be on the scene, he will be useful. You have done all the groundwork in establishing the investigation and there are people here that will grow the case. You can back off a bit."

Clett exhaled.

"Thanks Maggie. I might need to. Do you remember Russell, my brother?"

"Yes. his wife is Margaret. He has two girls still at school in Kirkwall."

"Aye that's right. He is going to organise most of the arrangements; getting the bodies…"

Clett coughed.

"…getting the bodies back to Papay, dealing with insurance and the will and the house, but I'll have to help. He is busy with a farm to run. To be honest, I could do with tomorrow off."

"I don't see a problem with that at all Roland. Keep your mobile switched on in case anything comes up, but take a few days if you need to."

"Thanks Maggie, that might be very helpful."

"Roland, you look after yourself. Let me know if you need anything else from us. Tell me when the funeral arrangements are made. Hugh and I would like to attend."

She touched Roland Clett's arm as he turned to leave.

"Thanks, Maggie."

Chapter 11

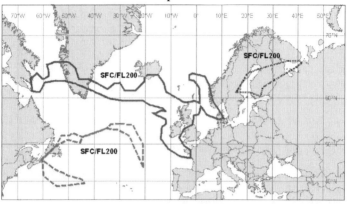

Friday, 23rd April 2010 midday.

Patrick Tenant came out of the pub and blinked in the clear Glasgow sunlight. He was drunk. He had been drinking since he got off the ferry, and at every bus stop en route. His head pounded and he felt nauseous. The lack of fresh air and the motion of the bus had not helped. He had continued to dream and perceive the world as conspiring, but above everything, through the confusion, was an overwhelming desire to do something that would compensate for the thing he had done.

On Great Western Road, he passed a bar where there was a wedding party. Three men in kilts were entering from the street. The second man bumped into Tenant and excused himself but then he looked at the gaunt figure in front of him. There was a fixed look in his eye that stopped the wedding guest in his step.

"I'm related to the groom, I've got to go in."

The wedding guest looked at the person staring at him. Tenant stank of old sweet beer and he held his hand out. It was cold and thin and he gripped the arm of the wedding guest with bony fingertips. Tenant's eyes were red from lack of sleep, the irises drilled out from the red veined white.

"Can ye no hear the wedding party? We are about to have the meal."

"The 'Amnavoe...."

"Let me go..."

Tenant released the guest's arm, but the man remained where he was, obeying Tenant's unspoken demand like a small child. Slowly, his shoulders drooped and he slumped and sat down on a low wall. Tenant spoke quietly, trying hard to control his slurred English Drawl.

"I left Scrabster on the 'Amnavoe. Everybody waved to the ship when it left ... and everything changed."

A couple stepped out onto the road, avoiding Tenant and the man in the kilt, staring as they went. They were distracted and a car swerved to avoid them.

"We passed the harbour lighthouse and the foghorn sounded."

In the clear air, on Great Western Road, a car blew its horn. People crossing the road looked away and quickened their step.

"The crossing of the firth to Stromness was good and the sun was warm."

The bride came out.

"Jim, are you coming in?"

She saw that he was trapped in Tenant's gaze.

"Eh, just come in when you are ready."

The wedding guest didn't answer, and the bride went back inside.

"Can I go in? I'm related to the groom."

Tenant continued, swaying, holding on to the low wall next to him. The guest remained where he was.

"I went to Orkney for my work and I met Dominic Byrd. Do you know that he took me out of myself. As soon as we spoke, we laughed. I laughed for the first time in years and he listened to me. *He Listened To Me*. You know what I mean."

Tenant paused and looked at the bright cloudless sky, blinking. He turned to the wedding guest.

"I don't know how long we spoke for. We shared so many things. We were both English, in this weird place, but he was so confident and I was, well I was lost mostly. He was working on an archa … an archae-o-logical dig and he invited me to see it. The things he told me…"

There was a pause. A stray dog squatted on the pavement and looked at the two men. Tenant gazed at the dog, and then slowly rotated his head slowly back towards the wedding guest.

"Did you know that Orkney has moved from the equator and they have had civilisation for more than six thousand years? The oldest things in the world have been found there. Dominic told me this. When Dominic spoke, I was interested. We took a ferry to his archae-o-logical dig on an island called West-ray. It was a lovely evening and we crossed on the water; we saw the front of the ship rise and dip into the sea. It was beautiful. We sailed with birds showing us the way, and with birds following us, and birds above us. Birds everywhere. The hills looked bright green in the evening sun and the ferry creaked and rumbled as we laughed and shared the conversation and silence. We drove to the dig and saw it in the last of the light. The sun was low in the sky and it lit up the site and the shadows were long; and we sat in a stone house five thousand years old and watched the same sunset people had watched all that time ago. We drank a bottle of whisky. God! Was it only two days ago, two days ago?"

The dog on the pavement shifted its position and yawned, and the traffic rumbled on Great Western Road. The two were alone. The wedding guest shifted uncomfortably. He tried to rise and go, but the man in the kilt remained seated. Tenant carried on in his slurred monotone.

"We told each other about families and our problems. The moon came out. He listened to me when I told him about my home and my job and my wife – my bloody wife. No one had ever listened to me before. It was the first time I felt significant and I was happy. And then I told him my secret, my first shame, my weakness, my

134

in-cap-acity, my failure. He listened and I cried. I rested my head on his shoulder and I wept and I embraced him. I felt so close, I touched him and he was suddenly shocked and he changed. He changed and he shouted at me and I'll never forget what he said to me."

Tenant wiped his eyes.

"I touched him and he said to me:

'No fucking way! No fucking way, you prick. Fuck me. You pathetic twisted bastard', he said to me. 'You fucking disgust me. God almighty!' He said this to me."

Tenant wiped his eyes again with an old crumpled paper tissue. He continued.

"He said that to me. I disgusted him. He carried on shouting and I was still crying and he wouldn't stop shouting and I picked up a rock and I hit him. I hit him again and again and again and his mouth still seemed to say those words and his mouth just got bigger and I kept hitting him and hitting him. I hit him for a long time."

The wedding guest sat, still. He could not speak. There was a squeal from a bus' brakes. Tenant got his breath back.

"I stopped hitting him, and it was quiet, but his words stuck in my ears, like when you stand too close to a bell and you hear the note long after it dies away. I couldn't believe I had done such a thing and I thought it was a dream, but there it was. I did a hellish thing."

The mongrel slowly looked down the road to something of interest. It raised itself lazily and walked away.

"I got off Westray and eventually off of damn Orkney, but it was as if I was alone in the whole world that mocked and cursed me. I don't know why they didn't catch me. surely everyone could see me for what I did. My guilt was written all over my face. Half way back to Scotland, the ferry stopped in the calm water due to an engine problem. It was probably only for a few minutes, but it seemed like an eternity. No-one spoke. We were in silence on the still sea. Our red ferry was motionless with the stationary sun in ther sky. I hadn't eaten or drunk anything for several days; the café was closed and there was nothing to drink. The sea was oily and smelly. We passed some kind of blue and green and white whirlpool that was stirred by witches to keep the sea salty. I carried the weight of my sin around my neck. People lay or sat, waiting, avoiding me. Across the water, we could see a ship with a cargo of black containers. Some people were playing cards at the next table and they looked at me and they laughed. In my confusion, I bit my arm and sucked the blood. I still have the teeth marks. Look."

Tenant rolled up his sleeve and showed the scab to the wedding guest.

The wedding guest looked at the wound and away again. He hung his head.

"Then I fell asleep. I was aware of the ferry starting up again and with the starting of the engines came the slow gabble of conversation. I slept again and when I woke, we had landed and I was the only one left on the boat. I looked out and saw the harbour lighthouse; and the church. Do you know that when I was asleep on that ferry, there were voices. They told me that I have not finished my penance."

The wedding guest gazed in silence at the ground. When he looked up, Patrick Tenant was gone.

*   *   *

Detective Inspector Tony Nelson arrived at the Burgh Road Police Station and was met by Clouston. They walked in to the office where Clett was talking to his brother quietly on the phone.

"Ah! Look who it is, bloody Snow White."

Nelson came up to Clett and slapped him on the shoulders.

"I'm sorry Russell, I'll have to call you back."

"Hello Tony. How are you?"

"Calling the seven dwarves, eh. Still fucking Grumpy, eh? Fucking grumpy, gettit?"

Nelson laughed out loud.

"You know why we called this lad Snow White in Glasgow? It was because he wanted everything so clean."

"That's not true Tony."

"Yup, Snow White here thinks that the world is such a place that you can remain clean. Well let me tell you sonny boy, this job makes you all fucking dirty."

Clett didn't reply.

"But our Snow White here learned his lesson when his snitch got shot in Blackhill. Eh Clett! Took your eye off the ball there, didn't you?"

"DI Nelson, that snitch was a young boy with a mother and a father and a family. His name was Liam Tumelty."

"Anyway, enough of this banter. I have some news that will solve your case *Inspector* Clett."

Nelson emphasised Clett's rank when he said it.

"Yet again, Nelson to the rescue, eh? – Snow White!"

Nelson laughed.

Clett could still see Liam Tumelty's body, legs bent unnaturally, surrounded by a puddle of dark red blood. He had 'Mum' and 'Dad' tattooed on his knuckles and a syringe still sticking out of his arm.

Was it only eighteen months ago? The sounds in the room became muffled and his heart raced. Nelson's laughter filled the room. When he stopped, there was a long period of silence. Clett became aware that people were looking at him.

He placed both hands on his desk and felt the grain of the old smooth cheap wood, and he looked out past the busy whiteboard to the spire of St Magnus Cathedral. Nelson was smirking and looking down at Clett and shakng his head from side to side. Clett cleared his throat and spoke.

"Well, Detective Inspector Nelson, what information do you have?"

"Right. I've been through the telephone trail and I can tell you that your boy Byrd was into some right heavy drug deals. We think he was couriering regularly between Holland and Norway, and he had recently made a connection here in Teuchterland. His connection was Torvald Arnsenn. Have you heard of Torvald Arnsenn Inspector Clett?"

"No Tony, I haven't."

"Well you bloody well should have. Arnsenn is potentially one of the biggest dealers in north western Europe. We have a file three feet thick on him and I'm waiting for further confirmation from Interpol. The long and the short of it is that Arnsenn was grooming your boy Dominic in the great mysteries of drug dealing."

Nelson tossed a newspaper on to the desk. It was a Norwegian tabloid and Arnsenn's name was in the headline. The paper was called *I Dag*. He continued:

"As you can see, the Norwegian press are on to him."

Clett looked at the rest of the front page. There was a picture of a young woman in a very short skirt getting out of a taxi with a glass in her hand. This really didn't look like quality journalism. Clett picked up the paper.

"Have you any more evidence than a cheap headline?"

"And you know all about cheap headlines, Inspector"

Clett carried on.

"There is no significant history of drug related crime in Orkney and there was no drug residue either on the body or in the hostel where Dominic Byrd stayed."

"Of course, you idi ..."

Nelson's voice trailed off. He resumed in a patronising tone.

"Inspector Clett, He is not going to leave his stashes lying around. I'm telling you that this boy was being groomed by the best. He was doing deals on the phone. There are more telephone connections with local dealers in Aberdeen over the last week."

"DI Nelson, we have forensic evidence that places Professor Trevor de Vries at the scene. Do you have any connections there?"

"Well, there it is sonny boy. The sucker punch. Do you know what a sucker punch is Inspector Clett?"

"Yes Tony."

"A sucker punch is when you dummy a right and then you come in with a left; the knockout blow. Here it is."

Nelson assumed a boxing pose and dummy Ied some punches at Clett, puffing exhalations.

"One, two, three."

Clett was finding his irritation hard to hide. The others in the room looked away as Nelson continued.

"Professor Trevor de Vries made a call to Torvald Arnsenn last Tuesday 20th April. Does that date ring a bell at all? Anyone?"

People were shuffling, but starting to pay attention.

"De Vries was turning out to be a further drug connection that would allow Arnsenn a foothold in the market up here on these lovely islands of yours that you claim are so free of drugs. Get it – Arnsenn plus Byrd plus Trevor de Vries equals new drugs distribution controllers."

"Is there anything else other than the log of a call between Trevor de Vries and Arnsenn? Why would this form a motivation for murder?"

"For God's sake Clett, wake up. It's obvious. Arnsenn wanted to start a new drug distribution network using your boy Byrd, and he was expanding his network to include de Vries; and Inspector, I'll tell you the last piece in the jigsaw is that Trevor de Vries is gay. Did you know that Inspector Clett?"

"It was recognised as a possibility."

"Yup. Gay as they come."

Nelson sniggered to himself.

"I've checked with Norfolk University and he had a string of relationships with young men at dig sites."

"Yes, DI Nelson, we also had that information, but we were not convinced how relevant it was. Any connection would be speculative."

"Speculative! Speculative! Well let me tell you sonny boy, it is very relevant indeed. Arnsenn is also gay. You didn't know that, did you? I'll tell you what happened. Trevor de Vries thought your boy Dominic Byrd was coming on to him, but all the boy wanted was to set up drugs deals. Trevor de Vries couldn't deal with the rejection and lost the plot. Bingo, Bang, bang. One dead drug dealer. No loss really."

Clett felt that Nelson did not offer a convincing motive, but now several people in the room were nodding their heads. To be honest, it was a better scenario than Clett's, which amounted to precisely nothing. However, Clett just didn't feel this was right, but he couldn't articulate his doubt. Drug crime on Orkney was virtually unheard of, but he couldn't rule it out as a possibility. He also felt that Rust was a far more viable candidate than de Vries, but he needed more time to make a case. Even if Rust wasn't a suspect, Nelson's case against de Vries didn't add up. He decided to give it more thought before issuing an arrest warrant.

Roland Clett left Nelson and the rest of the team at the Burgh Road Police Station and walked the three minutes it took him to get to the Kirkwall library. He went up to the Orkney Room on the first floor, and walked around the room. He looked out at St Magnus Cathedral. The muffled sound of cars came and went and there was the odd incoherent fragment of conversation that could just about be heard from the furthest table. This was a place of sanctuary for Clett. The Orkney Room had rows of books, cabinets with maps and pamphlets that represented old and new Orkney culture in microcosm. There were a few armchairs scattered about. It was a place out of time. He turned to the shelves and reached for a slim book he knew well. It had been re-bound in the last hundred or so years with burgundy leather. He felt the cloth paper between his fingers as he turned the rough edged pages. The book was

'Upon the Sentiment of Morals' by Archibald Clett (1721-1799). He knew this passage by heart. It was the first passage by Archibald Clett that he had found and its resonance for Clett had been immediate. It was as if Clett had written it himself. He turned to page 45 and his lips moved as he read:

> *"This fragile veneer of manners doth not bear load. What it bears is our commonplace stories of rule and of law. These are the tales we tell each other and upon which we agree, about the rules we make for our comfort and protection, and for the comfort and protection of those less fortunate than ourselves. It may be observed that when placed under duress, this veneer is damaged and the tale becomes disjointed. At such time, we rely upon a moral sense, a sentiment accessible to each one of us, and distinct from the civic order that is this veneer of manners. Consider that at times of famine, artificial rules have no place and natural sentiments reign. It may further be observed that when so damaged, the dynamism of human enaction is revealed. It can be seen that we do not act out of seeming rationality, out of motives of profit, even out of the improvement of the self. In their particularity, evil acts are almost never preceded by evil intent. We are not driven by a motive that is borne out of rationality. What drives us is love, jealousy, comfort and affection; and their lack".*

Love, jealousy, comfort and affection; and their lack. Clett mouthed the words.

"Hello Roland."

Before he turned, he knew it was Christine. He would have known her voice anywhere, with its beautiful Orkney lilt. He would always have known and loved her for her voice, even when she would be older, when she would lose her youth. Her voice would be constant.

"I knew I would find you here. Have you been having a hard time with the investigation?"

"No, well, yes, but why are you here?"

"I just thought I'd see how you were doing. Anyway, I saw you across the street."

"I've just spent time with Nelson, and Maggie has agreed to go with him on arresting de Vries. Tony Nelson really is a shit you know. It brought back all the problems at Glasgow and it has affected my confidence in my own judgement. You know, I can still see Liam Tumelty's face. They killed him for doing something that I asked him to do. He trusted me."

"I know Roland."

"He wasn't just a junkie."

Christine put her hand on Clett's arm and he looked at her.

"I'm sure it is Rust; but maybe Nelson is right. Maybe I can't see the nose in front of my face."

"No Roland. You must stick with your own way of doing things."

"Thanks Christine, but I'm not sure how my convictions will stand up to Nelson. I really think I've just lost this one. But the next victim will be that idiot Trevor de Vries. He is likely to face a long stretch for something he hasn't done. I don't think he could face life in prison, poor bugger."

"Roland, all this just has to find its own level and it will only do so in time. You have to let events take their course. It is how you work. You know this."

"I know Christine. Thanks."

"You're very welcome Roland." Christine kissed Roland on the cheek and turned to leave the library.

"Are we still expecting the boys this afternoon?"

"Aye. This afternoon's Hamnavoe crossing. I'll call. See you later at Stromness."

Clett looked again at the bound volume in his hand. He gently closed it and placed it back on the shelf.

*　　　*　　　*

"Russell."

"Hi Roland. Are you ok for time?"

"Sure. How are the arrangements going?"

"Ok. I've spoken to the minister and he says that Monday morning is fine. Mum and Dad are being brought home just now."

"That was quick."

"Aye; the funeral director didn't seem to think there was any problem."

"What about the rest of the family? Do you want me to put any announcements in the paper?"

"Only if you have time."

"I'll make time. You and Margaret have done so much already."

"Aye, and Christine has been a great help."

"Aye. Maybe some good can come out of all this."

"Let's hope so Roland."

*　　　*　　　*

Clett called '*The Orcadian*'.

"Hello, My name is Roland Clett."

"Of course it is. Inspector Roland Clett. I would know your voice anywhere."

"Janie Shearer. How are you?"

"I'm great. Have you called to give me an interview about the case?"

"The case?"

"Oh, come on Roland, You know me and you've seen me at the press briefings. I've just had your colleague from Inverness on the phone and he told us all about Professor de Vries. Watertight case isn't it?"

"Well, no, I don't really think so. Actually, I phoned about something else."

"Oh Roland, this is big news on Orkney. We both serve the community. People have to know."

"Janie, I called to place a death notice."

"For the victim, for Dominic Byrd?"

"No Janie, for my parents."

"What?"

"I phoned to place a death notice for my parents, Bill and Vera Clett."

There was silence at the other end of the phone.

"Your parents... Oh no, I'm so sorry Roland."

"Janie, can I just give you the details?"

"Of course Roland. God I'm so sorry. Please go ahead."

*   *   *

Ronnie Rust snipped the ribbon with an oversized set of shears to the accompaniment of applause. He beamed as he accepted the recognition for his support for the creation of this new community hall. It was his greatest civic achievement and one he would be proud of. Out here in Burwick, away from the usual focus of the tourist trail and business activity, the local population would have a facility that could be used as a focal point for ceilidhs, night classes, football and sports clubs. Here, where neighbours were once isolated from each other, reliant on intermittent and infrequent public transport, they could form a true community through self help and support. Ronnie Rust felt this passionately. Brought up on Papay, he saw first-hand the pressures on his own family of rural disadvantage: the fighting and the day to day struggle to keep a family that wore down both his parents. He had been removed from his family by social workers to be kept in care in a List D residential school in Aberamno, three hundred miles to the south. Ronnie Rust remembered how people spoke differently there. He remembered the disorientation and the beatings, and he had escaped the darker side of the abuse only because he had developed a talent that made people frightened of him. He used this skill to deliberately initiate violence at will and honed it until it was as easy as turning on or off a light switch. He learned how to choose to be angry, or to choose to be calm. This gave him control and more power and he liked it. Thus he learned to protect himself. He learned to control and frighten in Aberamno.

He remembered hearing of his mother's death and missing her funeral due to the distance and disorganisation of his enforced separation. He remembered the punishment he received when he smashed up the TV room. It was after this that he was allowed to live with his Auntie Brenda in South Ronaldsay, where he settled into the ways of that community.

But today, all that lay in the past. He placed it in a box. Today marked a milestone in the new life of Ronnie Rust. To be here today, to offer something to these communities, was a source of profound pride and at the same time, a privilege. Rust had had a struggle in his business and with the law, and it had been a long hard climb to get him here where he was today.

Roland Clett stood with Jamie Gunn and watched as Rust soaked up the acclaim and approbation. He was vigorously shaking hands with the Honorary Sheriff Charlie Sinclair.

Jamie Gunn turned to his boss.

"Inspector, Are you sure about Mister Rust? Just look at him. Everyone loves him; and what about that community centre. Out of his own pocket. The guy is pure gold. People are saying you are taking it personally, what with the failed prosecution and everything."

Clett turned to face Gunn and snapped at him.

"Constable Gunn, I would remind you firstly that I am your senior officer and that is not the way you should address me. Secondly, you know nothing about Rust's history. He almost killed a man while at sea for skimming profits from smuggled cigarettes."

"What, Mister Rust?"

Clett saw a different side to Ronnie Rust. He saw the bully who made Clett's early school life a misery, and he remembered the relief during the period of time that Rust was removed from Orkney. On his return he saw Rust's rise through petty crime and violence; the killing of livestock and fights with farmers and others in the community, to the fully developed charismatic violent thug, capable of spurious and extreme violence. Clett knew that Rust was a product of his unfortunate circumstances, but he could not hide from himself his hatred of the man whom he saw escaping from justice. In particular, he remembered his disgrace when Rust violently assaulted a fisherman. The incident was on a fishing boat in a force eight gale where Rust broke a man's legs after partially drowning him. Rust's defence, successfully promoted by his Glasgow lawyer was that it was an industrial accident at sea. Clett remembered only too well the humiliation of the fine. Rust had defeated him once more. Clett had been in charge of the case and had seen the effect on the victim and his family; the feeling when he saw the malicious grin on the face of Rust remained with him still.

"I spoke to the family of the man he nearly killed on that fishing boat, a family whose lives were very nearly ruined and a man who still can't sleep at night."

"You think that Mister Rust is a psychopath?"

"A psychopath? And what does that mean? that he ticks some boxes in some psychologist's toolkit? No, he is not a psychopath under any strict definition, not in any black and white sense, but there is no doubt that he is a manipulative, controlling individual whose every action is focussed on gaining benefit for himself and himself alone. Anyone or anything that gets in the way will always be disposable to him. He sees people as objects to be used. Empathy is totally absent from his character. Regardless of the label, constable, you should be aware of being taken in by someone with his history. Don't fall for his charm. He is not what he appears to be and he is not to be trusted; and he is a danger to the people in this community."

"Sorry Inspector. It is just that he seems such a nice guy and would do anything for anybody."

"You can't afford to be so naïve constable."

Rust walked towards the two officers and shook hands with Gunn.

"Jamie, isn't it? Nice to see you here with your newly promoted boss. Hello Inspector Clett. Good to see you here on this day. I'm glad that you have seen fit to attend this opening. Quite an achievement, don't you think?"

His tone dropped and then he spoke quietly in a soft, almost familiar tone that Clett had not heard before.

"I was so sorry to hear about Bill and Vera. They were decent people. Aye, very sad. How is Russell?"

"Eh, he is fine. How did you know?"

"Oh, you know Roland, I know everything that happens on these islands. When is the funeral?"

Clett hesitated. "We're not sure; it's not been organized yet. Maybe Monday."

"I'll have some flowers sent."

There was a moment's silence.

"Ronnie, I would like to ask you a few questions regarding your movements on Tuesday night 20th April."

Rust abruptly switched his tone and spoke, now deliberate and precise, as if shifting gear. The change was shocking.

"*Inspector* Clett, have you come to harass me again, on this day that marks out my finest civic achievement on these Islands? You know that all these people can see this intrusion for what it is."

"Mr Rust, we have reason to believe you were on Westray on Tuesday evening. Your car was logged on the MV Earl Thorfinn on Tuesday and returned on Wednesday morning. That places you at the locus of the crime."

"The locus of the bloody crime! You fucking tosser. I told you I gave my car to my nightclub manager. Look *Inspector* Clett, get real. I am not going to say any more to you unless you have a warrant and I have a lawyer."

He looked Clett straight in the eye and under his breath, said:

"Now fuck off and leave me alone."

Rust turned and smiled at a small girl and changed gear again.

"Hello dear. Have you had an ice cream yet?"

He took her hand, winking at her mother who smiled back.

"Thank you Ronnie. What a lovely man you are."

Clett turned to Jamie Gunn.

"Ok Jamie, I think we've done our bit here for today."

*   *   *

Magnus and Sandy Clett stood on the deck of the Hamnavoe looking east. They had had a clear crossing of the Pentland Firth and the Old Man of Hoy was peering out among the clouds and the cliffs.

"Do you ever think that a ferry is like an extension of an island?"

"You mean how the Hamnavoe feels like home?"

"Aye."

"What are you going to say to Dad?"

"After what he has done to Mum, I've no idea how I can look him in the face Magnus. When she came back from Glasgow, all I remember is her crying all the time and that bastard not answering her calls; and now he has the gall to announce that they are back together again."

"It's their relationship and we really don't have much say."

"I know but I can still have an opinion. We are their sons."

"I saw it differently when I was studying in Glasgow. After they split, I would meet him for a coffee and he was pretty well frazzled. He was under a lot of pressure at work. Did you know he did undercover work? When I met him he was easily distracted and really odd, not like himself at all. He said that Mum wasn't answering his calls. I saw him drunk once...."

"Dad! Drunk?"

"Aye, I know. He kept on talking about her coat and his selkie. He made no sense at all."

"But what about him not wanting me to go to Gran And Grandad's funeral?"

"That doesn't make any sense at all Sandy. Are you sure that's what he said?"

"Definitely. After he hit me with the bombshell that him and Mum were seeing each other; he came out with it; just you stay in Glasgow and do your studying."

"What did Mum say?"

"She took his side and denied he said anything of the sort."

"You and Dad are just not communicating right now. No matter what misunderstanding exists between you and Dad, he would never want you to miss something like this. You know how he is about family."

"Aye, except when he decides to dump his wife."

"Sandy, we don't know what went on between them. We will never really know and mostly it is not our business."

"But we are their sons."

"Aye, but as long as they have a good relationship with us, that's all that matters."

"That bastard is not making much of an effort, is he?"

"Sandy, this few days will only work if you and Dad try to get on. If you don't, it could spoil a good family memory."

Sandy looked away.

"Aye maybe. Can we talk about it later?"

"Sure Sandy, any time you like." Magnus touched Sandy's shoulder.

The Hamnavoe slowly left the Old Man behind. It turned right into the Flow and then left towards Stromness and home.

Roland and Christine saw the Hamnavoe round the skerry and pass between Ness and the Outer Holm. They stood on the pier with their feet amongst the ropes and creels and fish boxes. One of the large sea-going trawlers was moored nearby, unloading a catch into an articulated lorry. Further up the pier one of the dive support vessels was manoeuvring to a berth, its oxygen bottles stowed on deck and diving suits drying in a patch of intermittent sunshine. Gleaming like a pristine blue and orange beacon was the huge Severn Class Lifeboat. A seagull, perched on its stationary radar scanner, surveyed the scene. It had a fine view of its territory, of some of the familiar places it could eat, outside the bakery, and by the bench at the old well where people would half finish their lunch. It looked out to Graemsay and on to Hoy Hill in the cloud. Lazily, it opened its wings and stepped into the air, dropping into flight, picking up an updraught that took it into the sky. A ship's horn sounded and the sheets rattled at the masts of the smaller boats in the marina. The harbour entrance was filling with sunshine, lighting up the Ness and the Hamnavoe coming in to dock.

"Do you remember the first time wee Sandy heard the siren?"

"Aye."

"We were coming home from nursery after picking up Magnus from school. We were going home for lunch when the quarry siren went off. He jumped out of his skin and started screaming. Magnus put his hands over Sandy's ears and we all gave him a cuddle and settled him down."

"Aye, and Magnus explained that it was letting all the birds know that there was going to be a big bang. It wasn't frightening really. The siren is good. It clears the air before the tension goes."

As the Hamnavoe backed into its mooring, Roland and Christine stepped slowly over the hoses and power cables and ropes to meet their boys.

"Hi Dad."

Sandy couldn't maintain eye contact with his father.

"Hello Sandy. I'm so pleased you are here."

"Aye well...."

Christine moved forward to her son.

"Sandy Clett you have lost weight."

"I have not."

"You have so, you peedie skinny boy."

She hugged Sandy tight.

Roland grinned at Magnus.

"How was the crossing?"

"Och, no problem at all. we saw some porpoises in the firth."

"Lovely" said Christine. "Any kitticks[2]?"

"No. And no tammie norries[3] either, just rittocks[4] and cullyas[5] all the way."

They drove to Finstown in an intermittent babble of small talk.

"I hear you have a new girlfriend Sandy."

"Aye, Margarita."

"Where is she from?"

"Argentina."

"Argentina, sounds exciting. You will have to tell us all about her."

"Maybe later Mum."

"Pity she couldn't come back with you."

"Aye, well maybe another time."

"What about you and Jane, Magnus?"

"No Mum, you know fine that it is well and truly over."

"Pity. She was such a nice girl. Maybe you'll get back together."

"Mum…"

---

[2] Kittiwakes

[3] Puffins

[4] Black Headed Gulls

[5] Seagulls

The car rolled into the drive of the boys' childhood home. It had remained frozen in time for them. Some new paint here and there, but the furniture and the home had stayed the same. Sandy and Magnus stood in the front room, seemingly smaller than they remembered, among the football trophies and family photographs.

"It's nice to be back where nothing changes."

"What do you mean? The bathroom was decorated last year and the paintings are moved about."

"Aye, but mum, you know, it is still home."

"Thank you Sandy."

"Roland, would you put the kettle on please?"

The boys left their rucksacks in the hall.

"Roland, do you know what your plans are?"

"I have a meeting in Kirkwall tomorrow morning, but it shouldn't take long. I can meet you at the airport for the three o'clock flight to Papay. We will meet Uncle Russell and Auntie Margaret; then back to Granny and Grandad's house to spend the night before the funeral on Monday morning."

"Are the flights on again?"

"Yes, so I'm told."

"Dad, we were thinking of meeting up with a bunch of people in Kirkwall tonight. What do you think? Is it a bit insensitive?"

"No Magnus, no problem. Granny and Grandad would have wanted you to go."

"Thanks Dad. Can we borrow the car Mum?"

"Yes, of course. I'll give you money for petrol."

"Mum, there's no need, I earn money now you know."

"Sorry Magnus, I forgot how grown up you are now. "

Christine started to tickle her grown up boy."

"Och Mum."

Roland Clett smiled at the scene around him. All thoughts of Rust, of Nelson, of the pressures of the case had dissolved. This was where he wanted to be. Here. Now.

Chapter 12

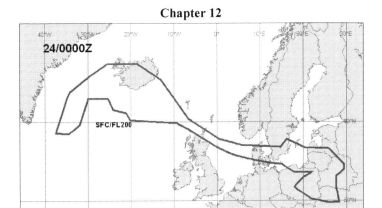

Saturday morning, 24th April 2010, 7.45am.

De Vries woke in his tent. He had overslept after a fitful
night. He had woken several times in a cold sweat re-living the
attack by Simon Byrd. His jaw was painful and swollen. This
morning he couldn't face his run and the meditation. He turned
over and closed his eyes.

*   *   *

Ronnie Rust looked down at something moving on the
ground. It was a spider, traversing a rock. He saw it scurry and
stop, a step away from his right foot. He allowed himself a small
smile as he settled himself into a frame of mind that allowed him
to focus on this moment; to forget the distractions of his quotidian
concerns, to forget the responsibilities and demands people were
making on him. He deliberately raised his shoe softly until it was
just above the spider; and he hesitated. He lowered his foot;
slowly, so patiently, so softly, so gently; and just at the moment
the spider would race for safety, at that judged instant, this was the
moment that the sole of Rust's shoe trapped it. Rust halted his foot

in its descent and was aware of the spider unseen, struggling for its tiny life. Rust stopped and looked up at the warming sun, at the changing beauty of his Orkney sky, and the sound of the breeze and the linnets. He sensed the small desperation under his foot. This, now, this moment, Rust was in sympathy with the rhythm of his nature. Imperceptibly, softly, he lowered his foot while breathing the fresh salt-laden air. He thought about the geometry of the action, of the angle of the descending foot, of the sole exactly parallel to the ground, of the way the weight of his lower leg felt on his knee and hip, of his straight back and head held upright. Details were everything. He would not be doing justice to this little piece of life; he would not be respecting it if he did not do the job with reverence and care. He tasted the air and very, very deliberately, he circled his foot around for a few seconds, and millimetre by millimetre, he lowered his shoe so, so slowly and compressed the life out of the creature. For what seemed minutes, Rust savoured this small assassination, this crunching out of a life. Once his foot came in full contact with the ground, he knew he had completed this now rounded little life. He stepped away and admired the smudge, the small rubbed out existence. He admired it for just a second, and then immediately looked around for the next thing to interest him.

His phone rang. He let it ring a few times, and then he answered.

"Ah. Torvald my friend. Good to hear from you. How is the progress on our little enterprise?"

"It is going well Ronnie. The paperwork is almost complete and the formal offer from me and my colleagues will be with your lawyer tomorrow morning. When they respond, the funds will be available to your Cayman account as you requested."

"Well Torvald, you will be the proud owner of the biggest nightclub north of Aberdeen; and, of course, the side benefits - well we will leave that until later. Good to speak to you. Are you still flying over to meet at the club on Tuesday?"

"Yes Ronnie. I look forward to it."

"Until then Torvald."

"Until then Ronnie."

Rust returned to his car and took a book out of the glove compartment. It was 'Chasing the Model' by Samuel P Winkler. Rust had read this book many times and had three copies around the place so he could refer to Sam's wisdom at a moment's notice. He considered the picture of the author on the front cover sitting at his successful desk with his square-jawed-tanned-blond success beaming against a sky blue backdrop. Rust had once flown to Edinburgh to hear him speak and the experience was electric. This talk was a turning point in Rust's life and since then he found direction and focus. Each day he would carry out Sam's exercise, the repetition of a phrase that signified success. He would repeat his mantra, honed over a period of several years. Rust had worked from the original phrase 'I must defeat them', which he now felt was imbued with negativity, through many iterations, to 'Today IS the next step'. Rust read through the chapter headings that he could recite by heart. The only part that Rust disregarded was the first chapter entitled 'Discovering Empowerment'. Rust had always known that he was in control, so this was not for him. Nonetheless, he recognised the process. He knew that in this respect he was ahead of Sam L Winkler, but it was what Sam did with this empowerment that impressed and inspired him. He realised that it was through Winkler's patently self-affirming psychological techniques, allied with the technical business methods, that success would arrive. The more specialist second half of the book was called 'Build your own MBA', and here Rust learned about the evolution of a successful business model. He remembered a key phrase from the book:

> *"The product is only a vehicle; look only to what it can bring to you. "*

Rust thus realised that he wasn't really interested in the drugs, but their allure as a vehicle was obvious. They would be a stepping-stone for all the good work he wanted to do in his community.

Rust had learned his craft and built his contact list in vodka and cigarettes, and was now ready for new horizons. Orkney was virgin soil for his ideas. He would start and grow the business from the manifest needs of this untouched market.

It was reading Sam Winkler that made Rust realise his errors in business, and he now understood how his previous attempts had failed. It was simple. Rust's failures in high level drug dealing and distribution were due to the lack of an appropriate business model. He knew that Orkney was ripe for the development of distribution. There were virtually no drugs on Orkney and Rust was in no doubt that the market conditions were now correct with the changing demographic. He just had to find his business model. The connection with Arnsenn was the way forward. A like-minded business partner to push it in the right direction. Tuesday's meeting would crystallise the goal.

*   *   *

Clett was discussing the facilities at the incident room with Clouston when Nelson walked straight up to him.

"Have you not issued that fucking arrest warrant for de Vries yet?" Clouston caught Clett's eye and left them alone.

"No Tony, I've got a feeling about it. There is the business of the car being driven off the cliff that doesn't fit in with your scenario. There is also the lack of any evidence of drug traces on the body, and the unknown contact in the Fraction Nightclub."

"Look, fuck the car, fuck the forensics. They just haven't found the drugs yet. These are distractions. For fuck's sake Clett, get a grip. He's our man. What is your problem? When are you going to learn? There are good guys and there are bad guys. We are the fucking good guys! Trevor de Vries is as guilty as fuck and is hiding something. Arrest him and get on with it."

Clett looked away, embarrassed, and out of the office window saw the ever present spire of St Magnus Cathedral, like a pivot around which his life and this case rotated. He walked out of the office.

" Where the fuck are you going Clett? You prick."

There was a long silence in the office. No-one spoke.

" Fuck", said Nelson.

*   *   *

De Vries stirred and looked at his watch. It was 9:50am. As he woke, he became aware of something back at the dig, a memory, something about the positioning of items at the newly exposed area. He rose quickly and drove to a patch of ground short of the site and walked over the hill, away from the road. His jaw was painful and the cuts stung as the sand blew at his face. He moved smartly across the rocks straight to the cleared area, away from the place where Dominic's body had been found, and out of sight of the single police officer on duty. He crept, hardly breathing, down to the freshly excavated earth. There had been something unusual about the lie of the rocks and the colouration of the soil. He took a brush and started work on a piece of compacted loam. He worked slowly and diligently; not wishing to disturb the beautiful coherence of the site. For forty-five minutes, he patiently brushed at this area the size of a loaf of bread. As he brushed, he became calm, engrossed in the task, blowing and brushing, blowing and brushing. Then it happened and the thing appeared out of the ground and he gasped. The texture of the object became clear, and the idea of it became crystalised. De Vries paused and savoured the discovery. All of the difficulties and problems seemed to him to point to this moment. It all led to this small beautiful few minutes. It was a whalebone mace head. His heart raced and his hands shook. He had only read about such an object and had never before held such an item in his hands. Nothing else now mattered and de Vries focussed on this sense of joy. He blew

157

and he brushed and more of the piece became visible, but he still could not prise it from the sediment. He took a spade and placed it under the mace head. He continued to brush and blow in an effort to release it from its five thousand year imprisonment. He blew and he brushed and he gently levered the spade, and slowly it became loose from the surrounding earth.

As he lifted it, he became aware that there was a problem. He could see a clear fracture in its structure. Nonetheless, he had to complete the excavation. He supported it on each side and continued to brush and blow. He levered with one hand and brushed with the other and then, as he lifted it free, it fell into two pieces. The mace head dropped into two halves, split each side of the central slot where it would have been attached to a handle. De Vries felt tears drop from his eyes. This object, so rare, so beautiful, so intact, had been corrupted by his action. He looked despondently at it, and then he looked again. The inner surfaces of the broken pieces of the mace were coated in compacted soil. These two halves had been placed together in the ground; he had not broken it. His sense of elation returned. But then, he thought, why would this ceremonial object ever have been split into two? Had it been deliberate? This thing was so all embracing, so composed and complete, representing a symbolic unity. It was manifestly not a weapon, but a ritualistic object full of meaning and coherence. What rending of their world would cause people to do such a thing? Why would they have broken it? What would have brought them to choose to create chaos over order? He held the representation of the destruction of a whole world in the palm of his hands, a world that had been torn asunder.

*   *   *

Clett pushed open the old oak door of St Magnus' Cathedral. He needed the free air of the red and white sandstone space with its height and solid pillars and its light to clear his head.

He walked over the flagstones to the south western corner where there were the names of various Orkney men and women of letters: George Mackay Brown, Edwin Muir, Stanley Cursitor, J Storer Clouston, Hugh Marwick, Robert Rendall, Eric Linklater, and Archibald Clett. They were individuals who were entwined with the collective, people who represented other people, whose lives encompassed each other. They were not strange names to the majority of Orcadians, they were as much part of the heritage as the ancient sites and the geology. These were writers' names that could be found on bookshelves all over Orkney.

Clett sat down on a pew and took out a photocopy of another of Archibald Clett's letters:

> *To Mr David Hume*
> *Edinburgh*
> *XIVth April, 1779*
>
> *Dear Mr Hume,*
>
> *Thank you for your letter. I should like to visit the next time I come to Edinburgh. Thank you for the claret which I imbibe as I write and look out upon my archipelago.*
>
> *Upon the subject of the artifice of justice and upon your argument for it being dependent upon its utility, I would like to offer some of my thoughts.*
>
> *I should assert that justice and morality are natural and are not the result of rules and artifice. There is a sentiment of morality that runs in our veins as deep as any animal feeling, as deep as love or hatred. Justice does not exist as a veneer; it beats in the hearts of men. If a man commits a crime, he desires punishment. When he does not receive punishment, he seeks it out. Retribution is a feature of the world and can be seen every day. This*

invisible hand of justice governs the domain of morals and is not an invention of men.

I would agree with our friend Mr A. Smith that:

'In every religion, and in every superstition that the world has ever beheld, accordingly, there has been a Tartarus as well as an Elysium; a place provided for the punishment of the wicked as well as for the reward of the just.'

I would not support, however, Mr Smith's reliance upon religion and superstition. Morality exists as do mountains and streams and birds and bats and it lives in each one of us. I regard an inclination for wrong doing to be punished as a sentiment, it does not require a first cause or designer to exist.

It is thus not possible to account for actions and accountability in any mensurable manner. Punishment cannot be calculated as in an equation. It is not rational but is an instinct or sentiment in each one of us; a need, a means of internalised moral regulation of the self.

Higher animals do not eat their young, and a pack will ostracise one that does not conform to its own codes of behaviour. In a similar way we intuitively desire punishment for our sins. This is not a spiritual phenomenon, but one that is natural. When a judge decides upon a sentence, he must not calculate the punishment upon a universal scale, upon some calculus of morals, he must rely upon his own feeling for the circumstances of the crime. Thus he is a judge, and not merely a moral accountant. When we do wrong, we desire punishment for ourselves and the regulating mechanism is the

> *feeling of guilt. We have answered the necessary retribution when the sense of guilt is alleviated. This accounts for the mechanism of self retribution in almost every man.*
>
> > *I look forward to our next game of billiards.*
>
> *Yrs.*
> *Archibald Clett of Canmore*

Clett put away the letter and in the dull light that filled the cathedral, looked up to the vaulted roof and considered the problems he experienced while he had been at Glasgow. All his colleagues there were assertive and had confidence in their convictions. They were so successful in their police work that it worried Clett that his approach was at fault. He had felt that he could not afford to be so sure of himself. Even the clearest piece of evidence might be flawed. Clett's approach involved the constant sifting and organising of material and the contemplation of a case. This was his strength, but it was time consuming. It did not produce outcomes as swiftly as the more inductive and dynamic methods required by police forces that demanded quick results. Clett just knew Trevor de Vries was not the murderer. He believed him. He recognised all the things that made him act the way he did and understood to a large extent his motivation. De Vries was fearful of being found out. He had become successful with his work in Mexico almost by accident, and he was thrown into an academic world of fame and visibility. He had to produce results in order to keep alive. He was simply not strong enough. His desperation was not that of a guilty man; it was the desperation of someone who wanted to get their career back on track. However, he could not yet present this in an articulate form in the face of the crisp, concise, coherent argument of Nelson.

Clett's phone buzzed in his pocket. He came out of the cathedral into the overcast and breezy afternoon.

"Hello Norman, what have you got for me?"

"Before I say anything else Roland, I wanted to say how sorry I was to hear about your Mum and Dad. Your parents were lovely people. Please let me know if I can do anything."

"Thanks Norman, just being a buffer between me and the bullshit will do fine for now. Any news?"

"Aye Inspector. Irene and Sanja have identified two fingerprints in the blood stained smudges on Dominic Byrd's neck. They were an exact match with Trevor de Vries's left hand middle finger and thumb."

Clett paused and looked out at the view, up to the cathedral spire and down to his shoes.

"Thank you Norman". Clett ended the call.

*   *   *

Trevor de Vries packed his tent in the back of the land rover. He placed the two bubble wrapped halves of the whalebone mace gently in his rucksack. He was heading for Rapness and the ferry. This investigation had become a joke and he had made a decision. The discovery of the split mace had been the catalyst that moved him into action. The unprofessionalism of these bumbling, inexperienced local police had caused him to halt the dig. He had a responsibility to his sponsors, to his career and to science itself to act with integrity. He would return to Norwich and get on with as much research as he could and work on the mace head. He would also be complaining to whichever idiots ran the police in this pathetic part of the world, and he would claim a refund for some of the lost costs of the project. In short, he had had enough. They had refused to accept his perfectly reasonable compromise to work side by side at the dig, and they had utterly ruined any chance of a surprise announcement that he could make. Everyone now knew where he was working and any of his rivals could guess at the significance of his findings. His only option was to get back and publish what he could as soon as possible. His spirits rose as he thought of the object in his rucksack. As he was about to start the engine, his phone rang. He knew it was Clett and let it ring.

*   *   *

Drever was moving his Charolais to a new field when he noticed a missed call from Clett. He went across the field to an area where he knew he would get good reception.

"Roland, it's Archie."

"Thanks for calling back Archie. We need to apprehend de Vries. He's not answering his phone. And I don't think it is anything to do with the poor reception. Fingerprint evidence has been identified on Byrd's body and it has been confirmed as belonging to de Vries."

"That doesn't necessarily mean that …"

"I know Archie, but this is the strongest piece of evidence we have. Can you hold him until I can get there?"

"Hmmm. No problem Roland. I'll get on to it."

As he ended the call, Clett's phone buzzed again. It was Russell.

"Roland, sorry to bother you, but we need to decide on coffins for Mum and Dad."

"Coffins? Eh, I …"

Clett stopped himself.

"Sorry Russell. Of course."

"No problem Roland. Why don't I tell you what I think and you can say if you agree?"

"That would be good Russell. Thanks. What do you think?"

"Well the undertaker only has two matching coffins just now. They are teak and have brass handles; kind of traditional looking. If we chose anything different, they would have to get them transported from Scotland and they might not get here in time. The other alternative would be to have different coffins. They can move handles around, but the teak ones are the only ones of the same wood."

"That sounds fine Russell. You are right, they have to match. Are there any other details?"

"No Roland. The flowers are sorted and I got the death certificate yesterday afternoon. I have emailed you the order of service and I've spoken to the minister about it. He thinks it will be fine."

"God, I should have been there. Sorry I've not been any help."

"No problem Roland. Don't beat yourself up about it. It's all in hand. Are the boys home?"

"Yes, they are staying with us at Finstown."

"All of you together?"

"Yes actually. This funeral may be good for Christine and me."

"Good news Roland. I have things to do, so I will let you know if there are any decisions to be made."

"Ok. Thanks Russell."

*　　*　　*

Clett's phone went again. It was Drever.

"Archie, any news?"

"Aye Roland. We've not been able to find de Vries. Angela heard from a local farmer that he was seen driving south towards Rapness."

"De Vries is catching the ferry back to Kirkwall. I'll get Nancie Keldie and Jamie Gunn to intercept the MV Earl Thorfinn at the Kirkwall terminal."

*　　*　　*

De Vries had an uneventful trip back to the Orkney Mainland. He had switched his phone off and sat on the outer deck wrapped up against the wind, contemplating the long drive to Norwich. He would catch the Kirkwall ferry getting him to

Aberdeen early on Sunday morning and then home to the sanity of his houseboat on the Norfolk Broads by late Sunday evening where he would salvage what he could of the project in the coming weeks. He was troubled by his altercation with Dominic's father, but he had no concerns that the police might be interested in him. The charge with regard to obstructing justice was trivial and further demonstrated their incompetence. He rubbed his swollen jaw.

As he drove off the MV Earl Thorfinn at Kirkwall harbour, he handed his embarkation pass to the purser and saw that there were two police officers in his path. Constable Nancie Keldie was speaking into her radio as she directed him to pull over to the side while Jamie Gunn approached the vehicle.

"What is this? More incompetence!"

Nancie recognised de Vries from the dig site.

"Excuse me sir. Please switch off your engine."

"Look, get out of my way."

Nancie stood at the side of the land rover and Jamie reached in to remove the ignition key. De Vries put the car into gear and accelerated away. Jamie found himself caught between the accelerating vehicle and the low harbour wall. One foot was trapped and he called out in pain. He threw his radio in through the open window at de Vries who ignored it as it hit him on the head. Nancie tried to grab the door handle, but her hand was wrenched as the car sped off. Jamie was left writhing on the ground. He shouted to Keldie, clearly in pain.

"Get after him."

Nancie raced to the police car, holding her radio to her mouth.

"Kilo two to uniform romeo. Code ten one zero eight, repeat code ten one zero eight. Officer injured at Kirkwall Harbour. Possible broken leg. Suspect in land rover leaving at speed from Kirkwall Harbour in a north easterly direction. Am in pursuit, over."

De Vries heard Keldie's transmission from Gunn's radio which was lying in the passenger footwell. He looked back at Keldie and Gunn in his rear view mirror.

"Damn, damn, damn!"

He accelerated, racing along the short stretch over the pedestrian crossing and braked hard at the Harbour Hotel, turning left into Albert Street, a narrow slabbed shopping street, and immediately found himself surrounded by pedestrians enjoying the mild evening. He sounded his horn, and then realised how much attention he was bringing to himself. He slowed and tried to drive at walking pace through the crowd, but ended up lurching between patches of people, alternately accelerating and braking. De Vries shouted and hit the steering wheel hard with both hands. He could see the clear stretch of street in front of the cathedral and accelerated towards it. The road narrowed even further at an old tree and people ran into shop doorways to get out of the way.

Nancie Keldie didn't feel pain in her hand, only the throbbing that made it difficult to hold the steering wheel. She gingerly crept through the crowd with the blue light flashing and siren sounding intermittently. People were getting out of her way and pointing in the direction of de Vries' land rover.

A young mother pushing a little boy in a buggy ran across the street to get out of the way of the careering vehicle, but she tripped and the buggy swung back into its path. De Vries braked hard and spun the steering wheel. The vehicle swerved but caught the buggy with the rear quarter, dislodging the toddler. Onlookers gasped in horror. The child rolled over and the mother was at its side in a second, protecting him from further danger. She cradled her child and other passers by stopped to help. De Vries sped away, but by this time was driving through an even denser crowd who were now shouting at him as he constantly accelerated and braked and swerved from left to right. As the crowd separated in front of her car, Keldie could see the young woman cradling her baby next to the overturned buggy and she recognised one of the doctors from the hospital with her. She stopped the car and silenced the siren. The sound of the crying baby cut through the mumbling of the angry crowd. Nancie called to the mother,

"Is everything ok?"

"Yes, keep going. Look!"

Keldie could see the brake lights of the land rover ahead. De Vries had found his way out of the pedestrian filled area and into the street. As he drove past the old town hall, he saw the flashing blue light behind him and accelerated once more, and again a pedestrian placed himself in front of the vehicle. De Vries swerved on to the pavement and drove over wicker baskets of knitting, scattering tourists who leapt back into the shop, tripping over toy puffins and fudge. De Vries got the car back on to the road again and saw Keldie behind him. At the last minute, he turned rapidly right into Tankerness Lane, but Keldie couldn't stop. By the time she had braked, reversed and turned into the lane, de Vries had got a lead. He turned left and south. He knew the only way he could lose the police was by staying away from the main streets. Keldie drove down Tankerness lane, couldn't see de Vries and couldn't tell which direction he had taken. She turned left and someone at the side of the street pointed west. She assumed he was heading for Stromness. She drove quickly along the clear road, but could see that she had lost him. She pressed the talk button of the radio to call in to Burgh Road and winced as she felt a sharp pain in her injured hand.

De Vries continued to listen to Keldie's report to base on the abandoned radio as he got to the southern outskirts of Kirkwall. He reassessed his situation. The police were clearly out to get him. To get to Norwich, he had to get a ferry back to the Scottish mainland, but they would be waiting for him at the terminal. There were only three roads out of Kirkwall and they would catch up with him sooner or later. He headed east until he saw the road to the distillery. He drove up the hill and saw that this road headed south in an almost perfect straight line. He was trembling and he tried to think. He knew he had to find a quiet place to rest and think through his next step. He came to St Mary's and crossed one of the causeways that linked the islands together. These were the Churchill Barriers that separated Scapa Flow from the open sea outside. He passed the Italian Chapel, up a hill and down towards the next causeway and then found a quiet road left towards a quarry and stopped the engine. He wound down the window and sucked in the cool air and tried to calm himself. He closed his eyes and felt ashamed; how sordid this whole business was. He now felt that he was losing control but for his possession of the whalebone mace, the constant around which this set of events rotated in an ever decreasing spiral.

*　　　*　　　*

Patrick Tenant staggered back in the direction of his home. It was raining and he had been thrown out of a pub. He had never been thrown out of a pub before. He was worried about returning to work and he did not know how to explain the loss of his car to the insurance company. He was making errors in the lies he was having to tell. If he was going to claim that the car had been stolen in Orkney, why had he not reported it to the police? He made errors about the time of the theft and the location from which he claimed it was stolen. When he spoke to her, his wife had berated him and he couldn't keep his story straight. He was having almost constant flashbacks to the scene of the killing and could not concentrate on anything. He just couldn't find the normality he so desperately sought.

He lurched along the side of a busy road, moving between the sodium streetlights. He turned into a grassy area under some trees to escape the rain. He was dripping wet and he was having difficulty with his balance. 'Dominic, Dominic', he repeated to himself. He hit his head on a tree to try to beat some reality into himself. He lost his footing in the wet grass and fell. He decided just to stay there. As he faded into a state of drunken unconsciousness, he was aware of breathing on his face. He opened his eyes and saw the muzzle of a deer about six inches from him. He closed his eyes again, oblivious to the soft rain falling about him.

Chapter 13

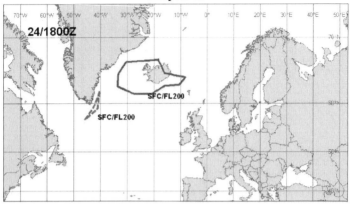

Saturday night, April 24th 2010, 9:14 pm.

At Balfour Hospital, Clett stood in front of Nancie Keldie and Jamie Gunn.

"Sorry we let de Vries get away."

"Don't worry about it Jamie. He'll turn up sooner or later. I've issued a general alert to apprehend and charge."

"Anyway, what about you two? It looks as if you won't be playing five a side for a while."

Gunn looked at his heavily dressed foot and he smiled sheepishly. Clett looked at Nancie's hand.

"Aye and you won't be playing the piano."

"I just feel so stupid, If only I had taken a different turning, I could have caught him."

"Don't blame yourself Nancie. You did all you could. It was a very dangerous situation and you handled it very well."

"Thank you sir. When I saw that baby and the upturned pram, my heart was in my mouth."

"Aye, the baby's fine, but the poor mum had an awful shock."

"…and what about the look on the faces of those tourists."

"They'll have some interesting photos to take home."

Jamie was using a pen to scratch beneath his plastered leg.

"And by the way sir, those new radios are just rubbish sir."

"Sorry?"

"Well I threw my radio at the suspect and it had absolutely no effect. Just bounced off him and he didn't notice. Now those old radios, well they were the business. If I had thrown one of them, it would have laid him out. Job done."

"I don't think that it was in the original design specification of these sophisticated pieces of communications equipment to have them function as a weapon."

"I know sir, but those old radios were great."

"Constable Gunn, have you been talking to Special Constable Drever?"

*   *   *

De Vries woke in the dark with the sound of a piercing voice that penetrated into his consciousness. There was a fierce red light blinking inside the car that had an intense aura making him look away and out into the dark evening. Intermittently, the headlights of passing cars came and went. He shielded his eyes against their brilliance. The pitch of each engine dropped and faded as it passed; until it came again with the next vehicle. Then there was that voice inside the vehicle, a woman's high voice repeating meaningless rapid syllables. The sentences were short and monotone and dropped with a cadence at the end of each utterance. He turned again to the source: it was Gunn's radio, lying where he had thrown it, illuminating the footwell of the car in bright red light with each transmission.

It was relentless. De Vries closed his eyes tight and put his fingers in his ears. He had to concentrate. "Kirkwall, Kirkwall. Kirkwall and the ferry to Aberdeen. No. No. No. No. No."

He knew he had to avoid Kirkwall, so he would no longer be able to catch the Aberdeen ferry. The police would be aware of his intentions. He would go for the Stromness ferry the next morning; the Hamnavoe was now back in service.

De Vries turned the key and the land rover engine started with a roar that made him shudder. He went back across the Churchill Barrier, changing gear gingerly to make as little sound as he could. He switched off his lights. The weather was closing in and it was starting to rain. He drove back along the long straight road in the direction of the lights of Kirkwall and then turned left and away from the town, down to the Coastguard station at Scapa and along the quiet road west in the direction of Stromness. He looked at his watch, it was nearly midnight. He had to find a secluded place to wait until morning when he could catch the Hamnavoe. In the murky night, vehicles passed him and he thought he saw a police car. He turned off to a quiet road marked 'Loch of Kirbister', and continued for a mile or two, peering out to the dirty night, to the rhythm of the windscreen wipers. He turned left down a lane, passed a farm and on out along the diminishing track into the moor. They would never find him here. He carried on and the rain became worse. The visibility was deteriorating, and he had difficulty identifying the track as the land rover crept up the hill. He wrestled with the steering wheel to keep the vehicle in a straight line. There was a thud as the rear differential hit a rock and the front wheels sank in boggy ground. The car became stuck fast. De Vries got out into the soaking night and attempted to push the land rover out of its rut, slipping in the mud. He pushed, and then tried to drive, but the wheels span with no possibility of traction. He got out again and and pushed until he was exhausted. Dripping wet and cold, he looked at his beloved land rover, stuck up to its axle. This was a four-wheel drive vehicle with a differential lock and low ratio gearbox, and de Vries knew how to drive it, but here in this filthy night it was immoveable. He shivered. He was weary and the cold penetrated to his bones.

The visibilility cleared, and he turned to look south, and out to the gas flare on the oil terminal at Flotta. It roared silently and lit up the whole archipelago around Scapa Flow with its orange glow illuminating the clear rain. It lit the lives of everyone encompassed by its radius. They were lit in all that they did and all they planned to do. In his exhaustion, de Vries somehow saw the flare as a metaphor, a moral illumination that could perhaps be relied on to justify some action or other. Some would just appreciate its presence and think it benign in the night sky. But tonight, de Vries was losing control of his life and he saw the flare as having a role in his actions he could not fathom. He tried to re-evaluate his situation. The fact he was stopped by the police at Kirkwall meant that they must want to arrest him. Did they think that he killed Dominic? Ridiculous, but he was no longer sure about anything. He had escaped from the police but they would have all the ferry ports watched. There was no way off the island. The land rover was stuck and he could not shift it. He was wet and cold and, despite his high level of fitness, was worn out with the chase and the time he had spent trying to cajole the vehicle into motion. He had no food or water and was exhausted. He reached in to the vehicle for his rucksack and lifted the whalebone mace and placed the pieces in his pocket. He looked around in the night sky and could see only the flare to the south. He peered at it and was sure he could feel its warmth, even at five miles distance. Then as he watched it, the flame on Flotta reduced in intensity and in an immense silent splutter, died.

*   *   *

Patrick Tenant arrived home to Somerston and let himself in. He staggered into the kitchen and poured himself a bowl of corn flakes. His wife stood at the at the sitting room door in a dressing gown.
"What do you mean the car was stolen? Have you reported it to the police? Where were you? How did you let it out of your sight?"
"I didn't, it was ..."

"Don't you realise I need that car for work? I can't rely on lifts until you decide to get your finger out and sort this mess. Are you crying? For God's sake Patrick, grow up. You are so pathetic. I'm going to bed. Don't bother coming up."

She left him weeping on the sofa. He went to the drinks cupboard and took a bottle of whisky and drank, alternating between the whisky and spoonfuls of corn flakes. He had no idea of the time. His watch had stopped. He looked at the hall clock and it too had stopped. He looked at his mobile phone and saw the screen filled with sea-water. He wept again. He finished the whisky and slept on the couch.

*   *   *

It was dark and Trevor de Vries was suddenly desperately cold. He was up to his knees in the bog and the wind had become stronger, blowing the rain from the west, or the north, or the south. He was having difficulties placing north. He knew the flare had been approximately due south, and that north should be in the opposite direction, but all he could now see was darkness and an enclosing mix of blown mist and persistent, penetrating rain. He had only taken several steps away from the land rover and shelter, but already it had disappeared in the fog. He knew that all he had to do was retrace his steps and he would find it; or he would merely wait until the weather cleared. He thought he knew this changeable weather well and that the wind would blow the mist away soon enough. He took several steps in the direction he had come. Within a few metres he had fallen flat into the bog. Angry with himself, he stood up and kept going, sure that he could find the vehicle in this direction.

He searched for what seemed a long time, each step increasing his exhaustion and hunger. The weather was showing no sign of change. He was very cold and he was shivering and all he could see was black mist and rain. There were now no distant lights, and there was no moon nor stars. All there was, was Trevor de Vries in this impenetrable world with no indication of direction. He felt for the whalebone mace pieces and he knew this could not last forever. All he needed to do was wait it out. He also knew he had to budget his energy. He had already expended much effort on trying to find the land rover. He looked at his watch. It had been exactly ten minutes since the flare extinguished.

"Ten minutes! My God, how could that be?"

He looked in disbelief at his watch. Yes, he had seen the flare go out and looked at the time. It had been 1.22 am. It was now 1.32 am. This was mad. Could his watch have stopped? What about the rain, what about when he fell into the bog? No, the watch was still going, and it was after all a Breitling. It was not going to let him down like this, but ten minutes. He might have to wait for hours for the weather to clear. This was madness.

De Vries tried to bring himself to his senses. He tried to control his rapid breathing. This was merely a situational awareness problem. He remembered his flying lessons when the instructor had placed covers over the windows and positioned the aircraft into an unusual attitude, pointing in a particular direction and at a particular angle. It had been de Vries' job to bring the aircraft back into straight and level flight. All that he had to do was ignore his senses and observe and fly by his instruments. When the covers were removed from the aircraft windscreen, de Vries found that he had placed the aircraft in a steep dive heading for the ground, from which the instructor had to recover. He had never been able to get over this. He had succeeded in a flight simulator, but he never managed to achieve success in this exercise in the real world.

He knew the theory, though. Ignore your senses and trust in the objective information in front of you. It had been ten minutes since the flare went out and when he knew where he was in relation to the land rover. All he had to do was analyse his movements in that time. First, he would meditate to calm himself.

175

He had meditated in the snow in the foothills of the Himalayas, so he should be able to settle himself here in this blowing Orkney mist.

He assumed the standing mountain pose and again tried to settle his breathing. He felt the cold wet air permeate his upper chest and lower lungs. He exhaled and let his shoulders drop. He inhaled again and felt the blood flow up his neck and into his head, and he shivered. He stopped and inhaled again; settling his shoulders once more, and again he could not stop shivering. He tried several more times, but could not relax into the simple exercise. He could not meditate because he could not stop shivering.

He looked above him and saw a patch of dark blue sky and a star traversing from left to right in the gap between the clouds. A moving star? Impossible. A meteorite? No it was moving at a walking pace. Had his senses fooled him so much? Was he seeing time move at a different speed? He looked at his watch again. It was now sixteen minutes since the flare had gone out. How could a star have moved so much in just a few minutes? The sky clouded over and he looked down. He was sure that two clumps of reeds below him were the two he had fallen over when he first left the vehicle. And, were those not fragments of tyre track he could see in the infrequent illumination from somewhere? From the moon? He stopped and thought of the orientation of the reeds and where the land rover had been. He went over it in his head several times and became confident of the direction he had to take. He walked for a few minutes and stumbled over more reeds and decided this was not correct. He would have to return to the point he came from, and start again. He felt one half of the whalebone mace head in his pocket. The other half was missing. He remembered taking it out of the rucksack, but now it was gone. Now it was gone. De Vries' despondency deepened. What had he done? Had he any control in this world with no markers? One half of the mace head was gone. Perhaps he could look for it as he backtracked? He returned in the direction he thought he had come from, but could not find the pair of clumps of reed. He wandered, looking for some kind of sign. The mist continued to persist and the dark was only occasionally broken by poor visibility of about five metres. He could see by the backlight on his Breitling that it was now twenty five minutes since the flare was extinguished. He was exhausted and confused, and he resorted to walking randomly with the hope he would somehow just come across the land rover in the dark. The heath was an area of several square miles with the nearest road about a mile away.

De Vries continued wandering, wetter, more confused and bewildered with each passing minute. The poor visibility and the persistent driving rain continued unabated. Frustrated and angry, he looked at his watch once more – it was still only thirty-five minutes since the flare went out. It had to be wrong. In exasperation, he threw it away. He wandered and stumbled over what he thought was a vast area. Aimlessly, and without realising it, he climbed to higher ground. He had heard the odd bleating of a sheep, or the twittering of some bird or other and tried to follow the sound. Profoundly exhausted, he fell down in the wet heather. He put his hand in his pocket and took out remaining piece of the mace head. The other half was now irretrievably lost.

Mixed in with this blowing fog, was a small amount of ash that gave the slight smell of sulphur. The fog was formed by the wind from the west, out in the Atlantic, driven across the ocean, colliding with the warm rising air over the Orkney archipelago. This blown mist, this gale of fog, would turn again into clear air only once it continued east over the sea. At this time, in this moment, it existed only over Orkney. It would not be blown away by the wind, but would persist as blown mist until the weather cleared.

*   *   *

Roland Clett was playing with Russell on Northwick Sands back on Papay, and his mother and father were sitting on old aluminium camping chairs, drinking tea from metal enamelled mugs. He knew they were too old for buckets and spades and he was getting sand in his shoes. He dropped his mobile phone and it disappeared as the tide swallowed it up. Russell smiled and threw sand at him. He started to cry and heard his mother call.

"Russell, stop throwing sand at your big brother. Roland, don't be such a cry baby."

Clett woke short of breath and blinked away tears. He got up and had a drink of water and sat down and regarded his reflection in the window. There was no view to be had tonight, just the grey wind obscuring everything and rattling the roof tiles, and the rain washing onto the windows. He continued to be troubled about the veracity of the evidence that connected Trevor de Vries with Dominic's murder. He simply did not believe that he had murdered Dominic Byrd. De Vries was an overly assured, self-obsessed, deceptive and unpleasant individual who had a possibly unhealthy interest in young men. He was connected with Dominic, but Clett did not believe that he had killed him. The evidence of his fingerprints on Dominic's shoulder was incontrovertible and Clett could not explain it. The existence of Dominic's DNA and body matter on de Vries' clothes and skin might be explained by his unbelievable interference at the body the next morning; and his height and build were consistent with the dimensions of the shadow in the body matter spatter radius surrounding the young man's body. Also, there was his obstructive behaviour at the crime scene. Could this really be some misguided professional motivation on the part of de Vries, or had Clett got it all wrong? More and more, despite Clett's feeling for the case, the evidence seemed to point to de Vries as Dominic Byrd's killer. He really had no choice but to have issued the arrest warrant for de Vries, but still he had serious doubts about this course of action.

Nelson would be pleased and it would be another tick in the box for him if a result came out of this; another southerner sorting out our problems. No, this was ungenerous, thought Clett. Christine would not approve of such thinking.

Clett went to his shelf and took down his own partially completed transcription of the correspondence of Archibald Clett, (1721-1799). He had copied these letters from the original documents held in the Orkney Room in the Kirkwall library. He chose a letter he had recently been working on:

To David Hume Esq.
1 St David Street
New Town
Edinburgh
23rd April 1770
Dear Sir,

While drinking the last of your fine claret I believe that I may have discovered a disagreement with your argument when you write of Miracles. In that excellent piece of work, you say that a wise man proportions his belief to the evidence. Upon contemplation of this notion, and with the greatest of humility to your skills in argument, I would state that this principle is faulty. It will never offer a satisfactory method of determining an outcome or explaining phenomena.

Before stating my reasons, I should say that I consider your method of using evidence to discover a state of affairs otherwise hidden to us is of use in many parts of life. and not only confined to your argument against miracles. In its particularity, I should like to see this subject spoken of in the use of evidence in the practise of the law, and in the judgement of guilt or innocence. I would opine that these subjects are more important than the discussion of mere religion. When we talk about the law, a man's life might be at stake, but when we talk about the truth or otherwise of religion, we repeat old arguments that will be repeated until my cows come home.

I digress, and so, I return to my argument. In the law, the proportionality of guilt comes under that banner of the calculus of morality, of which I have written before. It implies that we estimate the outcome of evidence by mensuration, that evidence is thus measured and the outcome dependent upon that measurement. I will contest this argument upon two fronts. The first is that if we apply this principle of proportionality to the veracity of the evidence, then it is clear that a secure outcome may not be attained because of the unreliability of evidence as demonstrated in your essay. Thus this method will never give an ultimate and definitive answer.

The second point is by way of an alternative. I would assert that the exercise of virtue is more satisfying in the decision of guilt or innocence than this mere calculus. The evil of the exercise of the calculus of morality must be avoided in every case. What must replace this calculus of morality is the exercise of virtue. This virtue is described by the great Aristotle and has been observed universally where humans congregate for mutual benefaction. From the height of the antient Greek civilisation to the littlest tribe in Africa, men practice the exercise of virtue. Judgements are made by one with wisdom and knowledge of life. In any place where one man stands in judgement over another, that judge should bring these factors to bear on the words being spoken. He should use his skills of the observation of character, of the ability to determine honesty and combine these in a judgement. This is to my mind a more honest judgement than where we employ a moral accountant to add up the premisses of an argument and come to a measured outcome. The virtue so exercised in my suggestion may be deemed as belonging within the realm of the sentiments. It is something we are born with and that we can nurture. It is as natural as the air we breathe. It is not a notion that is happy in our fashion for natural science, but I believe this to be a more satisfactory method of the determination of guilt than the notion of proportionality.

I fully expect sir, you to destroy my argument with the manifest flair you constantly exhibit. Nonetheless, my feelings lie with my position, even if I have not argued my case to your satisfaction.

I remain Sir, your most humble and obedient servant,

Archibald Clett of Canmore.

*   *   *

Trevor de Vries woke to a warm sun. Overhead a few crows were mobbing a kestrel. His back and neck ached and his feet were painful and blistered. He reckoned he had covered many miles. He felt for his watch and was surprised to find it missing. He stood up and saw the land rover, not twenty metres from him, the door open and the lights lit dimly. They must have been switched on all night. Mixed with the sound of a rising linnet, was the crackle from the police radio. He stumbled over and climbed into the driver's seat. The engine started with the first turn of the key, and there was no problem with the traction of the wheels. He simply reversed the car to a viable track and drove in the direction of Stromness and the ferry south. He did not plan his route, and several oncoming cars sounded their horns as he failed to maintain his road position. He was afraid of driving into a ditch and stayed as far away from the side of the road as he could.

He arrived at the Northlink Ferry Terminal where he meekly and silently complied with the police officers who had been waiting for him. He made no attempt to resist. He felt in his pocket and there was no sign of the remaining whalebone mace head. They took him back to a warm Kirkwall police Station and arranged for him to have some food.

DI Nelson advised Chief Inspector McPhee that he intended to interview Trevor de Vries. On her instruction, he advised Clett by text and accompanied Constable Jamie Gunn to Kirkwall police Station. He arranged for a recorded interview to take place.

De Vries sat in the interview room, shoulders drooped, waiting for whatever was to befall him. Nelson entered the room and brusquely carried out the formalities.

"Tell me how you met Dominic Byrd."

"I don't know, I, eh, he was just one of the boys on the dig."

"How do you know Torvald Arnsenn?"

De Vries did not respond.

"Are you involved in drug dealing?"

Silence.

"Were you involved with drug dealing with Dominic Byrd?"

De Vries shrugged his shoulders.

"Can you explain how a fingerprint of yours was found on the body of Dominic Byrd?"

De Vries gazed down at the surface of the table, examining the flow of its grain. He slowly lifted his half-closed eyes to Nelson. Nelson glanced at his notes.

"We have found particles of Dominic Byrd's blood and body matter on the clothes you were wearing when you returned to the scene of the murder the next morning, the 21st April."

De Vries returned to looking at the table.

"Why did you obstruct the investigation?"

De Vries remained silent through the continuous questions:

"For fuck's sake man, there was a tooth from the victim in your jacket pocket."

De Vries slowly turned in against the onslaught from Nelson. He leaned forward, hunched in his chair, his tall frame now compressed in a rounded form.

"Why did you instruct the dig team members to carry on working after the body was found? Did you kill Dominic Byrd?"

Constable Jamie Gunn observed de Vries' increasing disengagement.

Nelson continued the staccato questioning.

"How did you do it? What did you use to beat his face? Did you use a rock? Did you throw the rock into the sea?"

De Vries's whole demeanour threw Nelson. He had expected an assured and professional performance and the individual in front of him was wholly malleable and open to suggestion, but evidence was evidence. He continued.

"Look you piece of shit, we know you killed this boy. You have no fucking defence. We have your fingerprint on the body; we have his DNA on your clothing; there is your obstruction of the investigation on the morning of the 21st April; you have connections with Torvald Arnsenn and so did Dominic Byrd; and we have a good idea that the motive was a drug deal gone wrong."

Defeated and lost, de Vries looked at the floor and slowly nodded. He whispered:

"Yes."

"Yes you killed Dominic Byrd?"

"Yes."

Nelson came out of the interview room beaming. He punched the air and slapped Jamie Gunn on the shoulder.

"Son, we have a fucking result!"

Chapter 14

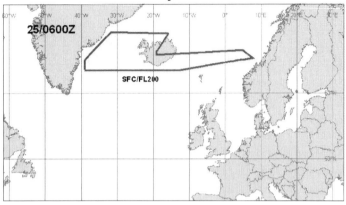

Sunday morning, 25th April 2010, 11:07 am.

Maggie McPhee and Roland Clett walked out of the Burgh Road Police Station and down towards Kiln Corner.

"How are the funeral arrangements going?"

"They're fine Maggie. Russell's done most of the work."

"Are you still looking at 11.00 tomorrow?"

"Aye. That'll give plenty of time for anyone who wants to get the Earl Thorfinn at 7.20 and we have booked the MV Golden Marianna to take people back and forward to Pierowall."

"The Papa Westray ferry?"

"Aye. We will be flying over this afternoon."

"Hugh and I will be on the morning ferry."

"That's good of you Maggie."

The two officers stopped outside the old Norwegian Consulate building.

"Roland. If you are up to it, we have to have a fairly high level discussion about the case. Here's Tony."

"DI Nelson. Thanks for coming."

"No problem Chief Inspector. Glad to be of assistance once more," he said, winking at Clett.

"Ok gentlemen, we are here to meet Anders Waitz who was the consular official and has been asked to intervene. Mr Waitz used to run the consulate and now works in Edinburgh."

"Why do we need to talk to him?"

"Because we are getting into murky waters here. We need the assistance of the Norwegian Special Branch who may have an insight that could help us."

"Why are we going through consular channels Maggie? Ordinary police work is all that is necessary."

"Well no, Roland. Let's go in."

Anders Waitz opened the door and welcomed the three officers.

"Ah Mr Clett."

"Yes. This is Inspector Clett", said Maggie.

"I beg your pardon. Yes, I know your wife, Inspector. She taught my children when I was the consular official here. How is she?"

"She is fine thank you. Yes, I think we met at a barbeque once in Finstown."

"Ah Orkney barbeques. They are not what I miss most about Orkney", Waitz laughed.

Nelson coughed.

"I believe we have some business to attend to."

"Yes Detective Inspector Nelson. I believe you have made a specialisation of the illegal drug trade in my country in particular."

"Yes, that is my area of specialisation."

"Well I have to say something that comes under the heading of classified information. You see Torvald Arnsenn has connections with the Norwegian deputy Prime Minister, Olav Gustavsson."

"What?"

"Yes. You might call him Olav Gustavsson's skeleton in the cupboard. The Norwegian police, and increasingly the press, are well aware of Torvald Arnsenn's drug connections."

"They are more than connections. We think he is running a drugs distribution organisation that has links to France, Holland, England, and if our investigations are correct, in Orkney too."

"That may well turn out to be the case, Detective Inspector Nelson."

"Mr Waitz, you know that we are involved with a murder enquiry and have uncovered a possible link with Norwegian drug gangs operating in these Islands."

"Yes, Detective Inspector, but I am here to make a request that any investigation of Mr Arnsenn is carried out with the utmost sensitivity. Our position is that he is a businessman making an investment in Orkney, with whose community we have had strong historic links for centuries."

"Mr Waitz", said Nelson, "We will deal with this case objectively and any action we take will be evidence driven. Frankly we do not care whether or not Mr Arnsenn has any connections."

Maggie McPhee cleared her throat.

"Thank you Detective Inspector. Mr Waitz, please be assured that we will be as sensitive as we possibly can be to the concerns of the Norwegian deputy prime minister. We will keep you up to date on any developments on this aspect of the case."

"Thank you Chief Inspector. That is very reassuring."

McPhee, Nelson and Clett left the Consulate and turned back towards the police station through the narrow Kirkwall streets. As they passed St Magnus' Cathedral, they heard singing Clett's mind drifted –

'…the kirk, in a gale of psalms'.

Nelson had been speaking.

"Chief Inspector, I have to say formally that I disagree with your approach to Mr Waitz's concerns."

"Your disagreement is noted DI Nelson."

"But we are not running this investigation for the Norwegians."

"No Detective inspector, but there is no point antagonising them. The connections between Orkney and Norway are very valuable to us."

The three officers moved to the side of the narrow road for a passing car.

"I'm sorry Chief Inspector, but Torvald Arnsenn belongs behind bars and I don't care if he is the President of the United States, I will collar him the first chance I get."

"Detective Inspector Nelson, I am going to give you a direct instruction. I want you to let me know before you take any action on Orkney and I want to know of any developments as they happen."

"Look Maggie, no need to be like that. All I want is a result. Of course I'll keep in touch."

They arrived at the Burgh Road Police Station.

"Inspector Clett, DI Nelson, I want to have a final review before we submit our report to the Procurator Fiscal who will prosecute this case against de Vries at the High Court in Edinburgh. DI Nelson, I believe you're satisfied with the outcome of your enquiries and optimistic about a successful prosecution."

"Yes Chief Inspector. I have successfully analysed the motivation and modus operandi of the charged individual. I believe that Dominic Byrd was killed as the result of a Norwegian drug organisation expanding into the UK. As you know, I've had much experience in the growth of the drugs trade and I have been following the expansion of the circle of influence of Torvald Arnsenn, based in Oslo. He has developed links with Holland and Thailand with the easy availability of opium from Afghanistan. He has had telephone and email contact with the victim prior to the murder. Furthermore Trevor de Vries and Arnsenn have had telephone contact. This leads me on to the unarguable conclusion that Arnsenn was setting up a new distribution route into the UK via Orkney. Dominic Byrd was to be Arnsenn's contact. He approached Trevor de Vries, knowing his weaknesses, to wit…"

Clett grunted

"…to wit."

Nelson continued.

"As I was saying, his weaknesses, to wit, a history of drug dealing activities and his homosexuality. On the night of the 20th April,

Byrd made his move on de Vries. De Vries misunderstood this and when confronted with the rejection, reacted by assaulting the victim with violence and did so murder him."

"Inspector Clett, I believe you have some doubts about this approach?"

"Yes Chief Inspector. I believe that DI Nelson's analysis relies too heavily on speculation. It does not take into consideration the missing car driven over the Noup Head cliffs, nor the lack of expected DNA evidence under de Vries' fingernails or on the body of Dominic Byrd. Also no drugs residue has been found at the site or on the body."

"Thank you Inspector Clett."

"Well, Chief Inspector, as to speculation, my analysis is based on years of experience in this area. I know how these networks work. This is a classic encroachment of a new drugs player on the UK scene. The car; well I think this is a red herring. I don't believe that any such vehicle has been identified. Anyway, why would anyone get rid of a perfectly serviceable car when it could have been used to escape from the scene? If it had been driven over the cliffs, then I think it is more likely to have been the work of young people messing about. As to the lack of drugs residue on the body, we are not talking about a street dealer here. We are talking about someone being groomed for the business at the highest level. I think the lack of drug residue is irrelevant and that some traces of previous exposure to drugs will come up sooner or later. That is, unless Inspector Clett has a more suitable candidate."

"Well actually yes. I still feel strongly that Ronnie Rust fits the bill and we cannot ignore the possibility that he is involved."

Maggie McPhee shook her head from side to side.

"Not Ronnie Rust, Inspector. We all know fine about the bad feeling between the two of you. Are you sure this is not just a chance to get back at the not guilty verdict he received as a result of your charge of attempted murder on Rust's fishing boat some years ago?"

"Yes, I know about this", said Nelson. "From what I understand, Rust is a respectable businessman that you stitched up. Didn't I see his name in *The Orcadian* opening a community centre somewhere? You don't seriously think he is a suspect."

"He was on Westray at the time of the murder and, regardless of the fact that he has conned many people on these islands, he is well capable of the brutality of this murder in a way that Trevor de Vries is not."

"OK Inspector Clett, do you have any evidence?"

"Not yet Chief Inspector, but I am still putting a case together."

"Thank you gentlemen. I think we shall go ahead with the initial presentation of the evidence to the Procurator Fiscal. On balance, I'm convinced that there is a strong case against Trevor de Vries. If you get anything on Rust, let me know, but Inspector Clett, please take it easy."

Both men left Maggie McPhee's office.

"Good result Clett. Glad to have been of help. We've done good work today. We've taken a step to put another one of these bastards away."

"Tony, I still have serious doubts and I still think that Rust is worth investigating."

"Serious doubts! For God's sake, look at the evidence! Look at de Vries' admission. Christ! Anyway, what have you got? Sweet bloody fuck all if you ask me. You can have doubts when you have a fucking case. Jesus. I'm trying to help you here, can't you see that? Your investigation was going nowhere until I turned up. My investigations have turned it around, and as a result, we have a case for the prosecution. What's the matter with you man?"

Clett didn't respond.

"Look Clett, I'm getting back to the Inverness office. Think on this. You can call me later to thank me."

Nelson slapped Clett on the shoulder.

"Have a safe flight Tony."

*   *   *

Roland Clett entered the bar area of the Fraction nightclub with its unusual daytime aura. The place, active at night, seemed strange during daylight hours. It was as if people didn't belong. Bar staff were hoovering and cleaning down tables for the evening's customers. The club smelled of stale sweet beer, of sweat and of last night's desire.

Clett knew one of the staff, a school friend of Sandy's.

"Excuse me, it's Barbara, isn't it, I'm ..."

"Oh Mr Clett, hi, how are you?"

"I'm fine Barbara, how are you yourself?"

"Oh I'm doing ok. Still working here though. How is Sandy?"

"He's doing well. He is in second year, doing Psychology at Glasgow Uni."

"That's great Mr Clett. I'll have to get chatting to him online, I haven't seen him for ages. Can I get you a drink?"

"No thanks Barbara, I'm here on police business."

"How can I help?"

"Were you working last Tuesday night, the 20th April?"

Barbara checked the roster.

"Yes."

"Can you remember this boy?" He showed her the photo from Dominic Byrd's facebook page.

"No, I don't think so." She showed the picture to the other staff member, a Chinese boy.

"Nope, I'm afraid not."

Clett looked up to the CCTV cameras in the bar.

"That's fine. Is Geraldine Work here?"

"Yes, she is in the office, I'll take you up."

Barbara showed Clett into the small office with yellow notes stuck to all available surfaces, and a number of folders and box files marked 'invoices 2010', 'correspondence', 'accounts 2009-2010'. Behind a large computer screen was a small woman, about thirty years old, dwarfed by the piles of paperwork. She was talking to a supplier on the phone. When she ended the call, stood up and introduced herself.

"Hi, I'm Geraldine Work."

"Hello, I'm inspector Roland Clett and I would like to ask you a few questions in connection with a murder inquiry."

"Oh, that boy on Westray."

"Yes. We have reason to believe that he was in this club on Tuesday night."

"Really?"

"Yes, we would like to interview some members of your staff."

"That shouldn't be a problem. I'll get you their contact details."

"Do you keep CCTV records?"

"Yes, on DVDs."

"Could I see the recording for the 20th April?"

"No problem."

Geraldine opened a filing cabinet and immediately found a DVD marked '21/4/10'. She handed it to Clett.

"Thanks."

Clett wrote a receipt.

"I've heard that the club is being sold."

"Yes, I think it has already been sold; to a Norwegian, a Mr Torvald Arnsenn."

Clett looked up.

"Torvald Arnsenn?"

"Yes, do you know him?"

"No, but I know someone who does."

So much for Rust's public spirit and generosity, Clett thought. The nightclub was being sold to Arnsenn, a known drug dealer. For the first time, Clett thought there might be something in Nelson's theory.

"Do you know anything about him?"

"No, never met the man. Mister Rust says I don't have to worry about my job – and the same for the rest of the staff. He has assured us all that our positions will be safe."

"Thanks. Just one other thing, how well do you know Ronnie Rust?"

"Mister Rust? He is like a father to me. He gave me the chance of this job when things weren't going well for me. I was brought up on Shapinsay."

"Ah, I see. Your name is Work. Were you related to Betty and Roger Work?"

"Yes, that's my mum and dad. They died when I was quite young."

"Ah, I think I remember now, it was a house fire wasn't it? Very sad."

"Yes. I don't know if you know, but I was involved in a violent relationship and I wanted out. I went away to London and got into a bad crowd. I was desperate and then I came back to Orkney, but didn't have any way of keeping myself and my wee boy Raymond. It was in the local papers. Everyone knows about it."

"Yes, I do remember. How old is Raymond?"

"He is seven now and in Primary 2."

"How did you meet Ronnie Rust?"

"I met Mister Rust here at the club. As I say, I was in a bad way and he just came over to me. It was as if he could see I was in trouble. He basically gave me this job on the spot. I'm just so grateful to him."

"I see. And are you or have you ever been in a relationship with him?"

"What? No absolutely not."

"Has he ever been violent towards you?"

"God, no, what a thing to say. He is a perfect gentleman. He is like a father to me. He looked after me and Raymond when I came back here. That man is a saint."

Clett looked at her honest face and then at his feet.

"Thank you Geraldine. That is very helpful."

*   *   *

Trevor de Vries paced the floor of the cell. Andy, his cellmate, swore and told him to settle down. Andy was awaiting a charge for assault while under the influence of alcohol. He had no knowledge of what had happened and he was worried that his wife would not know where he was. He constantly tried to attract the attention of the duty officer and was clearly very anxious.

De Vries was nervous and the atmosphere in the cell made it more difficult for him to settle. There was fading clarity and there were few choices left open to him. His career was clearly dead in the water and there was now no hope of resurrecting the most important dig he had ever been involved with, and he had lost the finest Neolithic artefact he ever had seen in his life. His world was collapsing. His paper would remain unpublished, and his position at Norfolk University would be lost after this. His whole world was now bounded by these four walls and the company of this man who was a constant distraction. Without natural light in the cell, de Vries could not tell which direction he was facing, or even what time of day it was. There was a clock, but who was to say if it is was correct. The ticking was irregular. De Vries repeated his options to himself and each time the choices reduced with each iteration of his analysis. His rational assessment as he saw it was that he was finished. What university would employ him, even if he was able to get out of this mess? The police were convinced he had killed Dominic Byrd and he was going to face a trial. To any other person, the evidence was damning. De Vries had supposedly killed Byrd in a fit of jealousy – there was his fingerprint on Byrd's shoulder; there was also the perception that he had deliberately obstructed the police investigation by contaminating the crime scene and that he had apparently misled them during questioning. As to his involvement with that thug Rust, that was a distraction too far and it was just as well the police did not cotton on to that. These idiots, how could they not see how unimportant this all was in the face of science? But what future did he have now? His science was a meagre narrative that could no longer direct him. He was convinced that he would continue to be imprisoned in this tiny world, this limbo with no sense of who or where he was, with no sense of the passing of time. These factors forced him to face up to the only choice he had. There was no point in wasting time. His decision was made.

*　　　*　　　*

Roland, Christine, Magnus and Sandy were met by Russell and Margaret and their girls at the grass airstrip on the island of Papay, or, as it is known to outsiders, Papa Westray. They shook hands and embraced and exchanged small talk. Margaret and Christine drove to Mayback Farm with the cases, and Roland, Russell, Magnus and Sandy took the ten minute walk.

At the front door, Roland Clett breathed in the air of his boyhood. The familiar musty aromas from old cupboards and curtains, and the books that were present in every room; the tired old houseplants and the particular smell of the old leather sofa. The late sun low in the sky illuminated the room with its tangential light that Roland and Russell each recognised as the light that lit their homework, or their reading, or just the quiet contemplation of their young worlds.

Magnus and Sandy got talking to their cousins Sarah and Carol.

"So is Mr Travers still teaching?"

 "Aye, the old fool. He is rubbish. Do you know he still wears a tie with food stains on it."

"I think it is his breakfast."

"And whit aboot Miss Scorray? Is she still knitting in front of the whole class?"

"Aye."

"Still the same then."

Clett coughed.

"Yes Dad."

"Are you ok about tomorrow's arrangements?"

"Yeah Dad," said Magnus,

"We'll play it by ear."

On the way up the stairs, Roland said quietly to Sandy.

"Son, you know I'm sorry for everything that happened."

"Aye Dad."

"Maybe we could just take it a day at a time, it's just great us being together."

Sandy coughed and looked away.

"Aye Dad, a day at a time."

*   *   *

Roland Clett opened his eyes. He had tried to sleep but his mind was running wild. The arrangements for the funeral, the progress of the case, his hatred of Ronnie Rust, and how to talk to Sandy over the next few days without starting an argument. He realised he had to concentrate on something he could have an influence on. He took out another photocopy of Archibald Clett's letters with its overwritten text and copied the words to his notebook.

To Mr James Sinclair of Gyre

My Dear Friend,

I was so very sorry to hear of your profound loss. Your wife, Nell, was the most sympathetic of women. While she dealt firmly with those who put against you and your family, she engaged with those who were in need of her help with no consideration for herself or for her own time.

I would say that many will say to you that time will heal your wounds of grief, as they said to me. I have to tell you my friend that time will never close such a wound as you have received. When I lost my Mary, some twenty years ago now, I lost a part of me. I still see some thing in a part of the house that was left by her, a letter, a picture, some small memory while eating a meal. Even in town, I will see a woman, not a young woman, but a woman who has grown twenty years past Mary's age when she died, and I see her and I still think her to be my Mary.

But it is the nights my friend, the empty nights when that warmth is no longer beside you. It is the very devil.

I have not the heart to tell you of other losses, of my four departed little ones, but in that, you are blessed. You have your children, and in them will live and be a visible and constant reminder of your Nell.

With my deepest sympathies at this time,
Your friend,
Archibald Clett of Canmore

*　　*　　*

Geraldine Work was completing the stock inventory. It was a job she enjoyed, making the relationship between the items held in the club match her records. She put a CD on the player and sang along with the song:
'Oh I knew, you'd love me as long as you wanted
And then some day, you'd leave me for somebody new'.

"Do you know the Willie Nelson version?"

"Mister Rust, I didn't know you were there."

"I was just passing. I love that song you know."

"Yes, since you told me all about her, I just adore Patsy Cline. She had just such a tragic life."

"Aye Geraldine, a true heroine. You know, my mother used to listen to her songs."

"Really Mister Rust?"

"Aye. She and I would sit together late at night and she would cry and I was the only one who could comfort her."

"That's beautiful Mister Rust. You must have loved her very much."

"She was the only girl for me Geraldine. No-one could ever match her standards; and those are the standards that I have always lived my life by, and I am reminded of them every time I hear Patsy Cline singing."

'Worry, why do I let myself worry?

Wonderin', what in the world did I do?'

*   *   *

Trevor de Vries had not eaten since his arrest. He was desperate and continued to pace the floor. He repeated the options he saw open to him but any sense of logic was now lost. He was delirious through lack of sleep and hunger. His cellmate was snoring gently. Trevor de Vries quietly tied sheets and pillowcases together. He tied one end to the top of the bunk bed. He tied a loop in the other end and put it around his neck. After considerable effort, he hung himself, quietly, without waking Andy.

Chapter 15

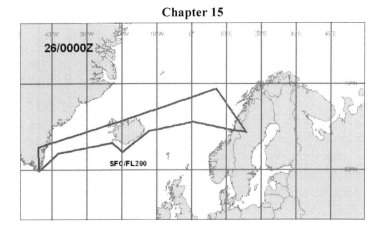

Monday Morning 26th April 2010, 8.50am.

At Mayback Farm, the two Clett families met over breakfast around the kitchen table. This was the table over which Roland and Russell had squabbled and played and laughed for that small eternity that was their childhood. Roland looked out the kitchen window to the view that he still dreamed about.

"Look Russell, there are grey seals on Dog Bones."

"Aye, and look, there are two on Surhoose Tang."

"Aye, right enough."

These two men, transformed into small boys, bickered about the number of seals and birds in front of them. Looking east from a kitchen window that would forever be their touchstone, they argued about the position of rocks and safe footholds from the Surhoose Tang in the north and then south to Dog Bones and the Holm of Papa, an island Roland and Russell had paddled over to many times.

Their wives looked at each other and smiled and the kettle whistled; it brought Roland and Russell back to the present. They realised what was ahead of them and went on to discuss the arrangements, while continuing to exchange memories amidst the uncertainty about the day to come. They finished their tea and faced the moment when they would say goodbye to their parents.

St Boniface church looked out to Westray and was lit by that inexplicable light that illuminates the archipelago. Bill and Vera Clett were to be buried in the family plot. Roland and Russell knew this space well. Here in these walls, they had played and sheltered before the church was roofed. Even then, the eleventh century church appeared to merge with the landscape, seeming as old as the brochs and 5000 year old homes that lay beneath the ploughed fields. It seemed as old as the second world war gun emplacements and military buildings that were only half decayed. It seemed as timeless as the rocks; as timeless as mothers and fathers and kitchen tables.

The two coffins took up a large amount of the space in the tiny building, and the minister and the congregation who came into the church had to squeeze past them; the proximity of life and death at this time became palpable.

Not all the people at the funeral could fit into the small church and they formed a group around the front door to hear the words that were to be said. Present were members of the island community, locals and newcomers, and Christine's mother. There were a few police colleagues, Maggie McPhee and her husband Hugh, Clouston and some of the rest of the team. Angela Fedotova, John Leask and Archie Drever had come over from Westray; there was Janie Shearer who shook Clett's hand warmly, and many more friends; and there were the local farmers. Clett said hello to Jessie Sclater from Noup Farm and thanked her for coming.

"It's the least I can dae son. Yer Mum and Dad were jist such lovely people. Ah'm so sorry fir yir loss son."

Roland's eye was caught by one of the wreaths. The card read:

'To Inspector R. Clett and Russell Clett and their families. From Ronnie Rust. Gone, but not forgot.'

Roland cringed as he read the message. Someone next to him said

"Isn't that a lovely gesture from Mister Rust, his lilies are gorgeous."

Roland reached down and rearranged the flowers to cover Rust's card.

The funeral service passed in a seeming moment as Roland and Russell's attention drifted in and out of the proceedings. The readings and hymns they had chosen with such care with the help of the minister were over in a blur, like driving along a piece of road and suddenly realising that one has not been aware of the passing of the last few miles. Russell and Roland each had their own memories: the turns of phrase, particular looks and odd little scenes with their parents. Roland remembered his first drive of a tractor and for the first time seeing his father from above; Russell remembered helping his mother bake marble cake. These fleeting wisps of memory came and went, some triggered by words or a face in the congregation. They would talk later about how they recollected differently, the events where they were present together: or completely forgot incidents that the other remembered clearly.

Russell rose and stood at the bottom of the pulpit and gave the eulogy. Roland was impressed how his brother was able to maintain his composure and speak so clearly about events and memories that were so close to both of them. He was probably never more proud of his brother than now. He blinked away the water in his eye and quietly cleared his throat. He listened as Russell read a poem that both had known from one of the collections on their parents' bookshelf:

Those who are dead are never gone;
They are there in the thickening shadow.
The dead are not under the earth;
They are in the tree that rustles,
They are in the wood that groans,
They are in the water that runs,

They are in the water that sleeps,
They are in the hut, they are in the crowd,
The dead are not dead.

Those who are dead are never gone,
They are in the breast of the woman,
They are in the child who is wailing,
And in the firebrand that flames.
The dead are not under the earth:
They are in the fire that is dying,
They are in the grasses that weep,
They are in the whimpering rocks,
They are in the forest, they are in the house,
The dead are not dead.

Outside, Bill and Vera Clett were to be lowered into the ground. Roland and Russell stood side by side at the graveside, shoulders and upper arms touching as they moved and breathed. Their wives and children stood close by. This was a silent part of the proceedings. The gravediggers, somehow not conspicuous in their overalls, stood in the background. Mourners found little spaces for themselves and avoided the mounds of earth and the rickety boards placed around the open grave. The minister read some words from the Bible. Neither brother knew what was being read, nor the significance that was recognised by many of the mourners who nodded at parts of the readings. The family and others present kept silent.

The coffins were lowered into the grave side by side. Each was gently laid into place by Roland and Russell and Magnus and Sandy who took the ropes that were attached to the ornamental handles, not to be used to lift the coffins. The undertaker requested that they let the cord run through their hands while the staff in the background took the weight. Roland and Russell both felt a little cheated. They felt they wanted to feel the last weight of their mum and dad; but they did as they were requested and performed their role. When directed, the two brothers took handfuls of soil. They held the heavy earth in their hands that had been the same earth that inhabitants of these islands had held in their hands for work, or for growing, or for burying for thousands of years. They each slowly let the grains drop from their fingers on to the coffins of their parents. The falling earth sounded first with a deep tone, and then as more fell on the coffins, the sound increased in pitch and fell in volume until it was inaudible. As the earth dropped, the assumption of their bodies into the Orkney ground became real and resonant.

The Clett families and the mourners returned to Mayback farm for tea and sandwiches, and for those who wished it, a dram. As the families mingled with friends and relatives, the words were repeated again, and again:

"I'm sorry for your loss."

"They were such nice people."

"What a lovely family you are."

"Your Mum and Dad would have been proud of you both today."

Russell and Roland both recognised the simple value in the inarticulacy of these words. These mumblings that came out of the mouths of people who didn't know what else to say; who could never actually say anything that could comfort or express any valuable mirror to the enormity of the fact that their Mum and Dad were dead. What words could possibly approach an adequate reflection of this fact?

People clinked cups and saucers and there was a pleasant murmur of conversation with odd words coming to the surface, some relevant and some nonsensical. This lovely babel, with all its contradictions and spurious small declamations, its slogans and statements, was all utterly meaningless, like a canopy, no, an aura over the circumstances of the event, that two loved people were that morning put into the timeless soil.

Roland Clett saw Maggie McPhee take a call and move outside. He looked at Christine and she nodded. Clett followed his boss out of the room.

"Maggie, is that about the case?"

"Yes Roland, But don't you worry about it."

"Please Maggie, I need to get my teeth into this. That is the way I will deal with it."

"Are you sure? What does Christine say?"

"Christine is ok with it."

"Oh. Excuse me Roland."

Maggie McPhee reached around and tucked in the label at the back of Roland Clett's neck.

"Sorry, I couldn't stop myself."

"It's ok Maggie, thanks."

A large flock of Golden Plovers landed two fields away.

"Well Roland, the first thing is Ronnie Rust."

"Is he going to make a complaint?"

"No, but you have to back off. I want you to be very careful with that man."

"Yes Maggie."

"Roland, there is a delicate balance to be struck here. I know about your history with Rust, and I know a little about his past."

"His past. He is a brutal thug Maggie. He is a brutal thug that is incapable of empathy and he has everyone on these islands dancing to his tune."

"Aye Roland, but if we are going to get anything on him, we need absolute and incontrovertible evidence. Roland, do you think he killed that boy?"

"I think he did."

"Why?"

"Because he is capable of that level of violence and he was on Westray on Tuesday."

"Is that all? Can you actually place him on Westray? Do you have any witnesses that saw him on Westray that night?"

"No. Sorry, you're right. His car was booked on the ferry on Tuesday morning and seen coming off on Wednesday morning, and there is an unconfirmed report that a silver BMW was seen speeding away from Pierowall; there is still nothing more at this time."

"Nothing?"

"I've been trying to put together his movements."

"What about a motive, and I don't want any philosophy?"

They both smiled.

"Well, there I might be on to something. Rust recently sold the Fraction nightclub to a Norwegian consortium that may have links to drug trafficking."

"OK, Roland, that brings me on to the second subject. Torvald Arnsenn."

"Yes. I know, the Norwegians want us to be delicate."

"Yes they do."

Maggie McPhee paused and turned away.

"Is there something else Maggie?"

She turned back and slowly looked him in the eye and then away again.

"Oh God Roland, I don't know how to tell you this; today of all days."

"What is it Maggie?"

"Look. Why don't we meet up tomorrow?"

"No Maggie. You have to tell me. What has happened?"

"Christ, what a mess. Ok Roland."

Maggie held Roland's elbow tightly.

"Trevor de Vries committed suicide last night."

Clett's head slowly dropped. There was a silence between the two of them. In the kitchen, not twenty feet away, was the continued rumble of conversation and the clinking of cups and saucers, but Clett and Maggie stayed silent. Roland looked up to the busy sky. Clouds were racing and patches of sunlight and shade ran along the ground. Roland placed his hand on one of the flagstone fenceposts that was covered in mustard coloured lichen. On the lichen, there was a bloom, a white powder that felt sharp when he rubbed it between his fingers. Above them, a linnet sang invisibly. Clett looked again into the sky.

"Roland. Are you all right?"

"Yes Maggie."

He paused and the clouds continued on their way.

"Poor bastard. All because …"

"Nelson says that …"

"I know what Nelson will say. He thinks de Vries is still guilty; but you know, I could have saved him. I could have saved him if I had made more noise. I could have spoken up for him and I didn't."

"No Roland. The evidence was always going to point to him. You can't blame yourself."

"How can I not Maggie? How can I not? Four deaths in one week. My God."

"Roland. I'm so sorry to have to have given you this news today."

"It's ok Maggie. I had to know."

"Why don't you take the next few days off? The investigation can run without you. We can get Tony Nelson back if you like."

Clett looked at his boss.

"No Maggie. I need to follow this up, now more than ever."

"Roland. Sleep on it. If you don't come in tomorrow, that will be fine. Hugh and I have to leave to get the ferry back. The Golden Marianna is doing another run in an hour and Russell has organised a bus to Moclett."

"OK Maggie. No problem. I think I will get back in to the family."

"Fine Roland. Look after yourself and keep in touch. I'm very concerned about you. You must look after yourself."

"Thanks Maggie. I just need to see this through to the conclusion."

Chapter 16

Tuesday, 27th April 2010, 3:25 am.

Patrick Tenant came to bed. He didn't know the time. His wife was asleep. He fell on to the bed and lay on his back. The room started to rotate as he had expected. He worked out that if he stayed still he might get to sleep before he threw up. He kept his eyes closed and the motion of his body rotating on his bed continued. He sank down and the spinning increased and then decreased.

He was looking out over the Bay of Noup towards a bright sun that inhabited the northern part of the sky, low down, and this was somehow normal. He felt warm in the growing heat of the sun and was aware of someone standing at his side looking out at the view. As they watched, two fish leapt out of the water. "Look! Look!"

His companion slowly turned towards him. There was a quiet shrill sound. It started like a small pulsating whistle and gradually grew in intensity. Tenant looked for the creature that would make such a sound. A cormorant stood on a rock with its long beak up in the air, drying its wings. The growing beat of the sound was incessant and impermeable and then became an ear piercing unstoppable throbbing scream coming from his companion's mouth. Dominic turned to face him. Patrick couldn't look, but then he couldn't stop himself. He saw what he knew he would see. Dominic's blood-soaked sweatshirt dripped hot blood all over Tenant's feet and legs. Dominic turned to him, spurting black foul smelling blood from the hole in his head that had once been a face. The rhythm of the spraying of blood was in time with the pulse of the scream. It was hot and Tenant could taste the salt on his lips. Dominic, still screaming, was beating him around the head. Patrick did not resist. This was the punishment he so desperately wanted. He stood and he let himself be beaten, all the while staring into the void that was Dominic's face.

"You dirty bastard. You dirty fucking bastard."

Patrick Tenant realised he was awake and that it was morning.

The sound of the alarm clock was waking him up and his wife was kneeling over him beating him around the head. He could still feel the hot blood and he was confused. His wife punched and scratched and slapped and beat at him. When he looked down at his body, he could see no blood. Where was the sensation of heat coming from? He had pissed himself. He had pissed himself and he was immediately engrossed with shame. The shame outweighed any objection he had to his wife beating him. It was welcome and he wished it to continue. He wanted her to continue beating him for ever. It was the best, most valid, most worthwhile thing he had experienced since before those words were spoken at the Bay of Noup. It was after those words that he had destroyed his own world.

Here he was lying in his own piss with his wife beating him and he was happy.

"You twisted fucking bastard you pathetic prick you disgust me."

Tenant was overjoyed. These were the words that framed his madness. They were the words that Dominic spoke to him at the Bay of Noup. He wept and his actions were now to him clear and authentic. This was his opportunity to end the madness forever. He could now close this torment and all would be finished.

He relaxed under the fists and nails of his wife and her manic onslaught. He knew now how she felt and he sympathised with her. He also knew that she would experience his misery unless he stopped her. This was the last act of love he could offer her.

He opened his eyes and looked at her.

She stopped and sobbed.

"You dirty fucking bastard."

"I know."

Patrick Tenant calmly put his hands on his wife's neck.

The alarm clock was still vibrating with the memory of the incessant pulse of Dominic's scream. Holding her neck with one hand, he reached over and shut down the alarm clock.

"It will be alright now."

He held her close as she sobbed.

"You fucking bastard."

"I know."

He held her tight and he said

"It will be all right now."

*   *   *

Sergeant Norman Clouston had been at work since six thirty. He expected a quiet shift with street duty. The previous day he had been back to the run of the mill community police activities. He had dealt with a stray dog and a shoplifter in the Kirkwall supermarket and he had informed a family of an accidental death. It had been quiet. Today he was keen to get back to the station to follow up some long-term work regarding fraudulent movement of money using online payment sites with a server that seemed to be present somewhere on Orkney. Clouston loved this work. He had made himself expert in financial crime.

He had started by teaching himself about inks and watermarks that show up in ultra violet light, or in coloured light, and holograms and credit card chips. He also learned about the movement of money across the internet; the ebb and flow into banks that had no front door, only an obscure website address; or maybe bank transactions that had a virtual presence in the Caymans, or Jersey, but where the transactions were done with a single trusted individual using a single phone number. These modern trends in finance and their links to criminals were what made Clouston's pulse race. At last, the intensity of the last few days looked as if it was dying down and he could get on with what he did best. He chased money.

He had become interested in this side of crime when he identified that Norwegian 100 Krona notes were being made in Burray. Among the farms and the bed and breakfasts and the tourist attractions and schools was a forger who made millions of Krona in a back shed. Clouston smiled at the memory.

Before leaving the office to walk his patch, he checked his emails and found a message from Harry Stout, the Kirkwall Harbourmaster, sent the previous night. It was a report from a fishing boat of a silver coloured car, washed up on the west coast of Westray. Harry did not have the registration number.

Norman Clouston sighed. He would have to follow the money later.

He picked up the phone.

"Harry, this vehicle washed up at Bakie Skerry. Could it be the vehicle driven off the cliffs at Noup Head?"

"Well first of all, they say the car is pretty much a wreck, but Norman, as you well know, the Roost around Orkney is a tidal pattern that is complex and unpredictable, especially over a period of several tides. If the car had been driven over the cliffs at Noup Head about 7 days ago, with the tidal reversals and eddys, the car might end up anywhere within a 40 mile radius. It is quite feasible that the car could have ended up at Bakie Skerry."

"Where is Bakie Skerry?"
"It's a promontory to the south west of Westray, about a half a mile from Langskaill and about six miles south of Noup Head."
Clouston found the site on the Ordnance Survey map and saw that there was a potential helicopter landing site close by.
"Yup, I see it. Thanks for your help Harry."
"No problems Norman. It is going to be choppy out there today, so be careful."
"Ok Harry. I'll keep in touch."
Norman texted Clett with Harry's information.

*   *   *

Patrick Tenant held his wife close.
"You fucking bastard."
She gasped, the last sobs from her were gone.
"You ....."
He raised himself from underneath her and went to the shower.
He cleaned himself, shaved and dressed.
He left his exhausted wife and touched her shoulder.
"It will be all right now."
He shut the front door behind him and walked out of the estate.

*   *   *

Clett was finishing his porridge when he looked at the text. He called back.
"Norman. Thanks for that information. That's good news."
"No problem Roland, I'll get in touch with ATC. The ash forecast appears to indicate clear air over Orkney today."
"Can you get Drever, Fedotova and Leask to meet us at the site and to take some photographs?"
"Us? What do you mean, us?"

"Yes us, Norman, it is about time you got some fresh air. If the helicopter is free, you and I can get to Bakie Skerry within the hour. See you at the airport. Give me a call if there are any hold ups."

*   *   *

Clouston called Anna McDonald at Kirkwall ATC:

"Good morning Anna, it is your mate Norman here."

"Good morning Norman, what can we do for you? Do you want to fly to Westray today?"

"Yes please. What are my chances?"

"Well Norman, you sly devil, it could be your lucky day."

"Aye Anna, but what about the helicopter?"

"Oh Norman, away with you. Seriously now, according to the Volcanic Ash Advisory SIGMET, the airspace in Orkney is today open for business."

"Great Anna. So you are open for business? When are you and I going to get together for our wee tete-a-tete?"

"Norman, behave yourself. It's nine o'clock in the morning. Do you want me to organise your helicopter for you, or do you want to phone Orkney Helicopters yourself?"

"If you could do it, that would be great Anna. We will be going to Baikie Skerry."

"Where?"

"It is on the south west of Westray. I've identified a possible landing site."

"Have you got the lat and long?"

"Yup, 59.2599 degrees north and 2.9816 degrees west."

"Ok Norman I'll set that up for you."

"Thanks Anna, you're a doll."

"Enough of your sexist claptrap Norman."

"Ach, you love it really."

"Bye Norman."

Norman and Anna both smiled as they hung up.

*   *   *

Patrick Tenant stepped gently on the kerbstones, now seeing clarity in their patterns. He observed how each foot felt, with the outside of the sole making contact with the ground first, and then the motion of the deliberate act of rolling his foot flat, feeling his foot make a solid connection with the ground before starting the deliberate movement with the other. He breathed the air. Some school children crossed the road in front of him, directed by a lollipop man, with a yellow high visibility coat and an aura of cleanness and honesty. The children were laughing and happy. Tenant smiled for the first time since the Bay of Noup. Passing a gorse bush, he was amazed at the yellowness of the flowers and breathed the coconut scent in the morning sun. The smell brought him back to the events on Westray and the bright redemption ahead of him. A bee, working the flowers, became silent as Tenant passed. Its back legs were solid with pollen weighing it down; it could hardly fly. A morning fox crossed in front of him, once wild, now appearing to offer a beautiful menace in this urban world.

*   *   *

Drever got out of his car at Langskaill and walked to Bakie Skerry. The wrecked car was in clear view, almost unrecognisable. It was in a precarious position. The tide was coming in, and it was in danger of being washed out to sea again. Angela Fedotova was arriving as Drever phoned in some pictures of the car. He called Clett.

"Roland. We've got a badly bashed up silver car. The front is almost concertinaed. It might once have been a Toyota, maybe a Corolla; no visible registration markings. Do you want the VIN number?"

"Aye Archie, looks like that is the way to go."

The VIN plate would give them the 17 digit number that could be used by DVLA to identify the owner.

"I'm at the helicopter with Norman; should be there in 20 minutes. Wait until we arrive."

Fedotova turned to Drever.

"Where is the VIN plate on a Corolla?"

"It should be at the bottom of the windscreen on the passenger side or on a door pillar, but we may have to find it under the bonnet, on the engine bulkhead."

Angela looked at the car on flagstone pavement, yawing and bumping and grinding against the rocks in the tide.

"I hope it is on the windscreen."

Fifteen minutes later, Clett and Clouston came down from the helicopter to where Fedotova and Drever were approaching the Toyota Corolla moving in the surf. The wreck was extremely unstable.

"This looks dangerous. Where's Leask?"

"He should be here soon."

"OK. Archie, no time to wait for forensics. Options anybody?"

"How much do we really need this evidence?"

"If the car is from the Bay of Noup and we identify it, we have a link between the killer and the murder. If not, we have nothing now that de Vries is dead."

In the salt wind and the approaching rain, Norman Clouston pondered the comfort of his desk.

"I can liaise with Sanja and Irene. They will want some photos and I can video until you need me."

"Aye Norman", said Clett.

"Anyone got a rope to secure the car?"

The officers shook their heads.

"Anyway, there is nothing to tie the car to. Let's just crack on."

Drever was itching to begin. Clett stopped them:

"We have to carry out a risk analysis."

"For God's sake Roland, forget all that crap, let's just get on with it."

Drever was right. He was wasting time.

"Yeah Archie, sure thing. Let's go."

Drever, Clett and Fedotova gingerly stepped on the wet rocks, dodging the surf. Clouston got pictures of the tyre tread pattern and forwarded them to Irene and Sanja.

The others clambered on to the rocks near the moving car. Drever climbed on to the bonnet and looked inside.

"No VIN plate in the windscreen."

Fedotova's heart raced. In fact, there was very little left of the windscreen. They tried to open a door to find a VIN plate on the pillar. The three officers pulled and tugged at the doors that were stuck, jammed from being repeatedly bashed against rocks. Drever gave the driver's door an almighty wrench and the car moved on an incoming wave. The underside of the car grated on the rocks.

"Shit."

All three jumped back from the moving car. Clett fell in the surf. Fedotova helped him to his feet.

When the car stabilised, Fedotova looked in to the vehicle through the broken window. There were a few CDs and a black folder.

"Is that a service book? It might have the vehicle ID. I'll get it."

Fedotova leaned inside through the window.

"Careful."

Clett called to Drever above the roar of the surf.

"No chance of fingerprints or viable DNA here. Only option is the VIN from the engine compartment."

Angela looked in horror at Drever, seawater glistening on his face, nodding. The Toyota was lurching precariously. Drever and Clett were working on the mangled bonnet. Fedotova was still inside the car trying to get the service book. Clouston got the axle spanner from Drever's car and passed it to Clett, who levered the bonnet as the car rotated by ninety degrees and slid a full four feet further towards the open sea. Fedotova was almost upended into the passenger compartment by the car's motion. She leapt clear of the car which was now lurching continuously while Clett and Clouston worked feverishly, attempting to manipulate the corroded bonnet catch. The spray had soaked them all and their hands were cold and the feeling gone. Drever's hands were bleeding.

Just as the car moved some more, the bonnet sprung open half way with a rusty groan. There, in clear view on the rear firewall, was the VIN panel. Clett leaned in to the engine compartment and shouted out the sequence of letters and numbers, rubbing at the corrosion with his fingers as he went. Clouston relayed the information to Irene and Sanja. The car was now almost continually moving. He was hanging on to the edge of the bonnet and his feet had no purchase on the rocks. The car was crashing from side to side and yawing in the surf. As Clett shouted the last digit, the car turned on to its side, depositing him on to the wet flagstone pavement. Clett was now in danger of being washed out to sea by the heavy surf, or the car could roll on top of him. As he scrambled towards safety, he watched as the car slipped and lurched away from him, groaning and bobbing on the open water. He was helped to his feet by Drever and Fedotova.

They looked out to the car, but there was nothing to be seen except the breakers and the open sea.

"And do you think a risk analysis would have helped?" said Drever.

Clett laughed and the three soaking officers walked over to Clouston.

"Well Norman, did you get any video? Are you going to put it on the internet?"

"Aye Angela, I think I might just do that. Irene and Sanja are on to DVLA with the VIN and they will get back to us when they have anything."

"What about the tyre pattern?"

"Ok inspector, just a minute – Sanja have you any information?"

"Yes. We're talking about 195/60 R 15 standard Continentals, consistent with the residuals at Noup Head and the Bay of Noup."

"That puts the car at the Bay of Noup. Superb."

The four officers were nodding and smiling.

"That was quick Sanja. Any data on the owner?"

"Aye. The car is a Toyota Corolla, registration mark FE04 MWG and the owner is one Mrs Victoria Tenant, 20 Fulmar Crescent, Summerston, Glasgow."

Clouston repeated the information to the other officers. They looked at each other anxiously.

"A woman?"

They had not considered that the killer may have been a woman.

"Surely our murderer is not a woman. What about the power of the assault and the repeated blows on the victim?"

"Hang on a second, the killer might be a woman, but the car may be registered in the name of a male killer's partner, or may be owned by someone not related. Let's not make too many assumptions here. With the tyre treads linking it to the murder scene, there is a strong chance of a connection with the killer. This result could lead to an arrest."

"Thanks Sanja. That looks great. Talk later."

Clouston called the ferry company, as the other officers warmed themselves in Drever's car.

"Inspector, the ferry company says that a car reg FE04 MWG had been on the 1630 MV Earl Thorfinn crossing to Westray on Tuesday 20th April. It was not recorded to have made a return journey."

"Thanks Norman. Can you call Strathclyde police at Maryhill Police Station to question Mrs Victoria Tenant in respect of her whereabouts between the 14th and 24th April?"

Clett called Chief Inspector Maggie McPhee.

"Yes Maggie, the car has been identified as the one at the Bay of Noup and at the cliff tops, so it places the car at the site. If

Strathclyde can get someone to Fulmar Crescent, we can put some of this together."

There was nothing they could do except wait for events to take their course 300 miles to the south.

*   *   *

Ronnie Rust met Torvald Arnsenn at Kirkwall airport. The two men shook hands.

"So, you got here despite the ash cloud?"

"Yes Ronnie, it would appear that we are back to business as usual."

"Aye, I wonder what all the fuss was about. We should go straight to the nightclub."

"Sure Ronnie."

They walked to Rust's BMW.

Chapter 17

Tuesday, 27th April 2010 Midday.

Roland Clett showered and cleaned up in the station. All he could do was wait and see if the lead to Victoria Tenant would be productive. He had done as much as he could and he just had to wait for the fates to play their game.

*   *   *

Meanwhile, Nancie Keldie was weary, staring at the stuttering frames of the CCTV images. Again she checked the date and it still said 19-04-10. This was the third time she had seen the footage and still she couldn't identify Dominic Byrd. She gave herself one last try before giving up. She looked again at the facebook profile picture of the smiling boy and started the sequence at six pm. She slowed the speed down, skipping the empty sections, and at 18:38, in the corner of one of the frames, she saw a figure she had not registered before. She played the sequence again and saw him come in the entrance to the nightclub, skirting the edge of the image. The figure was wearing a hooded sweatshirt and baggy trousers; not the clothes Byrd was wearing when he was murdered. She called Clett over from his desk to watch the clip. The two watched the silent whispery figure stagger from one frame to the next, to the bar and then to a corner. They chose the best shot to identify him, but the grainy image was still hardly distinguishable in the poor lighting.

"The height, the build are right; the hair colour looks right. If only he would remove his hood."

As Clett was speaking, the next sequence showed the man with his hood down.

"Look at the hairstyle. Could be the same as the facebook photo."

"Yup, I would say that looks like Dominic Byrd. Good work Nancie."

The two watched as another figure, a slightly older man joined him. The man had his back to the camera for the full time.

"That has to be Patrick. See if you can get him front on. What about the entrance?"

Keldie rewound the footage to Patrick's entrance. He was hidden by a group of people hanging about in the foyer. Patrick and Byrd could be seen shaking hands, smiling and engaging in lively conversation.

"They look friendly enough."

"Maybe, but we don't know what happens next. Nancie, make a copy for the secure drive and keep the original safe. Make an edited version and take a couple of screenshots for the whiteboard. This will be Patrick until we know otherwise; we need to confirm his identity and talk to him."

Clett walked to the Orkney Room in Kirkwall library and settled among the wood panelling and the books and the quiet. He sat in a leather armchair with his phone on vibrate. He lifted the box file containing the handwritten copies of Archibald Clett's letters. He stroked the timeless pieces of paper with their criss-cross writing and picked one that was written on the back of what appeared to be a tailor's bill. Clett became lost in yesterday, today and tomorrow, beyond progress and beyond history. He read the obscured words, with its over-writing and crossings out. He dug at the text and among the scrawl, with each iteration, copying out each word, he revealed the trace of the narrative.

To Mr. James Hutton.

St John's Hill,

Edinburgh

3rd June 1786

Dear Mr Hutton,

Thank you for your observations about the nature of our Orkney flag stones and their continual formation and dissolution by the elements. I should like to relate to you my own observations. Principally, it should be noted that our flags do not appear to lie with their grain in the same direction, even to other rocks in adjacency, for one would expect that the elements will have a similar efficacy towards rocks that are proximate. Is it sufficient that the erosion also moves the rock vertically and up and down within the strata? This would account for the granular discrepancy between adjacent rocks.

Rock it will rise or fall in this sea of moving stone that flows at such a slow speed as to make its movement invisible to human eyes. This notion is congruent with your plutonian theory which you explain within your fine volumes 'The Theory of the Earth' which sit happy in my library.

I should like to speculate further upon this subject and make some observations apropos the notion of North. If, as I have suggested, and you have demonstrated, the seeming solid rock we stand upon has been moved by forces at work in the earth, it would be a natural extension of your theory to look at the land as having been in continuous motion for – how long? For how long would such conditions persist? For an infinite period? Longer than 6000 years? Certainly. Can one ever perceive of a stable state from which these conditions have evolved? Might this mean that a piece of land on one part of the globe could have travelled from the other side of the world, or even have travelled the globe several times? I assert that this is incontrovertible. And more! How secure can be the rock upon which we walk? What of its orientation? Which way does it face? Which way is North? Is it the same direction that was experienced in ages past? How long does it take for these changes to take place? A hundred lifetimes; a thousand?

You see how the possibilities of your work lead us to inevitable uncertainty. This is not a reductio ad absurdum; it is not a contradictory outcome, nor is it nonsensical, it is but a consequence of your ideas. Thus we might consider that North was not always the predominant orientation that we have assumed. The land we walk upon may not have faced the direction that we see today. The very solidity of our world may be but a myth, the earth itself essentially insubstantial. Can we rely on nothing? Is there any fixed element that is constant? Where is our touchstone in this world we experience? If there is no such beacon of constancy, how do we live? How far can we take this? If the world is not fixed, how can we trust our own senses? How can we fix our selves?

Yes, my friend, how can we fix ourselves to this changing world? And does this lead to madness or to liberty?

I remain &c.

Yrs Archibald Clett of Canmore.

*　　　*　　　*

Arnsenn got out of Rust's BMW and looked up at the huge purple letters above him: 'Fraction'. He appeared happy with his acquisition.

Geraldine Work met them at the front door.

"Geraldine, this is Torvald Arnsenn, the new owner."

"Hello Mr Arnsenn I'm very pleased to meet you."

"Call me Torvald, Geraldine. I've heard great things about you and the efficient way you manage the club."

"Oh Mr Rust is too kind. He makes all the big decisions, all I do is keep it ticking over."

Rust patted Geraldine's shoulder.

"Now what have I told you about taking credit where credit is due. It is because of you I can concentrate on my other interests. I have very little to do with the club these days. Anyway, can you put the kettle on? Mr Arnsenn and I have some business to discuss."

"Certainly Mr Rust."

Geraldine left the two men in a corner of the lounge.

"So Torvald, we can now close the chapter on this bit of business, and talk about the natural next step."

"Oh really, Ronnie? Please go on."

"Yes Torvald, now you have your foothold in Orkney how do you intend to set up your distribution network?"

"Distribution network?"

"Yes Torvald, the real business that the nightclub is the foundation stone for."

"Ronnie, I won't be distributing anything, I've nothing to distribute. I just wanted to get an honest start here with a nightclub."

"Come on Torvald, what about the merchandise?"

"Merchandise? Ronnie I don't know what you are talking about."

"The drugs Torvald! The reason for buying this club was to get a legal home for your money and to start getting your drugs spread out using my connections."

"I'm sorry Ronnie, I do not know what you are talking about. I have no drug connections any more. All that is in the past. I just want to run a nightclub."

"What the fuck are you talking about, just run a nightclub? What about my connections, the promises I've made?"

"No Ronnie, I don't know where this is coming from. I never mentioned drugs to you."

"You didn't have to. I've seen the newspaper stories about you. We had an understanding."

"It doesn't really seem so, does it? Those newspaper stories have got it all wrong. That was in the past and plays no part in my life now. You didn't really think that …."

"Are you taking the piss? Are you fucking winding me up?"

"No Ronnie. I don't like the way this conversation is going. Could you take me back to the airport please."

"No I fucking won't."

"I'll find my own way."

Arnsenn rose quickly and left the club.

Rust was incandescent. He was shaking, almost convulsing in his anger. Geraldine Work had heard the shouting and entered the room with a tray of tea and coffee. He was sitting in a low sofa, hunched forward with his elbows on one of the large, low tables, He quivered and moved slowly from front to back, pivoting on his elbows,

"Mister Rust, Are you all right? Where's Mr Arnsenn?"

Rust did not answer immediately. He slowly turned and saw Geraldine through half shut eyes. She was intermittently lit by tiny moving glimmers of dull luminosity. He looked up to the slowly revolving mirrorball, reflecting bits of daylight from outside the club. Suddenly, he knew it was her.

"Don't you fucking talk to me you bitch. What do you know about this?"

Geraldine sensed danger and immediately turned away.

"Answer me you bitch."

Rust stood up slowly and inhaled slowly, as if growing into something. His anger powered every muscle in his body and caused him to shake, silently, but with small quick nervous movements; and only just perceptibly.

"Come here. I'm fucking talking to you."

Geraldine stood still, holding the tray, frightened, unsure what to do next.

"Look at me you piece of shit."

The mirrorball rotated above them, illuminating old corners of the room.

"Mister Rust, please, I don't know what you are talking about."

Rust reached forward and grabbed her hair. He was now less rigid and moved more flexibly.

He screamed in her face, spraying spittle.

"I said, what do you know about this?"

She gripped the tray tightly, trembling. The milk in the jug spilled over the tray.

"What do you know about that fuck Arnsenn?"

"Nothing Mister Rust, please let me..."

Rust wrenched her head back and she dropped to her knees and lost hold of the tray. It fell to the floor and the coffee and tea and milk and biscuits spilled on to the carpet. Geraldine looked away from Rust and to the mess on the floor. He grabbed her throat. She blinked through her tears and croaked.

"Please don't hurt me. I'm sorry. I'm so sorry."

Ronnie hit her across her face with his open hand and threw her to the ground. Geraldine looked at the carpet. A narrow beam of light lit up the cigarette burn marks and she wished she had replaced it for Mr Arnsenn. She felt the rough pile under her hands. Rust turned away and lifted a chair and threw it at the bar. The mirror smashed into a web of fractures and optics fell to the floor, adding to the mix of reflections in the dim room. Geraldine tried to get up and turn away but Rust saw her rise.

"What the fuck, come here you slag."

He lifted her up by her hair. In her pain, Geraldine did not scream, she whimpered.

"I'm sorry Mister Rust."

He looked her in the eye and saw her tears reflecting the dull light. He stood straight and still and he drew his arm back and he punched Geraldine in the face; and then he punched her again and then again and again. With the increasing intensity of his blows, he could sense his knuckles become wet and hot. She was limp in his grip. He threw her to the ground and kicked her in the body and head. He was breaking sweat. Dots of light slowly passed over them from the mirrorball rotating slowly above them. Rust was breathing heavily, but regularly, and he was experiencing that familiar mix of freedom and control. He looked away from her and observed the shards of light being cast about the room. Geraldine was curled up into a ball to minimise the injury she knew she was sustaining. She whispered through the pain,

"Sorry Mister Rust, sorry, sorry, sorry."

Ronnie Rust hauled Geraldine to the back door. He opened the door and gasped and blinked in the flood of bright sunshine. He dragged her into the yard at the back entrance to the club. He lifted a bottle from the open wheely bin and smashed it across her head. The fragments of glass exploded over the ground. Her eyes closed and her head dropped. He grabbed her hair and screamed in her face.

"Did you fucking speak to Arnsenn?"

Geraldine grunted. He raised the broken neck of the bottle to her cheek. Her head lolled from side to side as he gripped her neck. Out of the corner of his eye, Rust saw someone at the end of the lane moving away holding a mobile phone. He came to his senses. He considered the situation objectively. This was bloody pointless and it was also becoming boring. He let Geraldine fall to the ground and he saw the bloody mess he had made. She was twitching and the odd sound came bubbling through the bloody froth from her swollen mouth. He had to find Arnsenn.

Rust bent down to her and spoke calmly and softly.

"Geraldine, make no mistake. You will pay for this."

He sat in the BMW. He squinted and adjusted his visor against the midday sunshine and started the car. Arnsenn couldn't be far.

*   *   *

A few hundred yards away, Clett left the Orkney Library behind and was walking down to Broad Street. He had another briefing session with Maggie. He left the calm of the Orkney Room behind and was once more forcing himself to engage with the case. Rust, de Vries, Nelson, Patrick, was it all about drugs? All these factors were pulling at him. Which were the distractions, and what was he to focus on? There was Sandy, delicate wee Sandy; how was he going to cope? He could rely on Christine again – he would have to; his parents, God, his parents. In the ground just yesterday; and now another draining meeting about the case. He was late.

His phone was buzzing. He was about to turn down the lane when he heard two boys calling to each other. The sound of their voices rose above the babble of people in the street.

"Race you to St Magnus'!"

Clett looked around and saw two boys, about ten and twelve years old, running from Burgh Road. Their mother was behind them and shouted.

"Careful you two. Mind the road."

Clett stopped in his tracks, and all thoughts of the case became a fog in his head, the separate factors, the links and the names and times, all dissolved.

"Careful you two. Mind the road."

"Careful."

Clett stood among the swell of shoppers and tourists and young couples and children in the spring afternoon breeze, and a wave of sadness overwhelmed him. The sight of the cathedral blurred and he felt tears on his cheeks. He turned to the wall and put an arm out to support himself. And he wept. His shoulders heaved and he found a doorway to get away from the attention of people in the street. He tried to compose himself. When was the last time he had cried? There was no reason for this. He couldn't work it out. What started it? Two boys with their mother calling to them?

The more he tried to control himself, the more the waves of sobbing engulfed him. This carried on for several minutes; a passer-by glanced in his direction, turned away and quickened his step. Like the others walking by, he was embarrassed that a man in a doorway with his back to everyone, supporting himself with one hand, was weeping in public. A little boy walked past holding his mother's hand.

"Mummy, why is that man crying?"

"Shhhh."

After a few minutes, Clett settled and dried his face. He stayed in the doorway waiting for the involuntary gulps to subside. All he could do was to wait for it to pass. Christine had warned him something like this was going to happen. What had she said? You can only keep on working so long, ignoring how you feel. Your emotions will catch up with you. You can't lose your parents and expect to have no reaction. This must be what she meant. He was now breathing more regularly and he could feel his shoulders and neck loosen a little. His body relaxed a bit, but with every other incoming breath, he would still gasp and shake until he would relax. His headache had gone.

His mobile buzzed.

*   *   *

A police car and an ambulance arrived at the Fraction nightclub. As the paramedics lifted Geraldine into the ambulance, she groaned and mumbled incoherently through the pain and the swelling:

" … it must have been something I … … must have been me … My peedie wee Raymond … how will …"

Clett was trying to listen to Norman Clouston on his phone as the ambulance passed him. He asked him to repeat himself because of the noise of the siren.

"Ronnie Rust's club? You think it might be Geraldine Work?"

"Yes Inspector."

"I'm going over there. Let me know any developments."

*   *   *

Rust realised he was exposed, driving out in the open. He would deal with Arnsenn another time. He had some tidying up to do. He breathed deeply and calmly and headed for home. He was composed as he parked the car in the drive. He turned the key in his front door and called:

"Hello Auntie Brenda, it's only me."

He put on the football and poured a gin for himself. Real Madrid was playing Moscow Dynamo. He carefully placed ice in the glass, took a knife from the cutlery drawer, and cut himself a slice of fresh lemon. Some blood dripped on to the work surface. He took a cloth and wiped it clean. The game was just into the second half and there was no score.

*   *   *

Patrick Tenant was sitting on a park bench. He knew what he had to do, and he knew what was going to happen to him, and he was using this time to reflect. Some ducks swam over to him looking for food. A group of teenagers ran past shouting and laughing. On the other side of the park young mums pushed prams. He stopped and he took in this moment, savouring it. He tried to soak up each and every sensation. The green of the grass, the traffic noise in the distance, the birds singing, a barking dog. His sense of awareness was at a peak. He felt the end was imminent. His redemption was in sight. The leaves of the trees whispered something to him and he stood up and moved on.

*   *   *

Clett arrived at the Fraction nightclub and saw the broken glass and upturned furniture and the fresh blood in the service lane. His phone buzzed again.

"Yes Norman."

"We have a report of Torvald Arnsenn arriving at Kirkwall Airport a few hours ago."

"Good Norman. Put out an instruction to apprehend. We need to talk to him, but be sensitive. We don't want to upset the Norwegians. Let the Chief Inspector know before he is interviewed. Any more word from Balfour Hospital?"

"It does look like Geraldine Work has been the victim of a serious assault. A witness phoned in a report of a commotion at the back lane of the nightclub and a silver coloured car speeding away."

"Rust!"

"Well, em…, There is no definite ID."

"OK Norman, keep me up to date."

Clett walked back to the Burgh Road Station. He went straight to the whiteboard and peered at it, oblivious to the commotion in the office around him, trying to make the information make sense, trying to see the links between the sites and individuals and timings scattered over the board. Various photos and scraps of paper and yellow stick it notes were held in place with magnetic pins and joined with coloured thread. There was a photo of Trevor de Vries, with the word 'Deceased' written over it in red marker; there was the blurred image of the hooded man they thought might be Patrick; a photo of a suntanned Ronnie Rust taken at a pool somewhere with a drink in his hand, and to the side, there was the newly added picture of Torvald Arnsenn. Someone had written the word 'unlikely!!!' next to Rust's picture. Clett took the whiteboard eraser and rubbed the word out and replaced Rust's picture in the centre and circled it with a thick red marker.

He returned to his desk and as he sat down, he caught his trousers on a splinter sticking out from the wood. He looked at the small tear and grunted. He turned again to re-read the report of the retrieval of the car at Bailie Skerry when his mobile rang again.

"Yes Norman."

"Inspector, I have the initial assessment of Geraldine Work's injuries from the A&E department at Balfour Hospital. She has a fractured skull, broken jaw and nose, four broken ribs, fractured shoulder blade, multiple bruises and contusions, ruptured spleen, and possible kidney damage."

"My God, the poor lassie. Do we know anything more?"

"Only the passer-by I mentioned who called 999."

"The person who saw Rust driving away?"

"Well all that they said was that it was a silver car. They didn't identify Rust or his car specifically."

"It was Rust!"

"There was no specific identification of the assailant inspector."

"OK enough. I'm going to arrest that bastard."

Clett ended the call. He had not known how to tie Rust in to the new information about the car at Baikie Skerry, but right here, right now, this appeared to be an assault for which Rust could be charged. This time there was no messing around. There was a witness and what Clett thought of as a clear case. Rust's reputation would not survive this. However, Clett was quietly a little ashamed. He was horrified at the injuries inflicted on

Geraldine, but he was also he was overjoyed with the outcome. This time he would nail Rust. He got into his green polo and headed for the Olfsquoy Estate.

        After Clett rang the doorbell three times, Ronnie Rust opened the door holding a grubby glass in his hands. His FCUK sweatshirt was spattered with Geraldine's blood, his hands were filthy brown and his knuckles skinned to the bone. Rust spoke slowly and calmly.

"Ah Inspector Roland Clett, come in."

Clett could hear the football from the television.

"Ronald Rust, I am arresting you on a charge of assault. You need not say anything, but anything you do say will be taken down and may be used as evidence."

Rust leaned toward Clett and whispered in his ear through almost closed, tight lips.

"Aye. On you go you pathetic fuck."

Rust placed his bloody glass down on a low metal table next to a copy of 'Chasing the Model'. He called back into the house:

"Don't worry Auntie Brenda, your peedie laddie will be home soon."

*   *   *

Constables John Anderson and Jo Burns were leaving Maryhill Police Station when the radio in their police car issued a priority message. They scanned the information on the vehicle's mobile data terminal. They were to interview Mrs Victoria Tenant, of 20 Fulmar Crescent, Summerston, in connection with the murder of Dominic Byrd in Orkney. John Anderson read the rest of the case outline as they drove through the busy Maryhill traffic . They were two miles away and replied that they would respond. Detectives would also be responding. They accelerated towards Fulmar Crescent.

*   *   *

Sanja Dilpit began the final briefing.

"So, we have several conclusive aspects in respect of the murder scene at the Bay of Noup.

Firstly, the DNA identification and identification by the victim's father confirmed Dominic Byrd as the victim. The time of death was between 2200 and midnight on the night of Tuesday 20th April. The cause of death was trauma caused by repeated blows to the facial area, to the extent that facial and dental material was spread out from the site of the body. One fingerprint and a thumbprint were found and are those of Professor Trevor de Vries, now deceased. No other reliable biological evidence was found at the site that would give a positive ID on the assailant.

The car. Tyre prints were found which are consistent with the kind of tyres on the Toyota Corolla found washed up at Baikie Skerry. Unfortunately it was not possible to match the actual tyres to the car. They have been changed for standard non manufacturer's tyres in the last few months. It has not been possible to retrieve the car."

Clouston and Clett caught each other's eye and smiled. Irene Seath continued the presentation.

"So this particular piece of evidence remains in the circumstantial pile, given the large number of cars with these tyres. Therefore the car cannot be absolutely identified from the tracks at the scene of the crime or at Noup Head. However, the VIN of the Corolla was obtained by Inspector Clett and his team. Sergeant Clouston has obtained the vehicle manifest from the Earl Thorfinn and it indicates that the vehicle associated with this VIN arrived on Westray on Tuesday 20th April and did not leave the island again; this will be presented in our report to the Procurator Fiscal. The resulting efforts will be presented alongside the reports and evidence on the secure drive. The DVLA database identifies the owner as Mrs Victoria Tenant of Somerston, Glasgow."

Sanja took over.

"We would like to comment that the difficulties of obtaining precise data from the site were significant: the weather, the terrain, the effect of the sea and wildlife as well as the interference to the site by other parties."

Clett spoke.

"Thank you Irene and Sanja. I think we are all aware of the progress you have made under the difficult circumstances."

Clouston raised his hand.

"What about the blood spatter radius? Were you able to describe the physical characteristics of the assailant from that?"

Irene and Sanja looked at each other and smiled.

"Unfortunately, that data did not offer anything that could be used to describe any useful feature of the assailant. The approach was based on a paper submitted for publication by one of our colleagues, but has been proved on this occasion to be too unreliable. On a more positive note we might be able to offer information regarding telephone and data exchange in connection with the victim's mobile phone and social networking sites."

Sanja displayed a network of colours on the screen behind her.

"This shows that Dominic Byrd's phone was used for text and email communications with several Norwegian mobile numbers, one being Torvald Arnsenn. Similarly, he had several calls to an untraceable number – probably a pay-as-you-go mobile. It is identified on Byrd's phone as belonging to someone called Patrick. The first of these calls was on the morning of Tuesday 20th April. The network also shows that Trevor de Vries was involved in this cluster of calls. This data will require further analysis in order to be coherent enough for submission as evidence. That concludes the briefing. Any questions?"

There was a low rumble of conversation in the room. Clett stood up.

"OK, thanks Irene and Sanja. You've done sterling work here. Do you have any more to do?"

"No inspector, we are flying back to sunny Dundee to finish off the loose ends. We have to tidy up our report for the Procurator Fiscal. Thanks for your hospitality, by the way. We have had a lot of support from colleagues and from the community."

*   *   *

Constables John Anderson and Jo Burns arrived at Fulmar Crescent and rang the doorbell of number 20. This was their second ring.

*   *   *

Patrick Tenant walked lightly up the three steps and through the swing doors. There were posters on the wall advertising victim support and a number to phone if terrorist activities were suspected. There was also contact information for people who had relatives and friends stranded abroad because of the ash cloud crisis. He waited for the desk sergeant to finish his paperwork. He observed a spider creeping across the desk. The desk sergeant was about to place a book on the spider.

"Just a minute."

Tenant gently moved the spider out of the way. The desk sergeant waited until Tenant had completed this little task.

"Good afternoon sir, can I help you?"

"Thank you. I hope you can help me. You know that murder in Orkney last week?"

"Yes."

"Well, I am here to tell you that I did it."

The desk sergeant looked up at him with no expression.

Patrick waited on his response. The sergeant sighed and put down his pen.

"Would you like to come this way sir."

*　　*　　*

Victoria Tenant woke to the sound of her doorbell. She looked at the clock. It was now four in the afternoon. Had she slept the whole day? She cleared her head and remembered the events of the morning. She could not believe what she had done to her husband. Yes, of course he was a shit and incompetent and useless and she had punished him endlessly for it. But he was her husband, and she had been too hard on him this time.

She knew she had driven him to the drinking and the depression, but she had pushed him too far. His response when she had exploded with him this morning was terrifying. He had shown her what she would have been capable of. Her contrition was absolute.

The doorbell went again. There was a blue flashing light outside. She opened the door and a policeman and a policewoman introduced themselves.

*　　*　　*

The clapping died down and the MC took the microphone.

"Did you hear the one about when Margaret Thatcher came to Orkney. She was met by Jo Grimond and they sat together in St Magnus Cathedral for a civic function. Thatcher says to Jo Grimond do you want to see half the crowd go wild? Jo says ok. So Maggie stands up and simply raises her hand. Half the people in the cathedral clap and cheer. Very good says Jo. Do you want to see the whole crowd go wild? Yes says Maggie. So Jo punches her in the mouth."

The audience cheered and roared in approval. Roland looked at Christine and shook his head from side to side.

"These bloody liberals."

"Oh come on Roland" said Christine. "You are as liberal as the rest of them."

Roland smiled.

The ceilidh had gone well. Roland and Christine met old friends and blethered over the tea and sandwiches. People asked about each other's children, about their bits of business, the improving weather, and the warp and weft of everyday Orkney life.

They got talking to a visiting couple from Fife.

"You dance your steps differently here."

"How do you mean?"

"Well, every time when we have that move, you know, when the man holds the woman's hand up and she twirls underneath, what's it called? Anyway, you don't do that here. You seem to do a waltz style turn."

"Oh."

The next dance was announced.

"Would you like to join us to dance an Orkney foxtrot?"

"No thanks, we know when we are out of our depth. We can see that the locals know what they are doing when they change into their dancing shoes."

"Well if you don't mind, we will go up. It is our favourite; isn't that right Roland?"

"Aye, it is, right enough Christine."

They walked out among the other couples and a man sprinkled talcum powder on to the sprung floor around their feet. With the first chord, Roland and Christine struck an elegant pose in the room, erect and serene. Within a single step, they were synchronised with each other and with the music and they glided on the floor, moving as one. They dipped and drove each other in a way their friends recognized. Heads nodded as people around the room approved of their steps and their composure. They danced a beautiful inseparability that strangers might have mistaken for professionalism. Some people thought that their performance had come about through training, but Roland and Christine danced without preparation and without guile. They danced about this floor of friends, magically avoiding other dancers. They had such poise that everyone in the room could see their quality. Even people who did not know them saw the confidence and the nonchalance, and the beauty of each other's anticipation of the next step.

Chapter 18

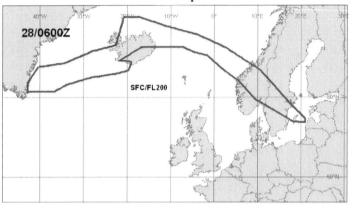

Wednesday Morning, 28th April, 7.30am.

Patrick Tenant woke crisply to sunshine which threw blurred shadows from the frosted window above him. He was in a large warm open cell with about eight other men, some still snoring softly. He lay with his eyes open and felt as if this opportunity, this road to redemption was at last becoming reality. He heard the solid thunk of the lock being turned. A policeman brought in mugs of tea in plastic cups and rolls with Lorne sausage.

"Vegetarian option off this morning, gentlemen."

The prisoners waited in a queue to use the toilet. The cubicle had no door. Tenant drank the sweet tea and ate the roll slowly. He experienced all this in a detached manner, as if watching it all from outside of himself. The sugar in the tea, the sound of the other men using the urinal, the crunch of the roll and sliced sausage on his teeth, the strong heat from the radiators, the intense green colour of the walls lit by fluorescent light tubes; and outside the sound of people going by, talking; the traffic, the buses and the electronic beep of a pedestrian crossing. All of these sensations he registered and considered as if someone else was experiencing them. In the next room there was the quiet roar of a gas boiler. These things, this small world that now consisted of these separate observations happening in this short duration, this world melded into one thing for Tenant that represented his current state. A state of worth, a state of satisfaction, all of these sensations amounted to his punishment. The wrong he did could now be paid for.

*   *   *

"Number Five, Mr Ronald Rust."

Rust stepped into the dock as the Clerk of the Court took her place. Ronnie was pleased that he had got the duty sergeant to bring a change of clothes. His blood-stained sweatshirt would not have created a great impression. He looked around and recognised the prosecutor, that big bastard Rostung. When he looked up to the bench, he saw his friend the Honorary Sheriff Charlie Sinclair wearing his wig and gown. He stood in the dock and nodded to his lawyer George Barr, Writer to the Signet.

The Sheriff Clerk laid out the charges:

"That on Tuesday 27th April, 2010, at approximately two o'clock in the afternoon, you did assault one Geraldine Jessica Work, of Ayre Road, Kirkwall, and that you did beat her head and body with various instruments and did cause physical injury to her person and did so place her in fear of her life. How do you plead?"

"I plead not guilty, Your Lordship."

Rust sounded confident and smiled at the Honorary Sheriff Charlie Sinclair who smiled meekly back. There was some quiet legal preamble among the lawyers and the clerk. The prosecutor, Sigurd Rostung spoke to the Sheriff.

"Your Lordship, I would submit that this assault is of the utmost severity and that the prosecution may be considering a charge of attempted murder following the consideration of evidence."

The Honorary Sheriff shuffled his papers and coughed.

"Mr Rostung do you wish to make such a charge today?"

"No your Lordship. We wish to consider ..."

"Then I shall speak for today."

The Honorary Sheriff spoke to Rust.

"Mr Rust, I cannot comprehend how this situation has come about; that a generous and upstanding member of the community has found himself in such a predicament. These charges are bewildering and I cannot for the life of me understand how you have come to be in this position. However, given the seriousness of these allegations, I have no option but to follow due process. I want a plea trial to get under way as soon as possible to minimise further inconvenience to all concerned. I am going to place you on bail pending trial because of your standing in this community and my own knowledge of your character. I do not see any benefit in keeping you in custody."

After a quiet exchange between the Honorary Sheriff and the clerk, the clerk announced:

"Mr Ronald Rust, you are to attend this court for a diet..."

She paused and checked her papers and nodded to the Honorary Sheriff.

"There will be a First Call where you are ordained to attend on Monday 3rd May. You must see the court administrator regarding your bail before you leave."

Rust smiled to his solicitor, and then to his friend, the Honorary Sheriff Charlie Sinclair.

"Thank you your Lordship."

Sigurd Rostung shook his head wearily and lifted the file for the next case.

Rust and Barr walked out of the courtroom and stood at the steps of the Sheriff Court and shook hands. From the court steps, they looked north, along Watergate to the spire of St Magnus' Cathedral, lit by the mid morning sun.

"Thanks again George."

George Barr, Writer to the Signet, noticed the cuts on Rust's hands.

"Been at the DIY again Ronnie?"

"Oh, you know how it is."

"Indeed I do. See you on the 3rd May. Give me a call if you need to."

"OK George."

Rust walked off in the direction of Balfour Hospital.

*   *   *

Back in Finstown, Roland Clett was taking a call in the hall, away from the rest of the family, still at a late breakfast.

"So that's the deal Inspector, The suspect is one Patrick Tenant. He has admitted to the murder of Dominic Byrd and he is in custody in Maryhill Police Station."

"OK Norman, I'll get the midday flight down to Glasgow, pick up the hire car, interview the suspect and fly back tomorrow."

Clett ended the call and returned to the kitchen.

"So you are going to Glasgow."

"Yes Sandy."

Clett finished his toast.

"And you are flying down today?"

"Aye."

"And me and Magnus have to get the ferry and drive all the way."

"Well, that was the plan Sandy, the tickets are bought now."

"And you don't want to come down with us?"

"Aye, Sandy, that would have been nice, but this is work. I fly down, do the interview and fly back again. Listen, why don't we get together for a curry later tonight? What about that place in Gibson Street?"

Sandy shrugged his shoulders. Magnus spoke:

"Great idea. You can sleep on my couch."

Sandy rolled his eyes.

241

"Meanwhile, we drive four hundred miles while you travel in style."

"Come on Sandy, it's the job."

"You are some piece of work Dad."

*   *   *

Ronnie Rust walked into Balfour Hospital and straight to the front desk, smiling.

"Annie Smart, how are you?"

Annie Smart looked up and was taken aback.

"Mister Rust. Hi. I, em, I thought you were ..., the news ..."

"No case Annie. My lawyer sorted out the misunderstanding with the police. They couldn't pin anything on me. I mean, do you really think that I could do that to a young woman? How long have you known me?"

"Aye, but she was so badly beaten. I saw her in casualty. It was horrible."

"I'm sure it was horrible Annie, but she was not beaten by me. The witness mistook me for someone else. Come on Annie. Use your judgement. You must know that I'm incapable of hurting anyone, especially a young woman that you know fine well I've helped for years. For goodness sake, how could I look wee Raymond in the eye?"

"Aye, well, right enough."

"That's more like it Annie. Now what room is Geraldine in?"

"Oh I really don't think..."

"Come on Annie. I'm really worried about her and I need to make sure she is set up for money and someone to look after Raymond."

"Well, I suppose so. She is in room G15."

"Thanks Annie, good girl. Say hi to your peedie Evelyn and her big sister Maggie. Lovely girls. Give them this from their uncle Ronnie."

He handed over two twenty pound notes, folded into small pieces that fitted neatly into the palm of Annie's hand. Annie smiled nervously.

"Thank you Mister Rust."

*   *   *

"Inspector. Norman again."

"Morning Norman. We're just seeing the boys off before I fly to Glasgow."

"Sorry to bother you, but there is something you should know."

"Oh?"

"Yes. You're not going to like it, but Ronnie Rust was released on bail this morning."

"What?"

"Aye, I know. I don't know what to say."

"How the hell did that happen?"

"You know Rust, sir. Friends in high places – the Honorary Sheriff Charles Sinclair."

"…who sits on the Burwick Community Centre Trust with Rust."

"Aye. He set a plea date for 3rd May. Sheriff Flett is on leave."

Clett breathed slowly. Christine watched him closely.

"Rust. Out."

He paused.

"I can't believe it. There was a witness for God's sake. That girl Geraldine is in a terrible state."

"I know sir. The witness couldn't identify Rust or the car, only that it was silver. Honorary Sheriff Sinclair this morning considered that there was not enough non circumstantial evidence to keep him in custody. Again, what can I say?"

"Nothing Norman, nothing."

Clett's shoulders drooped; there was a cracking sound inside his head as he stretched his neck from side to side. Ten thousand feet above, the volcanic ash cloud appeared to be diminishing. Aircraft now flew from departure to destination with no concern for the old restrictions, and as if nothing had happened. New rules of flight had been written and things were returning to the way they were before; before the invisible emergency that had caused so much disruption.

*   *   *

Rust walked into Geraldine's room. She was asleep and was barely recognisable beneath the bandages.
He touched her shoulder and whispered.
"Geraldine."
She woke up with a start when she saw Rust. Immediately she turned her head away from him and started whimpering and shaking. She couldn't move her jaw and mumbled something through her feeding tube. The tone from the heart monitor started to pulse much faster.
"It's ok Geraldine. It's ok. You're ok now, everything is going to be all right."
She croaked and spoke using only her lips,
"You're not going to hit me."
"Of course not Geraldine. What must you think of me? Look, it will all be fine now. I'm going to look after you."
She was still shaking, looking at the closed door behind Rust. Somewhere there would be an alarm button, but she couldn't see it. She looked wide-eyed in fear from between the bandages. She mumbled through the pain killers.
"Please don't hit me."
"Geraldine I don't want any more of that talk. You mustn't upset yourself. Don't say anything. Now let's get you sorted."
"But the club … bills to be paid … the stock orders and the functions booked…."
"I wouldn't worry about any of that Geraldine. Mr Arnsenn has that all in hand."

Rust knew that without Geraldine running the club, profits would disappear and Arnsenn would suffer. He allowed himself a small smile.

"Anyway, what about you? Who is looking after Raymond?"

"… with my Nan on Shapinsay."

"Good. How are you for money?"

She trembled in fear as she answered.

"I'll be ok."

The heart monitor accellerated. Rust glanced at it and back to Geraldine.

"Look. I'll take care of your bills and rent. Do you still have the same bank account?"

Geraldine nodded.

"And I will make sure your Nan has everything she needs. You just have to concentrate on getting back on your feet."

Rust turned to leave and smiled.

"Now. You won't be pressing any of those charges, will you?"

*   *   *

Sandy and Magnus were quiet in the car to Stromness.

"Have you missed any lectures Sandy?"

"Nothing I can't catch up on."

"And when will ye meet up with Margarita?"

"I don't know, I'll give her a call."

"When can we meet her Sandy?"

"Look. I don't know. Right! Enough!"

Roland gripped Christine's hand low down by the handbrake.

Magnus broke the silence.

"Will the case settle down now Dad, now that you have a suspect to interview?"

"I don't know Magnus, it all depends on what comes up."

Christine turned the corner and there was the Hamnavoe below them, blue and waiting for its fresh cargo. They drove to the ferry terminal in silence.

As they unloaded their rucksacks, Magnus spoke quietly to his Dad.

"Don't worry. I'll keep an eye on him."

"Thanks Magnus. We'll keep in touch."

Sandy said goodbye awkwardly and turned to his mother and gave her a hug. Christine held on to him.

"It will all turn out fine, my peedie wee Sandy."

"Aye Mum."

He sniffed and turned away to board the ferry. He did not look back at his father.

Magnus shook hands with his Dad.

"Look you two. Don't worry about us. We will be fine. Look after yourselves. I for one think it is brilliant you are seeing each other again and Sandy will just have to get used to it."

Christine blew her nose.

"Thank you Magnus. That means a lot to us that you think that, but it is just so terrible seeing Sandy like this."

"Don't worry Mum, we will all sort it out together."

"Thanks son. You better get going. Give us a call when you get to Glasgow."

"Ok. Bye Mum, Bye Dad."

Christine sobbed into Roland's shoulder as the Hamnavoe picked up speed and headed out towards Hoy.

"What a mess we have made of bringing up our boys."

"Christine, that's nonsense and you know it."

"No Roland, it's all down to us."

Her shoulders heaved as he held her.

"Christine, we have both made mistakes, but you know It is me that was responsible. It was my ambition, my unrealistic expectations and my inability to deal with things that was the cause of our problems. You, on the other hand, seemed to deal so well with things all through the bad times."

"Aye, but you didn't see me drinking and the hoovering not getting done. Poor Sandy went to school for a whole year with no breakfast. I'm surprised he can still talk to me. Oh Roland, if only I had stopped you going to Glasgow."

"Christine Clett you know well that you would never have stopped me. It was my blinkered doggedness that drove me, and that is where it went wrong between me and Sandy."

"And between me and Magnus."

"What do you mean Christine? You and Magnus get on like a house on fire."

"I do not, not the way you do with him."

"But you and Sandy will always have a special thing, forbye anything that happened when we split. I can never share that. We all have different relationships with our children and we can't have the same set of connections that the other one has."

"I suppose you are right Roland."

"Aye, well."

Clett paused.

"Sandy and I have a lot of fence mending to do."

"Well I can help. I'll supply the nails."

"Christine Clett, what will I do with you? Let's get back to the car."

As she turned the key in the ignition, Christine said;

"You know it was really nice having the boys back for a few days."

"Aye."

"Just like old times."

She wiped her eyes.

Roland leaned over and held her tight.

"It's ok."

"So it's just us now Roland."

"Let's go home for lunch."

*　　　*　　　*

Sanja and Irene looked east towards the high cliffs of Hoy. Seagulls followed in their wake and they felt the cold spray on their faces and the taste of salt on their lips.

"Ah shouldny a washed ma hair this morning. It'll need a guid dose o conditioner when Ah get hame. An this wind is playin havoc wi ma blusher."

"Jeeze if it's no yer mascara, it's somethin else."

"Whit aboot puir auld Keillor?"

"Puir auld nothin. His theory wiz shite an' you know it."

"Aye but ..."

"Aye but nothin. it means we ur stuck wi him."

"Och, he's no bad. Ye c'n get worse bosses."

"Suppose."

"Look at that burd."

"Orkney is nice so it is."

"It is a shag."

"Naw it's no, it's a puffin."

"Naw it is a cormorant."

"Aye, Ah'd like tae come back."

"An nice folk."

"Or is it a guillemot."

"Whatever it is, they don't hiv them in Dundee."

"There's an Aberdeen gemme oan in the lounge."

"Aye, an' Ah huv tae finish knittin that bunnet. Want a coffee?"

"Aye."

*　　　*　　　*

Clett tipped a large spoonful of instant coffee into a mug and poured boiling water into it. The mug said 'Yosemite'. Christine was standing beside him.

"I haven't seen that cup in ages."

"Well I've not been here to use it."

"I suppose."

"That was a great holiday."

"Aye. None of us will forget it."

"Do you remember Sandy's reaction when we heard that coyote?"

"We were all surprised. I'm sure it was right outside our tent."

"And do you remember that trout that Magnus caught?"

"It was a monster right enough. "

"Have you had enough lunch?"

"Aye, I better get that plane."

"Are you going to meet up with Magnus?"

"Aye, I'll buy him a curry in return for sleeping on his couch. Hopefully Sandy will be there too."

*   *   *

Roland Clett stepped off the plane at Glasgow Airport to a clear spring afternoon. The terminal was full of the remaining stranded passengers still waiting for information about flights delayed by the ash cloud disruption. The concourse was full of people in their holiday clothes, with crying children, and others sleeping across seats. People ate from plastic sandwich boxes and drank bottles of water. The cafes and restaurants were full and there were queues for the tables.

He left the terminal and picked up his hire car. He drove on the familiar old M8 in the direction of Maryhill, each signpost like another step into the past. The Kingston Bridge, the traffic at Charing Cross, the Mitchell Library, the old St George's Cross and up Maryhill Road to Glasgow Police Headquarters (North). Maryhill Police Station was a brown monochrome building right on the main road, next to a pedestrian crossing and across from the old barracks walls. He showed his warrant card to the desk sergeant, nodding to a few old hands who recognised him. He tried to avoid eye contact with some of his old colleagues. He was still embarrassed at the nature of his departure eighteen months before. He wanted to get this over with and get back to Orkney. His phone buzzed. It was a text from Christine.

'Hope interview goes well. Enjoy your curry with Magnus. Hope Sandy is there. C xxx'

Clett smiled and looked back at the face of the desk sergeant.

"Purpose of visit?"

"Inspector Roland Clett to interview Patrick Tenant. What room is he in please?"

The desk sergeant's phone rang and he answered.

"Look, I told you before. Just tell that numpty the score. We do the arrest and they find the accommodation and they do their own fucking paperwork."

He listened to a response.

"Look. I have not got the time for this. Tell me when you have something useful to say."

The desk sergeant hung up and he paused. He looked up at Clett.

"Sorry sir. Who are you again?"

There was the familiar sound of the jingle of the keys as Clett was taken down corridors to interview room three. He was buzzed through and he showed his day pass.

"Inspector Roland Clett entering interview room. The time is 2.17 on the afternoon of Thursday 29th April 2010. Could the other people in the room identify themselves please?"

"I am Ms Lorraine Tierney and I represent Mr Tenant."

"Have you had a briefing from your client?"

"Yes I am aware of the statement that Mr Tenant wishes to make."

Clett looked at the man sitting next to the recorder. He seemed like a small child, smiling, belying the fact he was thirty years old and five foot ten. His complexion was sallow, but he was clean-shaven and in a clean shirt. Tenant stood up and offered a hand.

"I'm sorry. That is not appropriate. I am the SIO in the investigation of the murder of Dominic Byrd at the Bay of Noup on Westray, in the Orkney Islands on Tuesday 20th April 2010."

"Yes. I did it."

"All right, we will get to that. Could you identify yourself please?"

"Patrick Tenant."

"Address?"

"20 Fulmar Crescent, Glasgow."

"Thank you. Can you tell me your movements from when you arrived on Orkney?"

Tenant related the story - meeting Byrd, going back to Westray, the murder, dumping the car, the walk to the ferry and the crossings, the failed attempt to get the Hamnavoe, the re-crossing of the island to get the Pentalina, and the lost drunken bus journeys back to Glasgow.

Clett listened. It all fitted.

"Why did you kill Dominic Byrd?"

"I don't know. I don't know how it happened."

"When you got to the Bay of Noup, what happened?"

"I don't know."

"You must know."

"We had a few drinks and he said something and I killed him. That's all there is to it. I'm sorry, but that is it all. Just send me for trial. I want to go to prison for what I've done."

"We have to know why you did it, a motive."

"There is no why. I lost myself and did it. I killed Dominic. That is all."

"Did you think about his family, or what would happen to you?"

"I didn't think about anything."

Clett looked down at his notes.

"Did Dominic Byrd scream when you killed him?"

"I can't remember. Yes, maybe."

"There was a witness that heard a scream at 1.40am, but the estimated time of death was nearer 11.00pm. Can you explain this?"

Tenant was silent. He remembered his scream when returning to the site. He remembered the feeling in his stomach and the sense that that scream had not come from him, but somehow was formed from something that was outside of him.

"I don't know; maybe it was me."

"Could you repeat that please?"

"It was me. I screamed when I saw the body."

"After you got rid of the car?"

"Yes."

"All right then, why did you get rid of the car?"

"I don't know. It seemed to make sense at the time, but I soon realised it was a mistake."

"How was it a mistake?"

"Well, obviously I could have used it to get away more quickly."

"Why did you give yourself up?"

"I had to. There was no choice."

"If you had to give yourself up, why didn't you do it sooner?"

"I just ran. I didn't know what else to do."

"If you had given yourself up, a man would still be alive today."

"What man?"

"You mean you don't know about Trevor de Vries? Don't you read the papers?"

"Who is Trevor de Vries?"

Clett told him about the suicide of Trevor de Vries. At the end of his story, Tenant was silent.

"My God, what have I done?"

Tenant looked up to the small window in the interview room. Outside, a beaten up old crow was watching. It ducked to get into the small space on the windowsill, darting from one side to the other. It pushed its scraggly head into the air, opened its beak and called three times, dipping its head and raising it to the sky each time. It dropped off the windowsill and flew away for a circuit and then returned to resume its observation of the proceedings.

Tenant folded his arms around himself and closed his eyes. He rocked slowly, back and forth.

*   *   *

"Are you sure you don't mind me sleeping on your couch?"

"Don't be daft Dad; any time. It is good to have you to myself."

"Thanks Magnus. Could you pass the naan?"

"Dad, you do know that the case has been getting a lot of coverage down here?"

"Aye."

"And your role has been getting a lot of attention."

"Do you mean the Terry O'Brien coverage in the *Daily Record*?"

"Aye Dad. He said terrible things about you."

"I know Magnus, but what can you do?"

"It is just so unfair."

"I didn't help myself with my performance at the press conferences."

"But Dad, you had just heard about Granny and Grandad. You were under a huge amount of pressure."

"It was them bringing up the Tumelty case that did for me in the end, but I just have to get on with things. I have to keep the focus on the investigation."

Roland looked out on to Gibson Street and to people coming and going. He tore a piece of the bread and dipped it in his raita.

"So what's next on the case?"

"Can't say for sure. Tenant has been charged and we will present our evidence to the Procurator Fiscal and if he sees fit, there will be a trial."

"You don't sound too sure."

"Well, the killer is a pathetic soul really, and there are more unanswered questions about Ronnie Rust and a drug connection in Norway."

"Surely Ronnie Rust would be too clever to expose himself in a drugs dealing situation. He is Mr squeaky clean these days isn't he?"

Clett told Magnus about the assault on Geraldine.

"My God, and he's free."

"Aye. Out on bail. There will be a trial, but Rust has a history of escaping justice."

"The sheriff who let him go, he must be corrupt."

"No Magnus, the Honorary Sheriff is an honest man, but Rust is a very feasible and persuasive individual."

"You know Dad, Ronnie Rust once came to our school and gave a motivational talk on self-improvement. He said that you have to recite a slogan every morning, you know, to improve your self-esteem. Things like 'I will not fail', or 'Find a new goal today'. He was very convincing."

"I'm sure he was."

"Did I hear he was running for the council?"

"Yup. There are rumours."

"You want to be careful around him Dad. He is a dangerous man."

The waiter brought two more beers.

"So you and Sandy didn't speak about anything else on the way down."

"Hardly a word. He listened to his i-player the whole way. It's ok Dad, he just needs his own space."

"I hope you are right Magnus. Anyway, tell me how your work is going."

"My work? Are you sure?"

"Of course. I want to know."

"Well, we are at a really interesting stage in the project just now. We are testing the coding for a new chip for our pattern recognition product. It uses a new algorithm to mimic a neural network that speeds up training times by about thirty percent. Quite exciting really. I've got this particular piece of code that I'm really pleased with. I'm sure no-one has ever done this kind of thing before. It uses an iterative fourier analysis in parallel to the training network and it estimates a best guess for the O.U.T."

"Oh?"

"You know - the object under test."

"Ah yes."

*   *   *

On flight BE6915, Clett settled into his seat and looked down over some part of Aberdeenshire he did not recognise. He was heading for home and an evening meal with Christine. He took out another photocopy of Archibald Clett's correspondence and a notebook and transcribed the interweaved writing into intelligible text.

To Mr Murdoch Mackenzie
Kirkwall
14 January 1749
Dear Sir,

I am glad to have been of assistance in the supplying of men to carry out your recent survey of the Islands of Orkney. This will be such a boon to future seafarers and to the trade of these islands. You must take your new charts to the Royal Society. I have written to Cpt. Cook of your successful project.

As I do, I have been reflecting upon charts, so forgive me for expounding. You cartographers have designed for us a representation of our world as if seen reflected in the canopy above us. This representation you have created of our Orkney Islands is recognisable only when the chart is held towards the north, as if seen by a bird flying in one direction only. Turn it upside down, or with east or west or any other direction to the top, and its whole relevance, its whole comprehensibility, its whole history, in short our economical engagement with natural philosophy is lost.

What is this northness? What is it about this direction-ness that encourages us to make sense of our world? Why do we only make sense of it when we look at it in this way? In antient times, charts were not produced in the same manner. So is it fashion that thus dictates this practice? If it is not, then all our charts now and in future times may represent only the one way of seeing our world. If north is our new marker, how do we make it fixed? If it was not so used in past times, there may be a point in time to come when it is not thus. My question is this; how do we rely upon North? How do we know it has not been changed? Where is our marker in this world, bounded as it is by a forever changing horizon?

Perhaps I am incorrect in my assertions. I perceive that your new chart has the meridian drawn through Kirkwall. In years to come when others extrapolate upon your exertions, will they keep this centre? A new Mappa Mundi with our Kirkwall at its middle?

Do you know that I still have the instruments you loaned for your survey? I will have them returned to your address at Kirkwall High School.

I remain, Sir, Yours, most sincerely,
Archibald Clett of Canmore.

The plane shuddered on a lump of air. Clett looked down to a cargo ship full of containers on the Pentland Firth.

*　　　*　　　*

As Roland and Christine were getting ready to go out, Clett's phone buzzed.

"That's Norman Clouston. Will I take it in the hall?"

"No need Roland, just take it here. I don't mind. Watch your time though."

"Ok."

Clett raised the phone to his ear.

"Norman, what's new?"

"We have just finished interviewing Torvald Arnsenn and it seems all that business about him being a big time drug dealer is well off the mark."

"Really?"

"Yes. He did some small time deals a few years back and spent three months in prison, but since his release, he has turned around. He has a basement bistro in Oslo, but he has had no drug offences for the last two years."

"But Nelson's research, his expertise, what about the Norwegian consulate's warning to stay clear?"

"Well, the discussion with the Norwegian consul reflected their position; that Arnsenn is a respectable businessman."

"And the connection with the deputy prime minister?"

"Apparently it was his family that gave him the loan for his bistro; but his main problem was the press. They ran stories about the deputy prime minister's brother being a drug dealer, along with interviews with men who were in prison at the same time as Arnsenn."

"Who were well paid, no doubt?"

"Aye, I would think so."

"So what put him on the straight and narrow then?"

"He discovered his daughter had been taking drugs and then he found Jesus. He volunteers in a rehab centre."

"So where did Nelson get the stuff about him being a big time dealer?"

"Straight out of Norwegian tabloids."

"Bloody Nelson. What a liability!"

"Couldn't possibly comment, inspector."

"What about all the mobile phone and email connections?"

"Not quite there yet Inspector, but it all looks innocent enough."

"How do you mean?"

"Well, on a more in depth look at the text and data connections, all we have is the two or three numbers with lengths of calls and the odd text agreeing to previous unknown messages. For instance there is one call made on Dominic Byrd's phone in the Fraction nightclub, which could have been made by anyone, and one more on de Vries' phone to Arnsenn on the previous day, but we can't prove who made the call. There were no other calls to this or any other Norwegian number from this phone. When it comes down to it, we can't question de Vries and all we have is Tenant's admission."

"Aye, it looks like that will be the basis of our case to the Procurator Fiscal. What we don't have is a clear motive, but there you go. That's often the way. Motives are often manufactured after the event. Anyway, what about Patrick Tenant? Why didn't we know about him? Did we really just miss him on the Earl Thorfinn and on the Pentalina?"

"Well I suppose it comes down to luck."

"Luck? Well don't tell anyone that Norman. We would be out of a job if people knew how many of our cases were won or lost on luck."

"Aye. True enough inspector."

"And there is no other link with Rust?"

"Nothing sir. There is only the fact that Tenant and Byrd met in his club and these inconclusive telephone contacts."

"And the assault on Geraldine Work?"

"Nothing more. The trial date for a plea is set for Monday. To be honest, the witness is not great. He doesn't know Rust and he didn't get the number of the car, only the fact that it was a silver BMW."

"Hmmm. Ok Norman thanks for that."
"Did your boys get away ok?"
"Aye. We're going to miss them."
"Well it's good you and Christine are on the mend."
"Yes Norman. Thanks."

*   *   *

Overhead, the diminishing volcanic ash cloud appeared to control men's actions less and less. According to the forecasters, its power was waning and the rules of everyday life would become more reliable. Predictions, we were being told, could now be relied upon and our future could be plotted once more.

However, there was a warning that the ash could yet return.

*   *   *

Christine's rocket, parmesan and partain salad arrived.
"What a week Roland."
They quietly clinked glasses.
"Aye, well, you know how it is. And there is still the court case. I was talking to Russell today. We have to see the lawyer to settle the estate. It's straightforward really and nothing changes. Actually, there's not that much money. Enough to pay Sandy's rent for the rest of his time at university, and maybe a nice holiday for us all. Russell will get some more for the farm which will help him out a lot."
"I don't suppose that another case like that will come along for a while. It'll be young drunks fighting and tourists who have lost their credit cards."
"And don't forget the lost livestock."
"And more time at home."
"Aye. That'll be nice."

"I'm quite looking forward to it really."

"I have a present for you."

"Lovely, what is it?"

Roland reached under the table and presented Christine with a small box. She opened it and inside was a tiny, almost spherical, carved wooden bird. The grain of the wood mimicked the texture of the feathers and there was a slight carved gap where the wing would be folded, as if it were about to take flight in the fluttering way of such a small bird.

"Troglodytes troglodytes!"

"I take it that's the posh name for a wren."

"Aye, oor wirran."

Christine held the small carving in the palm of her hand.

"If you didn't know better, you would say it was an ordinary looking peedie wee bird."

There was a bloom in the sky over Scapa Flow. The gas flare had been lit on the Flotta oil terminal. It flooded the whole night sky with its yellow glow. Outside and beyond the sounds of cutlery and conversation, seals sang in the flow.

'Compass of Shame' will be available soon.

25019456R00155

Printed in Great Britain
by Amazon